GW00600760

Fevreblau

Fevreblau

A Novel

Kenneth Mark Hoover

Five Star • Waterville, Maine

First Edition
First Printing: December 2005

Published in 2005 in conjunction with Tekno Books and Ed Gorman.

Set in 11 pt. Plantin by Minnie B. Raven.

Printed in the United States on permanent paper.

Library of Congress Cataloging-in-Publication Data

Hoover, Kenneth Mark, 1959–
    Fevreblau : a novel / by Kenneth Mark Hoover.—
1st ed.
      p. cm.
    ISBN 1-59414-361-7 (hc : alk. paper)
    1. Viruses—Fiction.   2. Moscow (Russia)—Fiction.
3. Women prisoners—Fiction.   4. Interstellar
communication—Fiction.   I. Title.
PS3608.O625F48 2005
   813'.6—dc22   2005027042

Acknowledgments

A writer never writes a book without outside influence. Many people over the years have, in one way or another, made this story possible. I would like to thank Stanley Schmidt who first suggested the more optimistic ending. Other editors who contributed in one way or another towards my education as a writer are (in no particular sequence of importance): Gordon Van Gelder, Warren Lapine, George Scithers, Kristine Kathryn Rusch, Algis Budrys, Edward J. McFadden, and Lillian Gohlke. Meeting and talking with other writers is always a source of inspiration and encouragement. Those who influenced me in some personal way by taking time to dispense advice or pass a few words are: Isaac Asimov, Harlan Ellison, Harold King (who will always be my best man), Hal Clement, James P. Hogan, Mike Resnick, James Van Pelt, Marion Poe, Sally Hamer, Dorie LaRue, David Coe, Terry Bramlett, Richard Parks, Shelley Powers and Randy Grigsby. I would also like to thank John Helfers, my editor, for his insightful comments regarding the novel. He made this a much better story than it already was. Finally, I wish to thank my wife, Sarah, for putting up with my various kinds of madness, and my three sons who also endure: Patrick, Matthew and Andrew. This book is dedicated entirely to my grandparents.

"Russia—a country
in which things that just don't happen, happen."

Peter the Great

Prologue

The running crowd surged past Mayakovskogo Plaza—a human tidal wave heading for Old Red Square. For one blessed second, the mob thinned. Nikolai shoved his way to the sidewalk, hoping to find sanctuary inside an abandoned church. But the crowds coalesced into a solid throng once more and swept him along like a piece of trash.

He passed a dead man. A tattered policeman's uniform still covered the mutilated corpse. There were shouts of "Hurrah! Hurrah!" as the mob glimpsed the oriental onion- and pineapple-shaped domes of St. Basil's Cathedral wreathed in neon. A brick soared over Nikolai's head and a plate glass window in a market shattered.

Shards of glass showered like hard rain. One boy fell, clawing his eyes. Nikolai glimpsed a sobbing man clinging desperately to a comlink post against the onrushing legion of men caught in a moment of hate and panic.

Terrified and gasping for breath, Nikolai tried to keep his balance in the press of sweaty bodies. To his horror, he trampled a man who went down in front of him. Across the boulevard, someone in a hydrogen-fueled three-wheeler systematically ran down victims, backing up to choose new targets. Shouting obscenities, several men rushed to the vehicle and lifted the back wheels off the filthy pavement. Hands smashed windows and pulled the driver out. Nikolai blanched as they pummeled the driver, one man sadistically lashing him with a severed limb.

The mob moved on. Nikolai cried out at the white-hot pain in his cramping legs and bruised ribs. Blood from his lacerated knees trickled down his shins. He ran through Pushkinskaya Plaza, no longer possessing the strength or the will to challenge the crowd intent on destroying Moscow.

"Hurrah! Hurrah! Hurrah!" The uproar was deafening. They were close to Moscow Square. Nikolai's group ran toward the thousands already packed between St. Basil's and the Kremlin. Among the waving arms he saw stones, rags and even bodies tossed in the air by the mindless crowd. A police barricade loomed ahead, strung across Sverdlov Square. Security men with red helmets and mirrored faceplates, armed with riot shields and mercy weapons, stood behind electronic sawhorses.

The barricade bore the full brunt of the onrushing wave. It fell back, but held as reinforcements came to augment the barrier. Like a sea, the wave of rioters fell back. The police moved forward, gaining ground. But like a sea, the mob came back, a living wall of human flesh crashing through the flimsy cordon to meld with the waiting throng in Old Red Square.

"HURRAH!" A thunderous cry of victory. Men waved paper handkerchiefs, shirts, linen. An ocean of men shouted, wept and cried oaths.

A stranger grabbed Nikolai by the shoulders and spun him around. "We've done it, comrade. We've made it!" The other man's eyes were wide, staring. "It's independence for us all!"

One

Two days before the Great Riot, it had rained in Moscow, and the streets surrounding Old Red Square glistened like waxed carbon beneath a dirty skin of rainwater. Fatly bundled pedestrians walked past the mag-lev terminal where he stood momentarily in the gloom, waiting.

Eighteen months. Nikolai Sholokhov, electronics technician second class, belted the raincoat around himself. Eighteen months on Dark Side calibrating the Shklovskii radiotelescope array for the Star Whisper Project.

Now, he was home for two weeks. Then Dark Side for another year and a half, along with a guaranteed upgrade to technician first class to reward his troubleshooting skills on the Project.

A porter struggled to unload his luggage from an aluminum rack on the side of the mag-lev.

"Home for long, sir?" the gray-haired porter asked politely.

"I'm afraid not," Nikolai replied. "Going back up in a couple of weeks."

"That's a shame, sir. Still, maybe it's for the best."

"Oh?"

"WeathCon says we're in for a brief Indian summer the next week or so, before the first snows hit."

Nikolai remembered the bitter Moscow winters of his boyhood. "Can't say I'm sorry to miss that."

The porter checked his baggage with a scrawled chalk mark. "How are you for accommodations, sir? There's always spare rooms in the old Rossiya Hotel, and the price is right."

"I thought it was gutted in the last riot."

"The Rossiya? Oh, no, sir. She's still standing like a proud lady. Clean rooms, and there's smoked fish, even on the meatless days of the week."

"Thanks, but I expect I'll stay at the Warren."

"I agree that'd be best for *you*, sir." The old man smiled and Nikolai caught a glimpse of yellow-stained teeth. "Just thought I'd mention the Rossiya. You see, I get a couple of tsars for every client I send over *nalevo*." On the side.

Nikolai nodded briefly. Obviously, things hadn't changed since his last visit two years ago. Moscow was still on a barter economy and suffering hair-curling shortages. The Russian economy was stretched to the limit to keep her offworld colonies viable, especially after the devastation wrought by the gender sensitive plague that had decimated her female population.

The porter handed him his bag. His thin arm seemed to bend under the weight. "Well, here you are, sir. Have a good stay. If you should need anything—tea, tobacco—I know a fellow. I'm always here at the station. Ask for Dmitri."

Nikolai hefted his pood over one shoulder. "Thanks. I'll remember."

He began walking. St. Basil's Cathedral, a gaudy mass of neon spires and gilded domes crowned with Russian Orthodox double-barred crosses, shone in the distance. Dying rays of sunlight gleamed off the golden cupolas. Further on, the red granite of Lenin's Tomb—now a strip mall—and the pale brick of the Kremlin faded into velvet shadow as the sun rapidly sank beneath a bleak horizon. Traffic was light, but with many more military vehicles than he ever remembered.

Government banners flapped in a desultory fashion from the towers of the Kremlin. Giant placards of the First Minister's taciturn visage hung from the shattered battlements. Nikolai splashed through standing puddles of dark water. Near Sverdlov Square he passed a dead cat in the gutter. Stiff and soaked, it looked out over the wet thoroughfare with white marbled eyes.

He quickly adapted the standard Moscow shuffle: hands deep in pockets, head down. He took deliberate, measured steps, unaccustomed to the demanding pull of gravity. Movement out of the corner of his eye brought his head up.

Men darted across Gorkogo to queue up near a temporary market. Instinct moved Nikolai. He trotted heavily to the other side of the wide boulevard and joined them. There was general pushing and shoving as they settled down in their places in line. He counted the file of men ahead. He was twenty-third. Behind him, the queue already extended three times as far, with Muscovites still assembling. Nikolai waited, listening to the excited rumors fly regarding what was on sale.

A man ahead addressed his neighbor: "Fruit is what I heard. And about damn time, too."

"They'll probably run out of it when it's my turn," a wizened man behind Nikolai groused sourly. "Wait and see."

"That fellow back there says they have cantaloupe. At twenty—"

"No, it's peaches. Peaches and cream! Or syrup!"

"Don't be foolish. When is the last time you saw a peach? It's strawberries, I tell you. Strawberries and cream for thirty-six tsars. Can you believe it?"

"It'll be gone by the time it's my turn," the old cobber growled again. "You watch and see."

Nikolai removed his glasses and rubbed rain droplets

from the plastic lenses with the fat end of his plain brown tie. He felt an odd sense of pleasure. This, and on his first day back on Earth! And in a few days he would have his Privilege. A queer, almost indefinable flush of well being settled over him.

The queue advanced rapidly. The aroma of sweets wreathed him. The street vendor, a stoop-shouldered man, subtracted thirty-six tsars from his credit disk and thanked him. Nikolai took a plastic spoon and left. Envious eyes watched.

He tore the cardboard lid off, ambling back across Gorkogo. Plump strawberries swam in cream that was re-markably fresh. He consumed it all. Before throwing the empty cup away in a compact recycling bin, he wiped his finger around the lip and sucked the remaining film of cream. He pocketed the plastic spoon.

There was a sudden disturbance behind him. A violent fight had broken out halfway down the queue. The argu-ment spilled into the deserted street. There were shouts and curses as men tried to take advantage of the absent spaces and advance in line.

A pair of bluecaps ran towards the disturbance, bran-dishing shocksticks and blowing whistles.

Nikolai continued on to the Warren. Street lamps came on to cast harsh pools of blue light on the plascrete side-walks. It began to rain again with nightfall.

"My name is Nikolai Sholokhov. I have a reservation." He pushed his ident card through the aperture. The con-cierge accepted it and deftly slipped it in a slot on his secu-rity terminal.

"Another one from Dark Side." It was a statement asking for confirmation.

"Yes."

The concierge swung the flat computer screen away from Nikolai's gaze as the information contained in his ID card scrolled on the security console.

"I'm from Kiev II, Korolev Crater, sector five block nine. I'm here on rotational leave. You see, it's my Privilege, so I made reservations two months. . . ." he stopped. The concierge didn't care, and besides that . . . Nikolai's legs hurt terribly. The brief span of days spent aboard Mir VII's one gee gymnasium in cislunar space hadn't adequately prepared him for the sudden burden of weight he now felt.

"Yes, yes. I understand." The concierge handed back the card and opened a barred-glass door. "Go to the front desk and ask for your room number. Give them this." The man held out a blue Warren-ident card with a holographic imprimatur and gold border.

Taking the card, Nikolai muttered "Thanks," and went on through. The glass security door hissed shut behind him, clicked.

A second man behind the lobby desk, bored and sleepy, checked him in and subtracted one thousand five hundred tsars from his credit disk for the night. He handed Nikolai a cheap, palm-lock key stenciled with a room number.

"Sixteenth floor. Pay for another day everyday at noon."

Nikolai nodded that he understood and entered one of the four lifts servicing the twenty-story building. Inside the car he leaned against the tarnished brass rail, feeling tired and alone. He ignored the security 'scope that watched him from the top corner of the car.

The elevator inexplicably stopped on the fourteenth floor. Its doors trundled open to reveal a plastic sign on a wobbly stand in the hall.

Lifts Inoperative Above 14th

Use Service Stairs

He groaned. Climb stairs, with his throbbing feet and legs? Murder. He shuffled down the brightly lit hallway and mounted the plascrete stairs. Halfway up the stairwell he had to pause and rest, and was huffing by the time he gained the sixteenth floor.

When he reached the stairwell door, it banged open and three small boys raced past. One bumped into him, causing him to stumble. The tow-headed boy didn't stop to apologize or help, he just flew after his companions, hooting and yelling. Their dwindling shouts echoed up through the stairwell.

Nikolai found his room, 1644, blessedly near the stairs. He unlocked the door, reached for the light pad.

His quarters consisted of one room with bath and a bed. He turned up the corners of a mattress that smelled of camphor. No bedbugs. In the kitchenette, a small portable refrigerator was bolted to the marred Formica counter, along with a two-range electric stove. The cabinets were bare. A dirty, worn rag lay in the sink. He surveyed the remainder of the barren room. Cheap Goya prints hung on the vanilla walls to hide the worst cracks and water stains. The yellowed lacquer on the wainscoting was chipped and peeled with neglect.

He shrugged at the surroundings. He had lived in worse.

He unslung the travel bag from his shoulder and gratefully collapsed on the edge of the soft bed. He kicked off his damp, rubber-soled canvas shoes. Massaging his burning calves with one hand, he keyed the vidphone by the bed and asked for Union House. Waiting for the call to complete, he switched on the computer terminal and punched in a string command for a local news/radio station. Mozart swelled from the speakers. He turned down the volume when a voice promptly answered his call.

"Union House. Can I help you?" A man in a neatly pressed uniform appeared on the flatscreen. Nikolai cued his own screen and consulted his official cablegram.

"My name is Nikolai Sholokhov. I have Privilege scheduled Thursday night, and I want to confirm."

"ID number."

He gave it to the operator, along with his work and social numbers. A brief pause ensued while the operator consulted his terminal.

"We have you down for 2230, Thursday."

"Yes. Yes, that's right." His pulse quickened as the confirmation came through. "Okay?"

"Fine. Bring the necessary identification cards and your State release, and final receipt of social duties paid. Be here a few minutes before your appointment so we can prepare you."

"Yes. I'll be there." The operator broke the connection.

Nikolai turned up the radio volume and lay back on the thin mattress. He removed his glasses, turned out the lights of the room from a master switch on the computer console, and threw a forearm over his hot, tired eyes.

He tried to think of whom else he could call while he was in Moscow, but no one came to mind. Most of the boys he knew growing up had moved on, or were working in one of the orbital factories. More than a few had been killed during the Encroachment War with Mongolia. Like most Muscovites, he had never forged close relationships. There was no emotional profit in it. People moved on when they could, forgot their past when it was convenient. Russia was a raped and barren country. Nothing like the vibrant nation of natural resources it was reputed to have been during the Mad Times.

He worked at a strawberry seed between his teeth with his tongue, half listening to the newscaster drone on and on about a large chemical spill off the Japanese coast, near Sakhalin. And the West had failed to reestablish contact with their experimental beam-rider spacecraft to Proxima Centauri, and heads were going to roll: Literally.

Another red tide bloom in the Gulf of Mexico: no surprise there. Word out of China was they had successfully integrated the thought-shards of an independent AI, but it had somehow got past its Turing horizon and was now running loose in the DataSphere. Scary stuff, if true. Scattered fighting around the world. Riots in Madrid. London was still burning; the dikes had failed and New York was flooding—again.

He fell deeply asleep while the radio played on:

"You are listening to Radio Moscow, the voice of the Confederation. The time is ten o'clock."

"Nikolai. Wake up, Nikolai. Nikolai, wake up."

He rolled over and keyed the appropriate button. "I'm awake." He rubbed sleep from his eyes. "What time is it?"

A dulcet voice said: "Twenty minutes past noon."

He grunted and kicked the harsh sheet from his naked body. He had stripped and set the alarm during the night. He twisted around and looked at the terminal.

"What name do you use?" He yawned and rubbed his sore calves.

"I respond to Sonya," the AI said. "I am a Metchnikoph VI model, room maid class, installed on May 7, 2125. I am directly plugged into State Central and the DataSphere. I will handle daily expenditures, remind you of any appointments and screen all your incoming calls. My Turing rating is—"

"That's fine. You needn't go on."

"I am here to serve."

18

He rolled out of bed while Sonya ordered his breakfast. Grabbing a clean pair of underwear, he hobbled to the bathroom where he showered and then shaved his three days' growth of beard. The mirror over the scalloped sink had lost most of its silver backing. His drawn, twenty-one year-old face with its wide-spaced gray eyes and thinning straight hair looked like a ghost. He washed the sink with a thin washrag, scrubbing at a ring of green-brown slime around the drain. He pulled on a worn pair of blue coveralls with a black nylon belt and canvas shoes that had dried over the tiny radiator by his bed. A knock at the door interrupted him. It was room service with his breakfast: powdered eggs, two small strips of real bacon, watered-down juice and two stale but thick slices of homemade black bread. The meal cost twenty-five tsars.

He pitched the paper plates in the incinerator chute behind the kitchen sink, but kept the plastic cup, rinsing it out for future use. He fished out his ID and credit chips from yesterday's pants, counting out his remaining money: five cards of ten thousand tsars apiece, minus what he had spent for the room plus strawberries and breakfast. He was doing okay. Warrens were set up strictly for the use of Confederation offworlders like him, and granted extra credit if one happened to run short.

He picked up his raincoat and shook it out. "I'm going out, Sonya," he said, preoccupied with hand-pressing some of the larger wrinkles. "I should be back around 2000 hours or so."

"Nikolai," she warned, "I suggest you not overtax yourself. You are not acclimated to the gravity yet."

New arrivals from Luna tended to overextend themselves the first day back on Earth. It was her duty to remind him of this.

19

"I'll be careful." He shrugged on his coat and left.

He went shopping, purchasing toiletries from the myriad stalls open to the fresh, clear air in the bright August sun. Other people were about, taking advantage of the good weather, or riding the electric trains to the wooded outskirts of the city to pick wild mushrooms.

He shouldered his way through the crowds without looking at anyone.

Late in the afternoon, he paid one hundred and fifty tsars to see a pornographic film featuring virtual actors. He had cautiously chosen one of the better-looking theaters, staying away from places that had too many boys hanging around.

It was warm inside the theater, and he had to remove his coat. The air stank of stale cologne. The soiled seat would not fold back, but it was comfortable and the armrests weren't begrimed. A ubiquitous trash of wrappers, cigarette butts, and punctured tubes of euphoria dollops littered the porous floor.

When the lights went up, an usher shuffled down the aisles to make sure no one tried to stay for a second showing without paying. Nikolai grabbed his coat and left.

Outside he blinked rapidly, eyes tearing at the swollen afternoon sun just touching the jagged rooftops. He took off his glasses and wiped his eyes.

He casually headed back to the Warren by way of a corner grocer's, but on impulse turned into a pop shop. He browsed unhurriedly, one of a score of men jammed in the stifling place. There were the usual magazines, videos, and interactive software. Another wall carried wallet-sized cards and 3V posters. He examined one of the manikins. He had never been able to bring himself to use one, although those who knew maintained one couldn't tell the difference.

Nikolai doubted that—and his mind veered to Thursday night. He went out to the cool evening air. This pop shop didn't offer anything the stores in Kiev II didn't have. Anyway, he would have to pay a steep duty on anything he brought back to Luna.

He pushed toward home, purchasing a few days' worth of groceries from various stalls, and a daily newspaper loop.

It was evening when he reached the Warren. Its steel and glass facade sparkled under the soft yellow bioluminescent street globes that illuminated the grounds. Almost as if twilight beckoned them, the boys were out roaming the streets. Many stood on the corners; some walked and worked the immediate vicinity of the Warren, looking for an outworld customer who might be interested in a new face, a new body. Most of them were tall gangling youths with long hair and diversified styles of dress. Their arms and torsos sported smooth, firm muscles. There were couples going out in the night to a restaurant or symphony. All were of mixed ages, all were men.

In Moscow, as in most of Russia and the entire world, the only women present were those of the giant Union Houses, and one had to have paid social duties to receive the privilege of accompanying one, if only for an hour. It had started with gender selection—modified centrifuges with separating electrical fields, glass tubes of filtering serum albumin, X and Y chromosomes. Female infanticide in population pressure spots: India, Central Africa, Asia, Hot West 'Merica. Men traditionally valued more than women. Then the gender sensitive virus with a shifting antigen hit like a firestorm: The *Fevreblau*. Some said it originated in the West, with the CDC in Atlanta, or from God, but who really knew? Trillions were spent worldwide to find a vaccine, bankrupting nations. A nightmarish sociological disaster no one had ever expected or imagined, had come to pass.

It was an apocalypse not foretold by any prophet of any belief system in any age of the world.

Women who survived the Blue Fever (roughly one in every five thousand) through some lucky genetic roll of the dice found themselves protected and sheltered. They supplied crèches with their ovaries that birthed male children to staff depleted armies, sustain the work forces, racing to keep a sliver of humanity from the precipice of extinction. Women were Exotics, used to prevent populations from dissolving in a shattered world. A history gone mad.

That night, Nikolai lay in bed, lights off, listening to Ohta's 9th symphony. The music washed over him. He thought of the boyhood friends he had once known. Names forgotten and lost. A life unremembered. When the music ended, he switched the radio off and tried to rest, forcing himself not to masturbate. He kept thinking of Thursday, and wondered what she would be like.

Choking back a cry, he bolted up in bed. He crouched over, propped on both arms, head down. His hair was stringy with sweat.

"Nikolai?" Sonya. A red light near her fish-eye lens intensified. She studied his configuration with her infrared screen. "Are you ill?"

He leaned on the headboard, slicking it with sweat.

"Bad . . . dream." He coughed. "Nothing else." His heart rate slowed. He looked at the disk of light on Sonya's console, tried to make a joke of it: "Nervous about my appointment on Thursday, I guess."

"That is a common reaction," she assured him in a maternal tone. "Most males experience it in countries with an unstable population ratio. Do not be alarmed."

He crawled out of bed and drank a cup of water. When he returned, Sonya asked, "Have you recovered?"

"Yes, sufficiently." Back in bed, he stared at the darkened room. His skin slowly dried.

"My psych program recognizes this as a classic anxiety pattern. Go back to sleep. Please, rest."

But the apprehension of what lay ahead at the Union House was too much for him. He got out of bed again and started dressing. The tattoo watch in the palm of his hand read 0415 hours.

Early, but he hoped a bit of food and the bright lights of the commissary were what he needed to chase away the last shreds of his anxiety attack.

He told Sonya where he was going, and locked the door to his room with the palm-lock. He trudged down the flights of stairs to a floor where the lifts were working. A few minutes later, he entered a well-lit cafeteria. The place was empty, except for one man sitting with his back against the wall and huddled over a cup of coffee as if trying to draw warmth from it. He used a blunt forefinger to push chess pieces around on a board painted onto the table.

Nikolai coolly inspected the stranger. Pale blue eyes. Blond hair with tight curls. Heavy jaw, and bushy eyebrows that crawled like wooly caterpillars across a domed forehead. An expensive coat with sable trim was folded carefully on the bench beside him.

Nikolai drew his own cup of the thick brown liquid from a samovar and was about to sit down at another table when the man spoke.

"Hello. Didn't see you come in. Thought I had the place to myself. Can't sleep either, eh?"

"Not really."

"You look like you could use some company. I certainly

23

could. Mind if I join you?" He started to get up, Nikolai waved him back down and slid onto a bench opposite the table.

"Name's Yuri Tur." The stranger held out a big paw. His handshake was dry and firm, his fingers thick with yellow calluses.

"Nikolai Sholokhov."

A look of surprise. "Say, you're not from Dark Side, are you? Working in Sharonov Crater?"

Nikolai suddenly became leery. The Star Whisper Project was an ultra-secret program. He knew everybody connected directly to the project, but this man was a complete stranger.

Still, he thought, if there's been a security leak I'd better find out who this cobber is and report him to the bluecaps.

He drew a poker-face. "Why do you want to know?"

Yuri inaugurated his next words with an easy-going laugh designed to put anyone at ease.

"Because, Sholokhov," he chuckled softly, "I've been contracted to kill you."

Two

"You've been hired to kill me?" Nikolai asked incredulously.

"That's right. But, don't worry. I'm only after your identity, not your actual life." Yuri divided his attention between Nikolai and the chessboard. He was trying to extract a black czarina from a white monk's pin. He moved the other pieces, trying to outflank the attacking monk.

Nikolai's face hardened. "Why are you looking for me? I don't know you—do I?"

"No, we've never met." A mischievous grin tugged at the corners of Yuri's mouth. He gave up on the chess problem. "But, I know what you look like." He fished a film slate out of his coat pocket and slid it across the table. "Have a look."

The film slate was a common type sold at any corner electronics market, or drug hut. Nikolai paged through a dozen different holographic pictures taken from various angles and perspectives, all dated within the last month. Buttons at the bottom of the film slate enabled him to rotate the view. The background was of corridors and eating halls in the Korolev Domes on Luna. Two were of him assembling hardware in a lab.

He raised an indignant eyebrow. "Where did you get these? Did you take them?"

Yuri slipped the film slate back into his fur-lined coat. "No, not me, but they were taken—let's leave it at that and say no more about it."

Nikolai frowned. "Who hired you?"

"Can't tell you that, either. Not because I don't want to, you see, but because I don't really know. The kind of jobs I take on—" he spread his hands apart. "I'd really like to tell you, but there'd be trouble if I said more."

Nikolai's throat tightened with fear. "Are you with Internal Security?"

The idea amused the stranger. "I have affiliated myself with them from time to time, or they with me, but I don't work directly for them, no." He chuckled affably at the thought.

Nikolai rose from the table. "I don't have time for puzzles. Whatever you're selling, I'm not interested." He made to leave, the other man half-rose, too.

"No, wait." Something in his voice, a plaintive note, held Nikolai back. "Sit down, give me a chance to explain. Please."

He did so, slowly. He was curious, despite himself. Who is this man? he wondered. What does he want? He's not an Outworlder, his accent was pure Muscovite.

"Let's see some identification first," he demanded.

Without hesitation, Yuri slid an ident card out of a leather protective holder. Nikolai curiously examined the recorded data. The card gave a local address, probably false. The biometric measurements for size and weight appeared to fit the other man, though.

"Do you work on one of the orbital factories?"

"Me? Ikon, no! I've hardly been outside of Moscow."

"I thought not." He handed the card back. "You don't have the look of an Outworlder. Who are you, cobber?"

"I told you my name. Yuri Tur."

Nikolai grimaced. "What I meant is, why are you here, looking for me? Why does someone want my identity erased?"

A sunny smile broke across Yuri's face. His teeth were white and evenly spaced. "Well, now, that's a different question altogether. What you really want to know is why I'm in the Warren at all, if I'm not affiliated with any space project. Right?"

Nikolai let stern silence serve as his response.

Yuri poured himself another cup of coffee. "I don't blame you for being suspicious, Sholokhov. Warrens are supposed to be secure and strictly off-limits to ordinary mudballers like me. However," he winked slyly, "even the best security measures can be outwitted, if you know how."

"And you have these talents?" Nikolai, dubious.

"I have my moments." Yuri drank his coffee. "The Warren is a self-contained arcology; everybody knows that. But even they have to get rid of excess refuse: they can't recycle everything. I have some drag with the chief operator who sends out the garbage cars at the end of the day." He rubbed a thumb over his fingers to convey the universal sign for a bribe. "These cars return once they've dumped their loads into the organic recyclers, and the process itself isn't very efficient. There's always some bits remaining in the bottom. One can hide oneself under that trash if he doesn't mind the smell. Once inside the Warren, I cleaned myself up and came here. I figured you'd come to the canteen eventually." He ended cheerfully, "My good luck it was sooner rather than later, eh?"

He put aside his coffee and lit a machine-made cigarette of makhorka tobacco.

"I started looking for you when I got word you would be entering Moscow on the 1715 hour train. Our contact on Dark Side alerted us as to your arrival. I had to spread around a few tsar notes until I found a porter who remembered your face. He told me you were going to the Warren.

That's when I slipped through the back way to wait for you." He crushed out the half-smoked cigarette. (Nikolai soon realized the man hardly ever smoked one past the midpoint before stubbing it out.)

Yuri continued: "I'm here for a specific reason, Sholokhov. My *vozhd*, my superior, sent me here to pick you up. He buys and sells information, you see. Somehow, he got wind of you and wants to talk. You don't have to go, if you don't want to," he added hastily. "I'm not going to force you. I don't work that way. It's not my style."

"What happens if I decide to report you to the bluecaps instead? They might be interested in someone who can so easily flout state security measures."

Yuri was unmoved by the threat. "You're laboring under the assumption I would still be around when you returned." He flashed another easygoing smile. "You have a name on me, nothing else. A man can change his name quickly if he has enough *blat* with the right officials."

Nikolai had no reason to doubt this man had recourse to that influence if he needed it. He was also fairly certain Yuri belonged to the Russian underworld.

He had the look: Smart clothes, well-groomed, self-assured manner. Who acted that way, other than state officials or high-ranking members of the criminal underworld?

And this fellow was no ordinary state official, that was for sure. Something in Nikolai's gut told him this was so.

He examined the problem from different angles. What can I do about it?

Only one way to find out. Go fishing.

"Why is anyone interested in me? I haven't done anything."

Yuri rolled his shoulders. "Like I said, my *vozhd* wants to talk to you. I don't know why. Forgive me, but you don't seem very interesting. Still, when he tells me to march, I don't ask how far; I just go."

"I think I'd rather stay here and have my breakfast, if it's all the same to you."

Yuri started gathering his things. "I'll tell him you weren't interested. That'll be the end of it as far as you're concerned, but I'll probably get a tongue-lashing for not bringing you in." His straight white teeth gleamed. "That's not your concern, though."

Nikolai mulled it over. Maybe this was the diversion he needed to take his mind off things. Today was Monday. In three days he would go to the Union House for his Privilege, but he wasn't doing himself any favors sitting around his room, letting the anxiety build.

Of course, these people wanted to question him about the Star Whisper Project. That much was evident. Hell, he wouldn't even be in Moscow if it weren't for the fact his Privilege had come due. Despite the security clamp down after the Project started gathering starsign, Nikolai's superior didn't have the heart to cancel his leave. A man had paid his social duties and earned his Privilege. No superior would stand in the way of that; not if he didn't want to find a metal shiv slipped between his vertebrae by a disgruntled employee.

Not to mention the fact Yuri could give Nikolai access to goods and services one couldn't get elsewhere. More than local and state governments, the Russian underworld had an air of authority and mystique about them most men admired.

Nikolai made up his mind. "Okay, I'll go with you, but if I don't like what I see, I leave. Fair enough?"

Yuri's smile broadened. "I couldn't ask for more."

The *elektrichka* trundled across the stone embankments of the Yauza River and sped past the rail line that branched off towards Kaliningrad. The canopy of the carriage was tuned to transparency; cold stars glinted through the trees speeding past. With the interior of the car dimmed, Nikolai felt like an animal inside a grotto, peering at the night sky from the safety of a warm den. There weren't many people on board the commuter train this early in the morning; he and Yuri practically had an entire car to themselves.

Fifteen minutes past the Yauza River, and after the conductor checked their passes, Yuri nudged him in the ribs. "Come on," he muttered under his breath. "Now that the conductor is gone. . . ."

Nikolai followed the man towards the end of the swaying car and through a sliding connecting door. They stepped outside into a blast of cold morning air. The train was chugging through a dense stand of birch and maple. The foliage had already turned and fallen, carpeting the forest floor in an amber and russet mosaic. The sky to the east was beginning to lighten. The woods had an eerie atmosphere of gloomy tranquility on the cusp of dawn. It was like something out of a fantasy story, surreal and magical.

The train slowed as it approached a winding grade.

"Here's where we get off." Yuri climbed down to a bottom rung at the end of the carriage. His breath frosted on the morning air. "Watch how you step."

The electric commuter train labored as it neared the top of the grade. At the right moment, Yuri swung off and landed on the damp ground with a couple of little hops. Nikolai judged the distance, had to wait for an outcropping of exposed rock to pass by before he too leapt from the bottom rung. Misjudging, he sprawled on the wet leaves. Getting up, he was relieved to see Yuri wasn't laughing at his clumsiness.

"It takes a bit of practice." He produced a couple of

string-bags from a pocket as the lights from the last car of the *elektrichka* disappeared around a bend. "We have to keep up appearances."

Nikolai took one. "Okay."

Yuri struck off into the woods, following an old game trail. They stopped to pick mushrooms here and there so they'd have something to show for their effort. Nikolai hadn't been mushroom hunting since he was a child. He'd forgotten how many species there were. Yuri helped him out from time to time by saying: "Those are poisonous," or "You don't want that one, try these."

They weren't the only ones turning over leaves and poking behind mossy rocks. Other men with caps turned inside out, or bulging kerchiefs swinging from gnarled hands, hunted in the early morning gloom.

Three young men saw them working the edge of a shadowed glen and cautiously approached.

"Any luck?" one called from behind a stand of bracken.

Yuri hefted his half-filled bag and pointed in the opposite direction. "We came upon a good patch of milk mushrooms over there. I think we got them all, but you never know."

"Thanks, uncle. We'll check it out."

"Yeah," Yuri said under his breath, "you do that." He turned to Nikolai. "Almost there. You going to make it?"

"I hadn't expected to do this much walking my first couple of days back. My legs are killing me. I'm not used to a one gee field."

"When we're done we'll catch a train back to Moscow on the other side of that grade, and I'll treat you to a bathhouse. How does that sound?"

Nikolai didn't want to be beholden to this man. It might

31

not be such a good idea, in the long run. "I'm all right. Let's keep going."

"It's not much further," Yuri promised.

To Nikolai's relief, it wasn't. Another two hundred meters found them in open wood. In the middle of the glen, among the birches, was a *posad:* a trading settlement comprised of a dozen carts and half as many trailers. There were pots and pans hung out to dry, and wet linen flapping heavily in the wind. The smell of wood smoke and frying bacon drifted through the camp. He saw people setting up stalls, yawning and scratching, preparing for a new day.

Someone in camp called out in a gruff voice: "Hey, leave some of that coffee, you shithead. I haven't had mine yet."

"Too late, that's the last cup."

"You bastard, I'll tell the *vozhd.*"

"Go ahead. He's the one who took it!"

A third man laughed, then they all joined in. Nikolai had the impression they were a tight knit group roughing it in the birch and pine. Close enough to the rail line so people could visit and shop for black market items, far enough from Moscow's environs to keep the bluecaps off their backs. A happy den of wolves.

"I didn't know this place was here," he said.

"These trading settlements spring up all over the place like boils, and then disappear about as quick," Yuri explained. "Once the location becomes too well known, the police have to do something about it, you see. That's when we pack up and move down or back up the line a few kilometers. Then we're back in business for another three months."

"Is this where you live?"

Yuri became evasive. "I visit here sometimes."

They entered the encampment. The wares set out for

selling were all top-notch. Mostly food goods, clothes and tobacco, along with electronic items like telecomps, suspensor harnesses (military issue), 'nocs, and the occasional music or televisor system. Nikolai recognized a Shadowlight dish, used to tap into and read the coded language passing between global satellites. He remembered Yuri telling him they sold and bought information here. If this was indeed the case, he realized, then they were more than adequately prepared for such a venture.

But what was the information sold, and who was the buyer? He couldn't fathom it. In this day and age, with bankrupt nations and depleted armies, there was no call for this type of international espionage operation, mainly because there was no way to finance it. He suddenly had a brainwave: Unless the intelligence bought (stolen?) from one Russian organization was turned around and sold to another.

That actually made sense. The organs making up the Confederation often vied with one another for more funding and control within their own fiefdoms. Hell, even the Russian Dark Side colonies were not above siphoning money from lesser projects to insure their own prosperity.

"Yuri! Good to see you, cobber." A lean Ukrainian limped up, a fully charged shattergun cradled in one arm. "How long have you been here?"

"Just arrived. Nikolai, this is Alek Petrovich, one of my compatriots. Alek, this is my friend, Nikolai; he's from Moscow."

Alek gave Nikolai a polite nod. "You want to see the boss, I suppose?" he asked Yuri.

"If it's not inconvenient. Why, something happen?"

Alek eyed Nikolai suspiciously, appeared to resolve some inner conflict regarding the security of the situation.

"About what you'd expect. We're trying to get ready in time, but. . . ." He spat on the ground. "You know what we're up against."

"Mm."

Another sidelong glance at Nikolai, back to Yuri. "Have you heard? We lost Ivanovich, I'm afraid."

"No!" Yuri was visibly upset.

"The MKD picked him up two days ago." Alek hawked up phlegm and spat. "There's been talk about going in to get him out, but we might not have time to mount that kind of operation before—"

"Yes, yes," Yuri hurriedly interjected. He scratched his head. "That's too bad. Well, perhaps something can be done for him afterwards."

"I hope so. He's a good guy."

"Can we see the boss?"

"Come, I'll take you."

Alek led them to a trailer parked in the middle of a copse of pine. Wood smoke drifted through the tops of the trees like a gossamer web. A large tarpaulin of shycloth provided protection from the elements, and, Nikolai guessed, camouflage from the air. Four men stood idly around, shatterguns riding on broad shoulders. No one looked directly at him or Yuri, but Nikolai had the distinct notion they saw everything that needed to be seen. This fact struck home when one of the gunmen, a glowering Uzbeki, inspected their string-bags. He lifted his cold gimlet eyes in mute inquiry.

"We did some mushroom picking on the way here," Yuri smiled, not at all intimidated. The gunman returned the sacks and resumed his post without a word.

Yuri mounted a flight of wooden steps and stomped his feet on a rustic porch built flush against the trailer. A handful of chairs were thrown haphazardly around a rough-hewn oak table. "Hey, you, Mintz." He banged a fist on the side of the metal trailer. "You awake yet? Get up, bastard."

A muffled voice called from within: "Be right out. Get yourself some breakfast, will you?"

Yuri pitched his string-bag down on the table and went to a side-tray laden with delicacies. He motioned for Nikolai to join him. "We'll eat first," he explained, "and then Mintz will talk to you."

"Is Mintz your boss?"

Yuri slathered caviar on a thick slice of brown bread and bit into it lustily. "He's more than that," he said, chewing. "He runs the twenty-seven *rayony* that make up Moscow. He goes by many names, but Mintz is the one I know him by. Does that surprise you?"

Twenty-seven districts, Nikolai thought grimly, the final clue—as if one were needed. He *had* fallen among the *blatari,* the men of the underworld. It wasn't completely un-expected; he'd had suspicions when he first met Tur. Still, having the fact validated was something of an event for him.

"I thought that was the case when I met you. You have the look of a scoundrel about you, you know."

Laughing, Yuri opened a bottle of Moldavian wine. He poured for Nikolai, too, and they drank a toast together to the rising sun and all scoundrels everywhere.

Nikolai was beginning to like this strong, charismatic thief he had befriended. He couldn't help it; Yuri always had a beguiling laugh for whatever situation he found him-self in. The man positively exuded goodwill and confidence. It was hard not to like and trust anyone with those charac-teristics.

"Yuri, tell me the truth. What does your boss want with me?"

He chewed another wedge of toast thoughtfully before

answering. "I don't know." He swallowed, lowered his voice a shade. "Listen, Nikolai, I've taken something of a liking to you. I think you're okay, understand? You're in no danger here; I want you to know that."

The fact Yuri saw fit to mention it gave Nikolai pause. "What kind of danger might that be?"

"I promise you no harm will come to you. It would be a great favor to me personally if you cooperated with my *vozhd*. Mintz is a very authoritative man for all of his diminutive stature." He leaned in close. "He's so powerful he has his own wo—"

A metal screen door to the trailer banged open. "Hello, Yuri. Glad to see you're back where you belong. You brought a friend with you, too. Good job."

Yuri brightened. "Mintz!" He threw his arms wide and the two men greeted one another with spine-cracking embraces and smacking kisses. Nikolai thought the scene had less an air between superior and subordinate than that of equals. When they parted Mintz asked him:

"Have you had something to eat, young man?"

"Yes, sir." He indicated an open tin of smoked salmon and a half-eaten package of crackers. "It was excellent. Thank you for your hospitality."

Mintz was a short man, wiry, with animated movements, deep-set eyes, and a strong mouth. His hair was stone gray and shorn close to his skull, military style. He sported a neatly trimmed beard, but dressed simply: dark blue trousers, brown shirt with the cuffs rolled to his elbows, and heavy boots completed his peasant wardrobe. He had a gold earring and diamond temple studs on either side of his narrow, feline face.

He jammed fists on slim hips. "Well, here we are! Sit down, I won't keep you long. I suppose Yuri has already told you why you're here?"

Before he could answer, Yuri said, "Not really." He pulled out chairs and poured a round of wine for everyone. "I thought I'd leave that up to you, Mintz."

The Russian underworld boss tugged an ear lobe. "Quite right, too. Nevertheless, you do have some idea, don't you, Nikolai?"

They settled into their respective seats. Nikolai cleared his throat.

"I expect you want to question me about the Star Whisper Project."

Mintz leaned back in his leather chair. "This is an intelligent young man here, Yuri. We were right to focus on him."

Yuri polished off the last piece of toast and caviar, and brushed the crumbs from his thick hands. "He's a good guy, Mintz. We can trust him."

"Nikolai, do you know what my business is?" Mintz sipped his wine, waiting for an answer.

"Yuri mentioned you buy and sell information."

"You saw the Starlight dish when you came into camp? Of course you did, with your expertise how could you not recognize it for what it was? It would be foolish for me to deny it; I won't even try. Yes, I buy and sell information. But not just to anyone, mind. I'm not a whore. Just because I have something someone wants doesn't mean I'll sell it to them, even if they meet my price. There is more to business—any business—than that. A man must trust another man. Especially in these times. Don't you agree?"

"As a matter of fact, I do."

Mintz lifted a finger to signal he wanted his wine glass refilled. Yuri complied, and then lit a cigarette and relaxed.

The *vozhd* said, "We know why you're here." He tapped

the oak table between them. "On Earth, I mean. Your Privilege came due, and despite the security measures enacted, you were given a pass to return to Moscow. Correct?"

"Yes, sir."

"That's when you became known to me. You see, Nikolai, a man in my position has feelers out everywhere. Naturally, my contacts are more reliable closer to Moscow, but I have men in all the Russian offworld colonies. That includes those on Dark Side which are military, or scientific, in nature. It goes without saying, I have eyes in the orbital factories as well—and not a few of the Western ones."

Mintz paused.

"I'm not a scientific man. My fields of expertise are economics and political science, not astrophysics. You must bear with me, okay?"

"No problem," Nikolai said.

"I know you are working on an ultra-secret project involving the construction of a radio dish in Sharonov crater. I'd venture to say it is the largest radio dish ever built."

Nikolai nodded wordlessly. "The crater is seventy-four kilometers in diameter. The dish will be half that."

"I understand the receiver won't cover the entire concavity of the crater, and will look like an asterisk when it's completed?"

"That's correct. A computer program, actually an enslaved AI, will integrate and refine the signal from the distant points of reflective mesh of the asterisk structure."

"That's a bit too technical for me, and probably not important for what I need to know," frowned Mintz. "It's located on the far side of the moon because that side always faces away from the Earth. Am I right there?"

"You are. There's too much electromagnetic radiation bleeding off the Earth, you see. That much interference swamps out faint signals, no matter what type of filtering devices you use. The far side of the moon also faces the ecliptic, so scientific study can be done on the planets of the solar system, as well as the sun." Nikolai didn't say: And other stars.

"And there's no atmosphere on Luna to attenuate a signal."

"That's true, it's a vacuum."

"Now, I want to be sure we're talking about the same place." Mintz squinched up his eyes as if he were recalling data unfamiliar to him. "Sharonov crater: an almost perfect bowl crater now that it's bulldozed and dug out with shaped-tactical micronukes. Latitude twelve-point-four degrees, longitude one hundred eighty-six-point-seven degrees. Is that the one?"

Nikolai said diplomatically, "Yes, sir."

"Call me Mintz, please. We strive for informality around here. Nikolai, I know a lot of construction is going on up there right now. Particularly since the von Neuman machines started mining the water-ice clathrate in the southern pole."

"Dark Side is a busy place, yes."

"The question remains, Nikolai, why Sharonov?"

"I'm not sure I understand what you mean."

"All Dark Side colonies are located near the South Pole and the open-pit ice mines there. Kiev II, the Apollo Shield Domes, the 'Merican underground complex in Mare Ingenii. That makes sense; it costs money and energy to transport the water-ice necessary for life support systems a great distance—one-sixth gravity doesn't change logistics *that* much. So why Sharonov? Why use a crater so distant from the other, more well established colonies, on Dark Side?"

"Well, the shape—"

"Is not that important." Mintz beamed a tolerant smile, one reserved for polite arguments. "I'm sorry, but there are other craters better suited for the engineering purpose in question. Racah comes immediately to mind, and it has the added benefit of being closer to the Pole than Sharonov. There are literally thousands of others; the far side of the moon is pockmarked with them. With very little maria there, the choice is unlimited."

His look was piercing. "It further begs the question why this was built in the first place. Extremely large for high resolution, ultra-secret, and camouflaged—oh, yes, I know the reflective mesh used for the dish is manufactured to resemble the Lunar regolith. Why build a radio dish like that in the first place? To study the stars? Bah! A volume of space two hundred light years in diameter around Sol includes something on the order of ten thousand of those stars. Will Sharonov study each in turn? I think not."

Nikolai sought Yuri's guidance, but he was staring off in the distance, absorbed in his own deep thoughts. No help there; the man was smoking cigarettes halfway down and stubbing them out with unconscious regularity. Nikolai doubted he'd heard or followed any part of the conversation thus far.

Mintz waited patiently. Nikolai squirmed. What should I do? How much should I tell him about the starsign?

He hadn't minded reaffirming what Mintz already seemed to know, or validating facts: the location and shape of Sharonov, for instance. But Mintz had delved into more sensitive territory and Nikolai wasn't sure he wanted to compromise what he knew.

He chose a middle ground. "You're unusually well informed."

Mintz made a throwaway gesture. "A man in my position has to be if he wants to survive." He pretended not to notice Nikolai's vacillation. "I will tell you exactly why the site was picked in one word: Security."

Nikolai gave ground. "It's no secret Sharonov crater is a long way from other Dark Side colonies. I'm afraid any modern Lunar map can divulge that much. Again, the problem is one of isolating oneself from other radio signals."

Mintz rubbed a contemplative finger around the rim of his wine glass until it emitted a high resonant whine. "Nikolai, what kind of experiments does a radio dish perform?"

This was safer territory, and he launched into a complete description to bide time. "It can investigate all sorts of natural phenomenon. Spectral analysis. Interferometry. It can even bounce radar signals off the planets in the Solar System." He shrugged. "The uses are endless."

Mintz's next question caught Nikolai off guard. "What is a radio dish's main purpose?" He reached out his hand, grappling for the right words. "What is its main function?"

Goddamn, he knows. He *knows*.

"A radio dish listens," Mintz stated with finality. A strange light welled in his deep-set eyes. "It is, first and foremost, a receiver that listens for signals from celestial objects, whether those signals be natural or man-made."

He leaned forward intently. "Or *alien*."

Three

Nikolai set his wine glass down, trying hard to retain his composure.

Yuri jumped up in a wreath of pungent tobacco smoke, grabbed the empty glass about to tumble off the table's edge. "You want a refill?"

"No, thanks," he mumbled back.

Yuri slumped down and continued chain-smoking. He appeared not to have heard what Mintz said, or if he had heard, he appeared not to care. He sat oblivious, chin in hand, one finger laid along the side of his aquiline nose.

At first, Nikolai toyed with the idea of discrediting Mintz's theory of alien signals, before slowly, grudgingly, he realized it would be a waste of time.

He knows, he reflected, but how? Surely, Lunar security is better than that? Precautions were taken. . . .

Yuri's words came back to him, belatedly:

Mintz is a very powerful man . . . he runs all twenty-seven *rayony.*

Yes, Nikolai realized, a man like that, bending all his energy and resources towards a problem, would have no trouble ferreting out secrets from any organization. He was a *vozhd,* a supreme leader of the Moscow underworld. Nothing would be out of reach if he truly desired it.

Where did that power originate? he went on to wonder. What was Mintz planning to do with the knowledge now that he had it? More importantly, what *could* he do?

He was still wrestling with these questions when Mintz

spoke. "This discovery is explosive and awe-inspiring: pick your own adjective, they all fit." He clumped to the wooden rail encircling the porch; loose boards creaked under his boots. His next words took on an evangelical air.

"What would the Earth give to know this? A world ravaged by plague, resources tapped out, hope gone, populations bled white by war, thinned by famine. What would a man pay to know it was possible to survive? And not only *survive*—" slanting sunlight highlighted the individual whiskers of his beard, giving a weird coronal effect "—but conquer what are now thought to be insurmountable problems? What can men do with such knowledge? Can you answer that, Mr. Sholokhov?"

"No, I can't. I don't think anybody can."

Nikolai had heard the same debate raging among policy makers and administrators involved with the Project before leaving Dark Side. For all he knew, it still raged. There were two camps: one wanted to release the information right away for the very reasons Mintz enumerated; the other was more circumspect. Not out of hubris, they acknowledged, but fear.

The signals were alien. No one knew what that ultimately meant for the sliver of humanity that remained on Earth. How would it affect the social dynamics of a world already on the brink?

Nikolai was a member of the first camp, but acknowledged the arguments of the second had merit. Nevertheless, he thought an official announcement should be made before another group noticed the signals and published the results, stealing Russian thunder.

Despite the shape the world was in, he believed the scientific process shouldn't be short-circuited. Discoveries had to be announced so others could verify or disprove the data.

That was the way science had worked for millennia. Purification of the truth was the only way to insure valid results.

But, with a discovery of this magnitude, and under this social climate, the old ways might prove more harm than good.

He sighed. For him, it was a moot point. No one in the higher echelons bothered to solicit his thoughts regarding the problem. He was a low functionary, a cog on a great wheel turning deep within the machinery. The only reason he came to the attention of the Project Director in the first place was because his Privilege came due at a most inopportune time. That had caused consternation enough in Sharonov. Nikolai counted himself lucky to have been released from his work contract and allowed his leave. He wasn't about to do anything stupid to jeopardize that now, if he hadn't already.

One of the camp guards loped up to the trailer, beckoning to Mintz. They spoke in engaged tones for several minutes. The *vozhd* nodded once towards the trailer. Nikolai had the fleeting impression someone was inside, perhaps listening or waiting for Mintz to finish interrogating him.

As the two men conversed, he marshaled his thoughts and planned how to extricate himself from this novel situation.

He had no illusions about diverting Mintz from the truth. The fact the man knew the nature of the signals was more damning than any technical facts Nikolai could describe firsthand.

It slowly dawned on him: Mintz might not know everything. He knows about the Project, sure, but he might not be aware of the final interpretation of the data. If that's true, then do I dare tell him?

An inner voice cautioned: No, keep a bargaining chip. You might need it later.

He decided to heed the advice. He knew he was taking an enormous gamble, especially if Mintz ever discovered he was withholding important details. Still, a lifetime of restrained social contact and mistrust of authority forced him to leave a flight square for the future. No other man would have done differently, he was sure.

Mintz dismissed the guard and resumed his seat and the thread of their conversation. "Am I correct, Nikolai? These alien signals were picked up by that dish?"

"You're right, Mintz. There are several point-like X-ray sources moving around Kornephoros—"

"Where . . . ?"

"In the constellation Hercules, the star that makes up his knee beneath Corona Borealis. It's a G-type, about 105 light years distant. More luminous than our sun. Also a close binary, if I'm not mistaken. There's little doubt these sources are spacecraft; they're crisscrossing one another and leaving radio wakes. They appear to generate X-rays because they're traveling close to the speed of light." He held his hands open at his sides. "That's all I know. Once the initial discovery was made, the Director of the project clamped the lid down. Any new data is shared among an echelon of scientists, and I'm not part of that group."

Mintz digested this news. The sun had climbed into the treetops to burn away the last of the morning fog. There was more noise in the camp, too, more movement now that dawn had lengthened into another day. People were coming in from Moscow to sample the wares.

The *vozhd* rose to his feet and thrust out his hand. "I want to thank you for your time," he said, friendly. "I hope I have not made you too uncomfortable with my questions, but what you have to say simply fascinates me. I want to show my gratitude. Please, stay as long as you want with our group."

Yuri awoke from his trance and stubbed out a cigarette. "Thanks, Mintz, but I promised to take him back to Moscow. Maybe we'll hit the baths and have a bottle of cold beer. That is, if you don't need us any longer."

"Whatever you think is best." Mintz steered him to the end of the porch, away from Nikolai. They talked shortly and in guarded whispers. He parted with a final instruction: "Ten minutes, no more."

"Okay, Mintz," Yuri promised.

The leader of the Russian underworld bowed curtly in Nikolai's direction. "Have a good day, Mr. Sholokhov. If you wish to visit us again, feel free to do so." He thumped down the wooden steps in his heavy boots. He met a group of men waiting in the center of the camp and began talking to them with sweeping, animated gestures. The men were dressed like government officials belonging to some secret organization.

"Who are those men?" asked Nikolai. "They hover around Mintz like honeybees around a bowl of molasses."

Yuri found Nikolai's statement apropos. "They're his Greek Chorus. They sing his praises." He uncovered a dish of sliced tomatoes and popped several into his mouth after sprinkling them with a pinch of salt. He gestured towards the retreating back of Mintz. "You did him a big favor, you know."

Nikolai down played his part. "I don't think I told him anything he didn't already know."

"True." Another slice went into his mouth. "But knowing something, and talking to a man who has experience, gives a new perspective. That's what Mintz wanted."

He wiped his hands on linen. "Now, he wants to show you his appreciation."

Nikolai was mindful of the breakfast table. "Well, I wouldn't mind having a couple of tins of smoked salmon for myself, if that's all right—"

Yuri's booming laughter cut him off. "Nothing so prosaic as tinned salmon for you." He sobered, clapped a big paw on Nikolai's shoulder. "I told you Mintz is a big wheel. Perhaps one of the two or three most influential men in Russia. You've really helped him out, and me, too, by coming here. He wants to show you how much he appreciates your talking to him about this space matter, by doing something extraordinarily special for you."

"What might that be?"

Yuri's voice sank. "Something he doesn't do for just anybody. He must really trust you, or feels that he owes you one."

Nikolai wished Yuri wasn't always so circumspect. "Come to the point," he said.

The other man softly tapped a knuckle on the screen door of the trailer. "Mintz has a Japper in there. God only knows where he got her. One of the Mongolian wars from a couple of decades ago, I'd guess, but she's worth her weight in gold."

Nikolai felt the blood drain from his face. "There's a . . . a *woman* in there?" His muscles tensed. The stunning knowledge soured the Moldavian wine in his stomach.

"I told you he was a wheel." Yuri glanced at the watchdisk implanted on the back of his wrist. "You'd better get going. You can't do anything you want to her," he cautioned with a wolfish grin, "but you can touch her; she's yours for ten minutes. Some men masturbate over her, you might try that. She won't mind. Well, what are you waiting for?"

Nikolai's mouth was dry. He trembled at the thought of Mintz's woman—any woman—on the other side of that wall. He started, stopped, tried to go through the door a second time. Finally, he gripped Yuri's arm.

"Won't you come with me?"

Yuri Tur was taken aback. "I didn't think you wanted someone watching you."

Nikolai blinked owlishly until he realized what Yuri meant. He removed his glasses and polished the lenses so his hands would have something to do. "I—I don't want you there for that reason," he stammered. "I'm not going to do anything like that to her, I couldn't." Pleasure himself while looking at her raw body? That idea was more alien than her actual presence.

He caught himself wringing his hands, stopped. Would he be this pathetic inside the Union House in three days? he wondered angrily. Paralyzed, like a sparrow?

He looked down at his muddy shoes, ashamed. "I'm afraid," he mumbled, surprised he had spoken the words out loud.

"Of a Japper whore?" Yuri's next question came soft: "Listen, have you ever been around a woman before, Sholokhov?"

"No," he croaked back.

"Ikon, you should have told me. When you go to the Union House they prepare you beforehand. I thought you were an old horse around women."

Nikolai shook his head dumbly, blood roaring in his ears.

"Well, don't be embarrassed; everyone has a first time." He slid an arm around Nikolai's neck and gave a reassuring squeeze. "I won't tell anyone. Come on, I'll introduce you." He opened the screen door and went inside the trailer.

Nikolai nervously tagged along, trying not to stumble on the doorstep and appear any more foolish than he already felt.

Yuri cleared his throat. "Yasu?"

They were in a large room with bulletproof skylights. The furniture was a mismatch of Asian and Western styles, the red carpet thick-piled, walls paneled in blond wood.

Nikolai noticed a low cherry wood table in the middle of the open space, with small porcelain bowls and chopsticks carefully laid around a black lacquer tray: remnants of breakfast. A hint of sandalwood hung in the air. A hibachi, fire damped, stood upon a bed of firebricks. Potted plants decorated the room, and brass sculptures of long-legged birds peeked between the long leaves. The air of the room was quiet, lived in. Bioluminescent lanterns hung like ripe fruit from cedar rafters.

Nikolai's heart hammered against his rib cage. A stray thread of smoke from the three-legged hibachi stung his eyes, and he wiped them clear.

"Yasu, are you home?" Yuri called again.

A noise from the far side of the room turned both men around. A shoji panel slid aside and a woman entered. Head bowed, she walked across the lush carpet. She knelt on a cushion in one fluid motion, flaring the embroidered hem of her silk kimono.

"Yasu, I want you to meet a friend of mine, Nikolai Sholokhov. He wants to spend a few minutes with you. Do you mind?"

The woman bowed her head a fraction deeper, held it there. Her hair was arranged with long silver pins, but long dark ropes slipped off her round shoulders nevertheless and cascaded forward. Catching his breath, Nikolai stared, rapt. His eyes jumped from her face to neck to arms to narrow waist, drinking it all in, almost savagely.

In her early fifties, Yasu's dark almond-shaped eyes and red bow of a mouth had a thin spiderweb of crow's feet at their corners.

Her dark lashes brushed her cheek, and once, when they fluttered, his heart lifted at the sight. The bone structure and planes of her face were exquisite: high, exotic cheekbones and a sculpted jawline. She wore no makeup, other than a thin dusting of face powder and perfectly applied lipstick. Her body was thin, curves lost inside the soft enveloping folds of a dark blue kimono with yellow nightingales flying across the front. A silver obi with gold interwoven threads was tied around her waist.

Yuri gently pushed Nikolai who stood transfixed. "Go ahead, touch her." He smiled encouragingly at the helpless look he got in return. "It's all right, I promise you. Here," he got down on one knee, "like this, in front of her."

Nikolai followed suit, feeling stupid and clumsy in the presence of this perfect creature—the first woman he had ever seen up close and in person. Kneeling, he became aware of something he hadn't noticed while standing: body warmth and a slight trace of jasmine perfume exuded from her skin. His mind swirled at the thought of her underneath the kimono.

He boldly reached out and took her hand. Cupping it between his, he bent over it, eyes closed, and inhaled the fragrance.

"*Krasnaya,*" he whispered, pressing the warm hand against his cheek.

"Yes," Yuri said with polite indifference, "I suppose she is beautiful, in her own way."

Nikolai examined, in minute detail, her hand. He marveled over the delicate bones, the slim fingers, their painstakingly lacquered nails. The blue tracery of veins lying quietly beneath translucent skin, the tender crease of skin where her wrist bent.

"Yasu," Yuri instructed, "show us your breasts."

Complying, the woman loosened her obi. She opened and dropped the kimono around her waist without protest. Her breasts were small with dark crinkled nipples that looked like plums. Nikolai felt his senses galvanize at the sight.

"I wanted to show you something," Yuri said to Nikolai. He carefully parted Yasu's lips with the tips of his fingers. Appalled, Nikolai saw they were sewn with gold wire from the inside, leaving only a small gap through which she could eat and drink.

"The Jappers did that to her," Yuri said. "We don't know why. They don't treat their women like we do over here, you know. They don't have Union Houses. And look at this," he took Yasu's shoulders and gently turned her around, presenting her bare back to view.

She had puckered scars on either side of her spine where rejuv nodules were implanted. Nikolai swallowed, grunted sotto voce: "How old is she, Yuri?"

"Mintz doesn't know." Louder: "Yasu, how old are you?"

She shrugged.

"She could be ancient," Yuri confessed. "There's no way to tell. The nanotechnology inside the nodules constantly repairs the chromosomal telomeres of her cells."

"She'll live for thousands of years." Nikolai, awed.

"Always protected, always loved." Yuri had a queer look on his face. "Locked forever inside a biological prison." He sighed, "Well, no one said our world was perfect. Everyone has his cross to bear, even Yasu. Even me. You too, I guess." He remembered his watchdisk. "Our time's up, we'd better get going."

The two men essayed to their feet. Nikolai bowed. "Yasu, thank you for allowing me to visit you here in your home. I'll always treasure this moment."

She bent her head to acknowledge his praise, the kimono still bundled about her waist. The silver pins in her hair reflected flickering candle flame.

"Goodbye, Yasu," Yuri said, in parting.

Nikolai thought her dark eyes followed them out. He wondered what she was thinking. Were they just more men passing through her life, and nothing more? Would she ever remember him, as he would forever remember her?

Yuri held the door of the trailer open. Nikolai stepped out into bright sunshine and blinked on a new world.

He couldn't stop talking all the way back to Moscow. Yuri said a word here and there, but mostly kept quiet as Nikolai rattled on about what he had seen, and experienced, inside the trailer.

As promised, Yuri brought him to the baths to put a perfect cap to a long and exhilarating day. They went to the private Sundonovski Baths housed in a three-story stucco-fronted building. Rows of large windows on each floor glowered upon the empty boulevard below.

They climbed a circular marble stairway leading to the private level. Huge neoclassical chandeliers marked the way. They changed clothes, showered, went into one of the many hot rooms. The steam opened Nikolai's pores, sweating the impurities from his body. His skin flinched at contact with the hot bench. There were others here, swatting themselves or their friends with dried twigs to promote circulation. The floor was a slick mass of decomposing leaves.

A couple of men recognized Yuri. "How are things going?" one asked, sweating joyously, a filthy towel across his thighs.

"Soon it will be going well," was Yuri's enigmatic reply.

This answer mollified them, and they returned to whacking each other's legs with birch twigs.

Nikolai sat near the red-hot fire bricks, but moved when one of the regular clientele poured half a liter of beer over them and roiling clouds of steam broke in his face.

He and Yuri talked little, each too engrossed in their own thoughts. Nikolai's mind lingered over the events in the trading camp, and Yasu.

When he could take the intense heat no longer, he wrapped a threadbare towel around his waist and padded through a set of double doors towards the showers. Gasping, he sluiced himself with cold water from an ancient spigot.

Drying with a towel that had lost its fringe, he told Yuri, "I'm going for a massage."

Yuri reclined on another bench, a towel draped across his lap. His normally florid face was beet-red and sheened with sweat. "I'll meet you in the pool room. We can talk there."

A masseur met Nikolai exiting the shower stalls and escorted him to a room furnished with long marble tables. Lying on his stomach, he speculated on what Yuri wanted to talk to him about.

Something cool and wet poured between his shoulder blades. Strong fingers dug and kneaded the oil into his taut muscles before moving on to the individually fatigued leg muscles. Nikolai grunted with pleasure as the soreness dissipated.

The masseur took a rough towel from the shelf below the

table and rubbed him down until the chafing brought a tingling rush all over his body. When he finished, the masseur wordlessly carried the soiled linen to a laundry bin.

Nikolai slid off the table onto his naked feet and wandered into the pool room. Marble walls and Corinthian columns surrounded an Olympic-sized pool. The place stank of old chlorine. Sometimes an occasional shout or peal of laughter echoed within the spacious room. He found Yuri paddling happily in one corner of the pool. Nikolai sank down to the edge, legs crossed.

"How do you feel?" Yuri asked. Chlorinated water slopped under his chin.

"Wonderful," Nikolai said, and meant it. He did feel good; better than he had in days, maybe years. "Listen, I want to apologize for going on and on after we left camp. I couldn't help myself, you know. It's just that I . . ." He finished in a wistful tone, "I'd never seen anything like her before in my life."

Yuri pulled himself out of the pool, arm muscles rippling. "Don't let it bother you." He slicked his hair back with both hands. "I was much the same way my first time, only it wasn't with a woman. Hey, it's the way things are now. You can't help that. No one can change what's happened."

"No, I guess not." He noticed an ugly scar on Yuri's right forearm. "What happened there?"

Yuri looked down. "What? Oh that. I used to be a sambo wrestler when I was a teenager. Pretty good, too, for my weight class. I made it all the way to the Moscow semi-finals until I met an opponent who wasn't focused." He rubbed the scar tissue fondly. "He broke my radius bone; compound fracture. It healed badly; that's why this arm is a centimeter shorter than the other. See?"

He stopped a boy in a white smock and ordered a couple of half-liter draft beers. When the drinks came, the two men retired to a marble table underneath a skylight.

Yuri drank down half and smacked his lips with satisfaction. "Ah, that's good. Your beer cold enough?"

"Perfect. Yuri, I want to thank you for everything you've done for me today. It's a steep price, for no more than I've accomplished."

Yuri's eyebrows crawled up his forehead. "How can you say that? You've helped me out a great deal, too."

"By telling your boss what he already knew. . . ."

"That's right."

He sat back in his chair. "I forgot to ask—what do you think about all this?"

Yuri swallowed a mouthful of beer. "About this space matter you discussed with Mintz, you mean?"

"Of course, what else are we talking about?"

Yuri spun his glass around and around on the marble tabletop, making circles with the beads of condensation. "I didn't pay all that much attention, if you must know. I had my mind on other things."

Nikolai started to laugh, stopped when he saw the other man was serious. "You don't think this discovery is important?"

Yuri jerked his shoulders up and down. "How is it going to change anything? Fundamentally, I mean. We're still going to be the same people, aren't we, with the same problems?"

Someone ran past their table and cannonballed into the pool. A few drops sprayed Nikolai in the face.

"Well, yes, but—"

"Mintz found it useful, that was enough." He called for another round of beer. "Even though I work for him, our interests don't always—" he interlocked the fingers of both hands "—dovetail. This time, however, things may be different."

"How are your interests different from his?" Nikolai thought it an innocent question. Yuri's reaction proved otherwise.

"I have several other projects I'm involved with. Areas of interest Mintz doesn't necessarily approve of, although he does finance them from time to time. But only when they suit his purpose."

Nikolai recalled the Ukrainian they met in the camp. "Like getting your friend out of the hands of the MKD?"

Yuri pursed his lips. "That's one—there are others." He lifted the beer to his mouth. "I'm always looking for people I can trust." He threw out a hopeful look before he took a long pull at the bottle.

Nikolai fell deep into thought. He was sure Yuri was trying to sign him on to an illegal conspiracy. I'm already involved with these people. If I don't watch my step, I'll get deeper and deeper. Is that what I want? How do I know where it will end?

"I doubt I can be of much help," he said at last. "I'm only here for two weeks before I return to Dark Side."

"I know, but you can help me get inside the Warren a little easier next time. I can arrive as your guest instead of wetbacking through a refuse train. That's all I'm asking. From time to time, while you're in Moscow. That's all."

Nikolai saw no harm in that. "Okay," he said briefly, "but only on one condition."

"I'm listening."

"Who do you *really* work for?"

"What's the matter, don't you believe I work for Mintz? Why would I lie about that?"

"You do work for him—but only when it suits you. Now come on, give."

The thief drank down the remainder of his beer, wiped his mouth with the back of his hand. "Those are your terms?"

"They are."

Yuri laughed guiltily, as if he remembered being a boy caught with a fistful of dirty pictures. "Okay, I'll tell you." He hitched forward, leaned both elbows on the edge of the table. A cigarette lay between his fingers, smoke laddering into the air. "Have you ever heard of the *Narodnaya Volya*, Nikolai?"

"The People's Will?" The underground movement had been around in one incarnation or another since 1879. "Are you telling me you belong to them?" He shook his head in disbelief. "I never figured you for a reactionary, Yuri."

Yuri appeared pleased Nikolai had misjudged him. "Well, that's exactly what I am, among other things. I oversee a resistance cell right here in Moscow, and I'm always recruiting new men. The men who work for me, or Mintz, have their identities erased from the DataSphere so the bluecaps won't catch on. Interested?"

"I'll have to think about it." This was a detour he hadn't counted on. Joining a reactionary movement was something altogether different from doing an odd job on the side for the underworld.

Nikolai had always been apolitical. Like most people, he found it easier to tack with the prevailing wind blowing out of St. Petersburg than against it. He had nothing personal against the First Minister and his Central Cabinet; actually thought the government was doing well in otherwise impossible conditions.

"Let's meet again, tomorrow night," Yuri proposed.

"There's a delicatessen in GUM, first floor. Tomorrow is a meatless day, but their vegetables are fresh and the vodka ice cold. How does that sound? That should give you enough time to mull over my proposal. What do you say?"

Against his better judgment, Nikolai replied: "I'll be there."

They shook hands to seal the pact. Nikolai exited through a swinging door to a locker room. He took his things off a hook in the wall, dressed, and ran a comb through his tousled hair.

Outside, he drew a deep breath, let it out slowly. What a day! He walked aimlessly, hands in pockets. The events of the day flitted across his mind like the frozen images of a film slate. He was still trying to sort them all out when he realized he had come upon the four-meter-tall iron fence surrounding Union House in Dobrynin Park. He peered through the narrow slats of iron at the grounds where the complex sprawled. It was dusk; bioluminescent security globes floated among the boles of the trees. Nearby, the muted hum of an invisible kill-field warned him and others not to penetrate the railing to gain the grounds. The side-walk underfoot was littered with the dead husks of insects that hadn't known any better.

Other men stood alongside and stared into the park be-yond the fence. Bluecaps ranged up and down the sidewalk, rousting them out if they didn't have proof of an upcoming Privilege session.

"Move along there, brother," one bluecap warned Nikolai. "No loitering around here. Go home."

"My Privilege is Thursday. Can't I stay a while longer?"

The bluecap considered his plea. "Go ahead, then." He ambled off, started shouting at another man. "You there! Yes, you! I've told you not to come around here again but you don't listen. When are you going to get your head out of your ass? You haven't paid social duties in years—" The bluecap applied his shockstick to the man's buttocks. "Now get the hell out of here. I won't warn you again."

The unfortunate man limped away. Men alongside the fence laughed at him. Someone sitting on the sidewalk got up to take the vacated spot on the railing.

Nikolai had enough and started to head home across Vosstaniya Plaza when he saw a line forming at the junction of Smolenskaya Plaza and Arbat Street. He instantly queued, but left when he learned it was only for writing styluses. He set out along Sadovaya Street, checking if he had any spare tokens for an underground tram, when it happened.

Cries of "Thief!" shattered the tranquil twilight. A young man sprinted out of an open bazaar, clutching something in his right hand, casting frightened looks over his shoulder. Two men from the bazaar ran him down and proceeded to beat him savagely. Patrons broke from a market stall and ran to see. Other men joined in and soon it was a free-for-all.

Men with nothing better to do emerged from communal apartments and stores to watch, crowding the streets. Cars honked furiously at the rapidly growing brawl. One three-wheeled Zil edged forward, blaring a single blast on its horn. Suddenly, its windshield starred. Stones and bricks rained down upon the car. The driver stumbled out, dodging and running. A long line of snarled traffic gridlocked the intersection. A hundred men clogged the street. There was a lot of noise.

Someone overturned a vegetable stand. Potatoes and yellow peppers rolled into the street and gutters. Two bluecaps hurried past Nikolai, one barking loudly in a field radio clipped to his helmet. Nikolai whirled to follow the policemen, thinking he would be safer with them. More people arrived to witness the melee, completely blocking the street, hemming him in. One of the officers went down, half-hidden beneath stomping legs. The other bluecap disappeared, too.

Arms and bodies jostled Nikolai. He fought to get away from the center of the throng. An elbow smashed into his stomach, doubling him over. Something cracked across the small of his back and he slumped to his hands and knees, head swimming. Glass cut his knees. He panicked as the full weight of the rioting multitude threatened to crush him. He flailed out and struggled to his feet, heart hammering. The acidic taste of fear scorched his throat. His breath sawed in and out of his lungs.

Several hundred people now clogged Sadovaya. In the distance, sirens wailed helplessly. Nikolai, seeing no other recourse, let himself be swept along with the mindless crowd past a burning Volga sedan. The nauseating stench of burnt flesh made him retch and he was blinded by the billowing black smoke of melting tires. Many cars were on fire or overturned. The hydrogen fuel cell of a Trabant two-seater exploded, splintering and cracking the fiberplas body like an eggshell. Torn and mangled bodies fell away.

To his left, fire ravaged a large Georgian tenement. Its skeletal plaswood frame sagged as load-bearing supports collapsed. The fiery debris tumbled into the street, smothering helpless men caught in its path. Fiery smoke roiled into the street.

Nikolai crawled away on hands and knees from the holocaust, an incoherent scream tearing from his throat. Someone yanked him to his feet, and everyone started running again.

Four

The crowd surged past Mayakovskogo Plaza and Novoslobodskaya Street—a human tidal wave heading for Old Red Square.

For a blessed second, the mob thinned. Nikolai shoved and fought to reach the sidewalk, hoping to find sanctuary inside a church, but the crowd coalesced into a solid throng once more and swept him along like a piece of trash.

He passed a man recently killed. A tattered policeman's uniform covered the mutilated corpse. There were shouts of "Hurrah! Hurrah!" when the mob glimpsed the oriental onion- and pineapple-shaped domes of St. Basil. Something soared overhead and ended in the shivering sound of a huge plate glass window shattering. Shards of glass from a market showered everyone. One boy fell, clawing at his eyes. Nikolai glimpsed a sobbing man clinging desperately to a comlink post like an anchor against the onrushing legion—men caught in a moment of hate and destructive panic.

He sucked in terrified, ragged gasps as he tried to keep his balance in the pressing, sweaty bodies. To his horror, he trampled a young boy who went down in front of him. Across the boulevard someone in a three-wheeler systematically ran down victims, backing up to choose new targets. Shouting obscenities, men rushed to the side of the car and lifted the back wheels off the filthy pavement. Hands smashed windows and pulled the driver out. Nikolai blanched as they pummeled him, one man sadistically lashing the driver with a severed limb.

He cried out at the white-hot pain in his cramping legs and bruised ribs. Blood from his lacerated knees trickled down his shins. He ran through Pushkinskaya Plaza, no longer possessing the strength or the will to challenge the crowd intent on destroying Moscow.

"Hurrah! Hurrah! Hurrah!" The uproar was deafening. They were close to Moscow Square. Nikolai's group moved toward the thousands already packed between St. Basil's and the Kremlin. Among the waving arms he saw stones, rags and even bodies tossed up in the air by the mindless crowd.

A police barricade loomed ahead, strung across Sverdlov Square. Security men with red helmets and mirrored faceplates, armed with riot shields and mercy weapons, stood behind electronic sawhorses.

The barricade bore the full brunt of the onrushing wave. It fell back, but held as reinforcements augmented the barrier. Like a sea, the wave of rioters fell back. The police moved forward, gaining ground. And like a sea the mob came back, a living wall of human flesh crashing through the flimsy cordon to meld with the throng in Old Red Square.

"HURRAH!" A thunderous cry of victory. Men waved paper handkerchiefs, shirts, linen. An ocean of men shouted, wept and cried oaths.

Someone grabbed Nikolai by the shoulders and spun him around. "We've done it, comrade. We've made it!" His eyes were wide, staring. "It's independence for us all!"

Others lit campfires against the night, scrounging whatever they could find for fuel. Men huddled around the flickering fires, arms clasped, singing, drinking, sometimes weeping. Sporadic fights broke out but these were allowed to die out between the participants. There was an orange glow in the southern sky as a fire swept across the older tenements there. It added illumination to the Square but made the skyline of Moscow into a black frieze. Many wondered aloud if it would be put out soon.

Night deepened, slowly revealing distant starfields. Nikolai wound through the crowds, seeking safety in numbers. He knew if he tried to reach the Warren alone he would more than likely be set upon by roving packs of hooligans. Hours crept by; he kept moving, zombie-like. Long after midnight he remembered Yuri saying there was a coffee shop or eatery in GUM.

Maybe I can pass the night inside the department store, he thought. Yuri might be there, too.

He slipped between the encampments scattered like so many stars throughout the square. An old man with a tattered blanket pinned around his shoulders offered him a bottle of syrupy vodka that smelled of fusel oil. Nikolai waved it off, pushed his way towards GUM.

A big crowd milled around the baroque-style entrance to the department store. He started to go inside when someone guarding the doorway grabbed his collar and pushed him back.

"Where do you think you're going?" The man had a black eye and bruised cheek. A shiverknife at his belt glinted.

Nikolai knocked his hand away with a snarl. "To hell with you. I'm not going back out there. I want to sit down."

They exchanged stares. Nikolai refused to back down. Desperate, hungry, he hoped it would come down to a fight.

The man in the doorway dropped his eyes first. "Look, I have to be careful who I let in. We don't want any trouble here." He jerked a thumb towards the people outside. "If that mob starts up again. . . ." he left the thought unfinished.

Nikolai ran his bluff to the end. "That's your problem, cobber. Now, get out of my way." He shoved the other man aside and entered the emporium's noisy interior.

There was a fountain in the middle of the main walkway. He stopped long enough to splash water on his face and neck before moving down the long aisle. He asked around if anyone knew of a delicatessen on the first floor. Most either shook their heads or pointed in a direction he had already searched. At one point someone shouted to him from one of the iron bridges linking the upper floors, but when he looked they had either gone or realized they didn't recognize him after all. He forgot about it and searched on.

He was about to give up when he saw grim faces behind a curtained window in one of the corner shops. He had to walk around another retail store to find the entrance he wanted.

The delicatessen was packed shoulder-to-shoulder and filled with tobacco smoke and the noise of clinking glasses. Men sat along the baseboards and on counter tops, some lounged under tables. The place looked like it had been torn apart then put back together by someone who didn't care whether the pieces fit.

"Do you want something?" A man, fat forearms resting on a rail behind the counter, asked.

"I'm looking for someone," Nikolai answered presently. He raised his voice so everyone in the shop could hear: "His name is Yuri Tur. Does anyone here know him?"

"I do," a gravelly voice claimed in the back, where the more expensive booths were located.

"Do you know where I can find him?" Nikolai asked.

"No, I've been looking for him, too."

Nikolai gave up. "Can I stay here?" he asked the proprietor.

A man propped against the window answered, "Why the hell not?" He cast a satirical eye over the men hunched in every available square meter of the shop. "—Everybody else is."

General laughter rolled around the stifling room, died. The proprietor swept a welcoming hand. "Sure, go ahead. The more the merrier."

"Have you got anything to eat?"

"Sliced cucumbers."

Nikolai started counting out kopecks. "I'll take a plate."

"You'll take what I've got, and it's not enough to fill a plate."

"All right, then."

A small dish was passed. "Put your money away; it's on the house."

"Yes." A man at the counter puffed away on a briar pipe. "We've already eaten the bastard's larder clean. He doesn't have the heart to gouge you for a dish of wilted cucumbers nobody else wants."

"Thanks." Nikolai wolfed down the half dozen slices.

"What's it like out there, cobber?" a middle-aged, heavyset man next to him asked.

Nikolai chewing, swallowed. "Bad."

"Is that all you have to say?"

"Can't you see he doesn't want to talk about it?" the man with the briar pipe growled. "Leave him alone."

"I was just asking—"

"Well, forget it, will you?"

Everyone went back to what they were doing, which was mostly drinking and talking. Nikolai wedged himself down along the far wall. His head fell wearily between his knees.

I'm so tired, he thought, closing his eyes. If I could only get to the Warren, I'd be safe there.

A sharp kick on the sole of his shoe woke him up. "Hey, you."

Nikolai deliberately brought his head up slowly, counting to ten. "Kick me again," he said between clenched teeth, "and I'll knock your goddamn teeth out, cobber."

The fellow standing over him had a balding head and a hawk-nose that crooked over a thick mustache.

"My name is Feodor Zim."

Nikolai's eyes smoldered. "That gives you the right? I'm not moving, friend. Go somewhere else before I wipe the fucking floor with you."

"I'm the bloke who knows Yuri Tur. We were shouting at one another a few minutes ago over the length of this sardine can. I thought you wanted to talk. I didn't mean any harm."

Part of Nikolai's anger dissipated, but he hadn't liked being kicked. It served to put this stranger in a bad light as far as he was concerned. He scooted over to make room.

Feodor squatted on his heels, a peaked cap folded in his back pocket. "Were you supposed to meet Yuri here? I was."

"Tomorrow night. I hoped he might be hanging around so I came here anyway."

Feodor rubbed a bristly chin. What hair he had on his head lay close to the skull like curled wires. "I've been looking for him, too." He grimaced. "Never find him in this chaos. Still, he knows how to look out for himself."

"I suppose." Nikolai's anger still rankled towards the man.

They heard a sporadic rattle of gunfire from outside.

"It's getting worse out there," Feodor observed. "How about yourself? Where were you headed when all this started?"

"The Warren. I don't think I'll get there now."

"Not tonight you won't," Feodor agreed. "Maybe you'll have better luck tomorrow."

Another burst of gunfire made everyone flinch.

"It's begun comrades," one man, wedged under the counter, said. "You hear it?"

Others nodded fearfully, expectantly.

Nikolai asked Feodor, "What are they talking about? Someone grabbed me in the Square and said the same thing."

"Revolt." Feodor picked his teeth with the edge of a dirty thumbnail. "It's been planned for some time now. They've been waiting for the right moment. Of course, it's doomed to fail, but they knew that ahead of time." He returned a critical glance. "Don't you keep up with the news, comrade?"

"I've been on Dark Side for the past eighteen months. Kiev II. We don't get much political news up there. At least not current."

"Ah," Feodor said, "that explains it." His voice sank to a low rumble. "Are you with the *Narodnaya Volya?*"

"No. Yuri wanted to recruit me, but," he shrugged, not knowing what else to say. His ego was still bruised from the kick. "Are you part of Yuri's cell?"

Feodor revealed a row of nicotine-stained teeth. "That's how we met. What's going on out there," he jerked his head towards the far wall, "is part of a faction within our group. As I said, they will fail, and we will let them. That's for the better because the men who make up the core of the People's Will are more deliberate, more careful." He raised his voice a notch or two so those sitting nearby could listen in if they wanted to. "We are waiting for the right time when success will be assured. We sympathize with the Faction, but do not see profit in throwing our hand in with them at this time. Of course, if they are successful, we will gladly move into the resulting power vacuum. If they fail, as I think they must, we are left the stronger. For us, it is a win-win situation."

"But something must be done, and soon," a rotund man sitting at a table said. "We have already given too much land for peace to those animals in the East. And the Euros are no better; they can't be trusted."

"Yes," another echoed. "Why can't the First Minister understand that for our culture to survive we must fight to keep what we have?"

"We still have Siberia," came a comment from the back of the room, "and some of the older provinces like Kazakhstan."

"Lucky us."

"What we need is a strong man in St. Petersburg," the rotund man proclaimed. "A man of iron, like they had in the Mad Times."

Others were drawn into the debate. The proprietor, still leaning against the railing, offered his own thoughts. "Perhaps the West—"

"The West has no direction," Feodor snarled, clearly not wanting to align himself in any way with that political movement. "Every two years their government is liquidated only to have the office infested with a new nest of fat rats. No, *nasha luchshe*," ours is best. He then told his audience why.

"The borders of our country remain inviolate. We have industry, commerce, even a strong space program. This man here can attest to that; he's from Dark Side. What other nation can lay claim to such riches? Ever since the plague, we have been the strongest country because our people have always been tempered by adversity. A Russian knows what it means to suffer; our history is replete with examples."

The crowd around him nodded and grunted their assent.

A telecomp behind the bar beeped urgently. A message was coming through the global DataSphere.

"Shut that goddamn thing off," the man with the briar pipe grumbled. "I'm trying to doze."

The proprietor checked the incoming signal. "It's the First Minister, fellows, he's going to speak."

"Oh, well, then, let's hear what our esteemed leader has to say," said the sleepy man in a sarcastic tone.

The projector on the telecomp activated. A blue sphere one meter in diameter ballooned over their heads. Black horizontal scan lines lay like jagged grooves on its surface. They were replaced by a holographic ikon representing the Russian Confederation of Democratic States. The ikon dwindled away to a vanishingly small point in the middle of the sphere. Slowly, the familiar visage of the First Minister emerged:

"Citizens. As you are no doubt aware, a coup was attempted today against the lawful government of our Confederation. It is my duty to inform you this action has failed, and those responsible are now being arrested and detained. These anarchists—part of a revolutionary movement known as the Faction—sparked a riot in several cities and intended to use the resulting chaos as cover for their illegal actions. Now that the crisis is—" the image in the sphere buzzed and blinked with static "—rioting and hooliganism will not be tolerated. Return to your homes before any more damage is done. Citizens, I expect everyone to work together for the general well being of our Confederation. Until that future is achieved, we must all be willing to give our blood and our lives to maintain the security of our country. I bid you peace, and ask you to do your duty."

The sallow face melted away until only the eyes remained, then they too slowly faded out. The bold structure of the governmental ikon blazed forth, signifying the end of the government-sanctioned transmission. The projector snapped off.

"Well," somebody said in a defeatist tone, "that's that."

"Shall we go home?" one asked. "It's almost dawn."

"The riot isn't over yet," another cautioned. "It will be dangerous outside."

Nikolai asked Feodor, "What do you think?"

"It appears to be over, but I agree we should wait." He tapped his watchdisk. "The sun will be up in a few minutes; we'll be safer then. Say, do you want my social number? If you happen to run into Yuri, we can get together."

Nikolai saw no harm in that. Perhaps he had been too hard on this fellow earlier. They traded information.

"Hey," a man sitting under the window exclaimed with alarm, "does anyone smell smoke?"

"That's only Petrov's pipe. Or his farts."

"Fuck you."

"No, I'm telling you, I smell smoke."

"You're daft."

A couple of men rose anxiously from the floor. "I smell it too," they cried.

"So do I!"

Nikolai tried to get up off the floor, but got knocked down again. Feodor reached out a hand and he took it, then they lost each other in the maddening shuffle. Men shouted and shoved for the entrance, blocking it. Through the greasy window he saw men running madly down the long aisles of GUM.

"Calm down, calm down!" a teenager came in to the shop and shouted at the top of his lungs. "The fire is at the other end of the building but it's already been put out. I'm telling you—gawp!"

Somebody had rammed an elbow into his solar plexus. "To hell with you, I'm getting out. Bust that fucking window out, you."

A chair bounced off the panes.

"Goddamn plasglas! The shit won't break."

"Break it, or I'll kill you before we roast."

Repeated smashes cracked the super-strong translucent ceramic. Heads and arms groped for freedom. Nikolai scrambled over the broken shards, tearing his blue coveralls. He didn't look back. White, poisonous smoke from burning plastics and carpets treated with disinfectant roiled throughout GUM. He felt the hot flash of heat on his unprotected face and hands as he raced under one of the iron bridges connecting the upper levels. Flakes of burning ash skirled through the air and, landing, smoldered on his clothes. He ran, slapping at his sleeves. The interior of GUM was a cacophony of shouts and screams and thundering feet.

He saw doors rising up ahead. The gray light of dawn washed over the terrified faces of the huffing men running through the fiery tunnel. His legs screamed at him, but he knew that to fall was to die. Somehow, he kept going.

Later, he tried to remember exactly how he escaped GUM. His memory was a collage of fists and elbows, fights and screams. There was no real substance to it, other than the bruises he acquired to show for winning his life. The only thing he remembered clearly was gasping with soul-lifting joy when he ran out under a blue sky that arched over his head like a benevolent tent.

He felt himself carried forward into the milling crowd. More people had entered Old Red Square during the night and the place was packed. Tens of thousands. Half a million? He didn't know.

The bond that compelled the mob and swarming crowds to the square voiced its approval, but it was soon fed by rising panic as impossible metal insects rose behind the domes and glowing neon spires of the Cathedral.

Five fragile machines painted in camouflage gray-green with long, wasp-black tails and silver windows flew above the multitude.

"Disperse! Disperse! We will fire on you! Disperse!"

Nikolai covered his head as one of the helicopters thundered by ten meters overhead, whipping paper and clothing into a maelstrom.

One of the lightweight machines buzzed the crowd, forcing people to scatter. Another descended in the middle of the waving sea. Eager arms groped for it. Men clung to its landing rails like barnacles. The helicopter tried to rise, carrying them up with it. More men reached, grabbed hold of those who held the straining machine. It wobbled, tipped over.

The carbon-fiber blades ripped off in whistling arcs, cutting swathes. Amid the screeching metal of the downed machine came the shrieks of dying men. A fuel cell ruptured and chunks of sizzling debris spiraled up, trailing white smoke.

The four remaining machines dropped clusters of stun gas. Armored windows along the sides of the helicopters opened and soldiers fired into the crowd, killing indiscriminately.

Pepper gas canisters burst around him, saturating the sea of bodies. Nikolai clutched his burning eyes. He had lost his glasses. He was blind. People surged back and forth in a tide.

Nikolai felt dizzy, the air sucked out of his lungs. He sank to his knees, cradling his head in his arms. A gale force tore at his body and he heard the rhythmic thump of rotors overhead.

He threw himself down and crawled to escape the black underside of a helicopter sinking straight towards him. He rolled over and over, expecting the massive weight of the landing rail to crush his spine. He came up against legs. Clawing hands hauled him and others to their feet. Troops poured from the metal body of the craft. An Army lieutenant carried a red baton in one white-gloved hand. Whenever he pointed his baton an assault rifle cracked and someone fell. He did this again and again.

Armored trucks rolled into the Square, water cannons spouting white jets to break up the solid mass of the crowd. Shilkas, armament bristling, rumbled behind them. Men broke like rats to seek shelter from the subsequent arrests.

A silver Tupelov, appearing over Moscow River, sleeked a hundred meters overhead at Mach 2. The tremendous concussion of the jet's shock wave had the desired effect. People fell back, running from Old Red Square, leaving behind the mangled bodies of a helicopter and their comrades. More helicopters and a couple of VTOLs appeared while the jet curved upward in the porcelain-blue sky, afterburners glowing.

Nikolai ran, lungs laboring. His only thought was to escape the arrests that would follow. He slipped and dodged, once striking a man who temporarily barred his way.

He slowed, loping on towards Gorkogo, intent on getting back to the Warren. He combed his sweaty, lank hair out of his eyes with his fingers when he saw a makeshift checkpoint blocking the intersection ahead. He drew nearer with the other bedraggled men intent on fleeing the carnage of the Square.

He smoothed his clothes and discovered his glasses in a pocket. He must have put them there while caught in the flow of rioters, but didn't remember doing so. The watch tattoo in the palm of his hand was smudged; the crystalloids had gotten smashed in the conflict.

About two hundred people were gathered around the checkpoint across from a construction site. It looked like the bluecaps were letting them through. No, they began questioning that one, but dismissed him after checking his papers.

He took short steps as the knot of people slowly trickled through the aisle of electronic sawhorses and state police prominently displaying loaded side arms.

He followed a man to the opening of the checkpoint, and was about to go through, when a grim-faced officer thumped his breastbone with the business end of a shockstick.

"Papers," the bluecap demanded.

Five

"What is your name, and occupation?"

"Nikolai Sholokhov, electronics technician second class."

The bluecap heard his accent. "Dark Side?" Others craned to listen to the interrogation.

"Yes. Kiev II, Korolev Crater. Sector five block nine."

"Were you involved with the rioters? Did you vandalize?"

"No. I was crushed in between them. I had to follow or be trampled. I tried to get away." The truth sounded pathetically lame to his ears. "I harmed no one. I tried to escape."

A second bluecap punched in his responses on a field notebook.

"Kiev II?" The interrogator squinted sharply, challenging the data.

"That's right."

"ID, work and social numbers."

Nikolai gave them.

The bluecap handed back his ident card, pointed to a spot where a dozen men sat in a makeshift corral of sawhorses. "Climb over there. We'll confirm your identification through Dark Side Central."

Nikolai swung over the railing top. "How long will that take?" He allowed no hint of exasperation to enter his voice.

"You be quiet and wait," the bluecap said, and started letting people through the barricade again.

Nikolai sat down in the center of a solemn group of men. Other Outworlders. Most were from the orbital factories. He hugged his knees and let his head drop forward, snatching dicey bits of sleep. During the next six hours seventeen more Outworlders were detained, then the trickle of souls stopped coming through the checkpoint.

"How long do you think we're here for?" a nervous fellow beside him asked. He kept glancing up and down the deserted street as if he were waiting for a late bus.

Nikolai shook his head slowly, tiredly. "I don't know. Perhaps all day."

"I don't like this. I'm afraid something bad might happen. We should get out of here."

"How?"

"Slip between these sawhorses while the bluecaps are looking the other way. There's only two, and we can outrun them."

Nikolai turned the problem over in his mind. The bluecaps were huddled over the field computer, asking it questions. "Maybe we should chance it," he agreed.

"I'll go first." They edged around a row of captives hunched in front of them. The stranger started to swing a leg over one of the electronic sawhorses. The sawhorse sounded a shrill metallic-sounding whistle through its voice-crystal. The bluecaps turned around and shouted.

"What the hell do you think you're doing, shitheads? Get back over there and sit down before I shatter your fucking skulls open." The bluecap waved his shockstick threateningly.

Chastened, they returned to their places and crouched down.

"I didn't think it would work," his companion said, wiping sweat from his upper lip.

Nikolai tried to be optimistic. "We had to give it a try."

"I suppose so. My name is Lev, by the way."

"Nikolai." There was no room to shake hands in the press of unwashed bodies.

Lev was clean-shaven with brown soulful eyes. "What do you think's going to happen?"

"I don't know, but like you, I'm worried. This doesn't look good." He looked around significantly. "They didn't detain anybody but Outworlders. They let everybody else go."

"I know."

A column of twenty urban assault vehicles rumbled past, knobbed tires singing on the pavement. The backs of the vehicles were filled with bluecaps decked out in riot gear and laminar armor. The column turned a corner and disappeared in the direction of Old Red Square.

"I bet there's still some fellows who won't leave," Lev proposed. "Those bluecaps are going in to roust them out."

"I can't let myself worry about that," Nikolai said.

He was too concerned about his own safety.

Later in the day, his throat burned with a fierce thirst. Everyone was suffering. When an automated street cleaner passed by, they all stood up and spread their arms, letting the water spray over their parched faces and tongues. When it was gone, one of the bluecaps ordered, "Okay, now sit back down. And no talking!"

Nikolai sat in miserable silence. Lev poked his ribs. They held their heads bent together, mouths down, and talked low without moving their lips.

"I'm trying to get to the Warren. . . ." Lev began.

"Me, too."

"I was out with a boy I'd picked up. We went to a steam house and rented a cubicle so we could be alone. Just as he got down on his knees the bluecaps came in and forced everyone out of the building. I think they were planning to use the place as a control center to coordinate their activities." He cast a cautious look at the two bluecaps who had detained them. "This is a hell of a way to end up my leave."

"Where do you work?"

Slight pause. Lev had the usual Outworlder skittishness about telling a stranger on Earth too much personal history. "I'm a life-systems engineer on *Tereshkova*."

Nikolai had heard of the orbital habitat. Privately owned by a consortium, it was one of the largest factories at L5. They were always looking for experienced men and dependable service personnel. The population was right around five thousand. Outworlders jokingly referred to it as the Foreign Legion of space stations because cellbuses rarely visited. The men who worked there were an iconoclastic breed; self-dependent and tough, but law abiding. There were rumors that women were aboard, too, but no one had any proof of that.

"They manufacture zero gee medicines, don't they?"

"All sorts of chemicals." Lev clearly wanted to change the subject. "What's your story?"

Nikolai told him, in bits and pieces. Lev waggled his head back and forth. "You've been in the thick of it, then. Uh oh. What's this?"

A dark blue unmarked van rolled up outside the cordon. Two security men got out of the cab and signaled to the bluecaps. They spoke for a minute or two before the taller of the two security men said something into a collar mike on his uniform.

A panel in the side of the van slid open and a whipcord lean man emerged. He wore a black knee-length coat and a peaked cap pulled forward to hood his ice-blue eyes. His long black hair flowed over the fur-trimmed collar of his coat. A black cigarette with a gold filter hung from his lips. A pair of black and tan mastiffs stayed alert at his heels.

"Internal Security," someone off to Nikolai's right said fearfully.

"Worse," commented another, "that's Stinnen."

The first man sucked in his breath. "What?!"

"Your brain pan has become fried sitting out here in the sun all day," Lev whispered to both of them furiously. "What the hell would the Grey Executioner be doing here?"

"Take another look if you don't believe me, uncle."

Nikolai did, and his blood turned to ice slurry. It was Stinnen, the head of Internal Security, reviewing the list of Outworlders the bluecaps had detained during the day. He pointed a skeletal finger at one of the names on the field notebook and made a sharp inquiry. A hush fell over the prisoners. The bluecaps pointed the man out.

"Abram Kalita."

The accused stood up in the middle of Nikolai's group. His hands and forearms were scarred with thin white lines. Probably works in one of the penal outposts, Nikolai thought, stringing razor vines. The genetically altered liana always left a distinctive signature on human flesh if one became careless handling it.

"Come here, you," one of the bluecaps demanded. Stinnen and his dogs watched with bland interest.

The man was questioned at length. Cold sweat rolled down his face as the bluecaps searched his pockets and checked the heels of his shoes for contraband. Stinnen remained composed, self-possessed: a counterpoint to the hot denials issuing from the captive man.

Nikolai couldn't hear their actual words, but the tone told him all he needed to know. Stinnen used a stylus to tag information on a palm slate. He showed the evidence they had gathered against Kalita and snapped one final question in the man's face.

Kalita hooked his thumbs in his belt laces, craned his head back. He seemed to be studying the clouds for an answer to his predicament. Seeing none, he motioned impatiently for the palm slate. A security man held it and Kalita pressed his broad thumbprint on the signature block.

The confession had been signed.

The first security man removed what looked like a trilobite on steroids from a holster under his arm. He held the device in one hand and led the condemned man away from the group towards the construction site.

"They're going to give him sleepdeath," Lev's voice was tight. As much as he wanted too, Nikolai couldn't tear his eyes away from the unfolding execution.

The security guard made Kalita kneel on shattered brick. He placed the smooth black head of the sleepdeath module against the back of the skull, flipped the safety cover off and pressed a button with a dull click. Kalita pitched forward like a dirty bundle of rags and lay still in the dust.

The two mastiffs trotted forward, tongues lolling out of their red mouths. They sniffed over the dead man thoroughly before returning to Stinnen's side. He lit another black cigarette.

"Viktor Agranov."

The scene was repeated twice more, with slight variations. One man protested to the end, the other went to his death as if emotionally disengaged from the proceedings. Each time a name other than his was called Nikolai almost wept openly with relief, only to go through the gut-wrenching experience again when Stinnen reviewed the list following each sickening execution.

Nikolai felt drained, wiped out, when the men from Internal Security began packing up their gear. He couldn't believe he had managed to escape with his life. The late afternoon sun looked somehow brighter, the blue sky more vibrant than he had ever seen it before. Between his shoes he saw each and every pebble in the empty lot, could later recall their exact shapes and sizes, even how the heat shimmered off the sidewalks and the road.

How the bodies had crumpled lifelessly.

"I wonder who those men were?" he asked Lev.

Lev wiped sweat off his upper lip. He, too, was glad to be alive. "Who knows? *Blatari,* maybe, or Factionists."

Stinnen hesitated a moment before pulling himself back into the body of the van. His eyes ranged one last time over the men huddled between the electronic sawhorses. For the first time in that long dreadful afternoon Nikolai heard his voice clearly:

"Release them all." The van door slid shut behind him and the vehicle rolled off in a plume of blue exhaust.

"They're letting us go," Nikolai said dully. "I can't believe it. It must be a trick."

"Stinnen isn't interested in us," Lev reminded him. "He's only interested in his quarry. And he got them."

They stared at the three dead men.

Despite the fact the bluecaps had been ordered to release the prisoners, they took their time going about it. Names were read off slowly, in twos and threes. When Lev's name was called he told Nikolai, "Maybe we'll see each other in the Warren." He walked away quickly into the gathering dusk.

When the officer at the console of the field computer obtained further clearance he read more names from the list. Nikolai refused to wait for his name to be called; it was getting late and he had to get to the Warren before curfew. He got up, ducked under a rail. No one shouted at him. He didn't linger to see if anyone else remained behind.

The streets had grown dark. Many corner lamps were broken, or flickered intermittently. A bluecap stood at each intersection, keeping an eye on things. Car traffic was re-routed in a one kilometer circumference around the square.

He kept near the buildings and storefronts as he passed invisibly along the dark streets. The streets themselves were nigh impassable. A single car burned furiously in the middle of the road. Bottles, garbage, bits of brick and yellow stone cluttered Gorkogo. In one alley he saw a file of electronic sawhorses marching along, their articulated metal legs clicking. Finally, the glittering glass and metal exterior of the Warren beckoned him. He drew near, relieved to be walking in a well-lighted and policed area. A skeletal borzoi, its long hair matted, crossed his path. The greyhound dis-appeared into the shadows on the far side of the boulevard, slipping between bushes.

"Hey." A voice issued from the deep indigo of a cul-de-sac to Nikolai's right.

"No." He went onward.

"Please," the voice implored.

Nikolai stopped and stared back. "I'm not interested." He started.

"I don't have a place to stay." The speaker partially edged from the concealing shadows, showing his empty hands. He said with a hint of grief, "I'm not a prostitute."

Surprising himself, Nikolai directed, "Come out of the shadows so I can see you."

A young boy, fourteen or fifteen years old, cautiously obeyed. Pale, thin, but dressed reasonably well. Fine brown hair tucked under a cap with a warped bill. The boy positioned himself so the lamp over Nikolai's shoulder bathed his fair, bleak face.

"Who are you?" He studied the disheveled boy.

"Piotr Borod." The boy didn't impart additional information.

"Why are you hiding? What have you done?"

A siren sounded. The boy half-glanced at the distant wail. "Curfew." He bit his bottom lip. "If I'm caught out after curfew I'll be shot." He thrust his hands inside his short, stylish jacket. "I have money."

"That's not the point. I don't know you. . . ." Nikolai left off.

"Hundred tsars."

"Listen to me," he began again, but was interrupted by the second siren.

"Two hundred from a gold Czarina debit-chip. It's everything I have."

"It's not a question of money. I don't know you."

"Please."

Silence grew between them like an immense block of ice. The siren wailed a third and final time. Nikolai thought of the men coldly murdered by Stinnen's crew, and all the others in Old Red Square who had died that day.

He relented in a clipped tone, "Come on, then."

They walked quickly to the Warren's entrance. One of the glass doors had been smashed and repaired with steeltape. Nikolai flashed his Warren ID card at the door guard. Two bluecaps standing nearby and swinging their shocksticks from leather loops paid them no notice.

They went up in the lift. Nikolai frowned at the boy standing on the opposite side of the car who was staring mutely at his scuffed and muddy shoes.

"You don't have any money." He tried to keep any hint

of accusation out of the statement.

"No."

"Doesn't matter," he said and got out, heading for the stairs. The boy tagged after, keeping his distance.

Puffing, Nikolai unlocked his door and entered. The boy shut the door after.

"Nikolai?" Sonya asked.

"You can wash up in there," he pointed Piotr to the bathroom. "Yes, Sonya. I'm back."

"I was concerned. There was a riot in Old Red Square and the mayor has called a curfew. Who is with you?" Her fish-eye lens swiveled to follow Piotr inside the bathroom.

"A friend. Any messages?" Nikolai wasn't sure if he might hear something from the Union House about Thursday night, or from Yuri.

"No, but I will have to contact Warren Central and bill you for the extra occupant. The evening news is on. They are discussing the riot. Do you want me to tune in?"

"Yes, but no visual." He'd seen enough of that hell for a lifetime. He unlaced his canvas shoes. Piotr came out of the bath, appearing less rumpled, his cap stuffed in his back pocket. His hair barely brushed his slim shoulders but tapered longer in the back. He listened to the newscast from the kitchenette, occasionally looking toward Nikolai for direction.

Nikolai summarily ignored the boy. He pulled out a change of clothes and locked himself in the bath. He studied his face in the mirror: One side was caked with dirt, forehead bruised. He washed his body thoroughly, standing under the stream of hot water. He leaned against the wall with the palms of his hands, arms straight, head down, and wept for several minutes under the hot shower as the tension slowly drained from his body.

After toweling himself dry (he had no three-kopeck tokens for the air blower) he sprayed disinfectant on his lacerations and gingerly applied strips of regenerative tape to the worst cuts and scrapes. He finished by brushing his hair straight back.

He opened the door. Piotr, who had been sitting on the edge of the bed, got up in his presence. The radio had been manually switched off. A light on Sonya's console glared.

"I didn't want to listen to it anymore," Piotr explained.

"Are you hungry?" Nikolai watched the boy drift closer to the locked door, a frightened animal.

"Yes," Piotr's mouth curled expectantly at the offer.

Nikolai dismissed the terse reply to nerves and prepared supper. He opened two tins of borscht, rummaged in the refrigerator and picked half a dozen eggs, cheese, onion and mushrooms. He made an omelet. Piotr watched. Nikolai divided the omelet and scraped the portions onto paper plates. He carried his half and a mug of cold soup over to the bed.

Piotr ate in the kitchenette, ravenous. When he finished he drank water from the tap by cupping it in his slim hands.

"Thank you," he said, turning the tap off and wiping his mouth.

Nikolai finished his own supper, grunted noncommittally.

"What started it?"

The boy's question took him unawares. He shrugged his ignorance. "Who knows?" He shrugged a second time, with less confidence. "It's something that happens in the world now, since the *Fevreblau*."

"I've never seen anything like that before." Piotr absently hugged himself. "All those men hurting one another."

Nikolai remembered the swaying helicopter, rotors scything down people in cruel swaths. He yawned with creeping fatigue. "Listen, I've got to sleep." He tossed a pillow and a heavy blanket at the boy.

Piotr folded the blanket in a crude pallet in the kitchenette and lay down with no question.

Nikolai got in bed, slats creaking. He turned off the lights and lay back, exhausted. Sleep lapped at him. He rubbed his face and wondered about the people outside who hadn't found shelter tonight. The executions that would follow. Reprisals, pogroms. The destroyed tenements, the shattered lives. Moscow in gloom.

The small bedroom was dark. All the Warren was dark.

"I can give you some money," he said out loud, blind.

A voice answered smoothly from the kitchenette, "I just need to stay the night."

"Where are you going to go tomorrow?"

"I'll find something."

"Don't you have a home?"

The boy didn't reply.

Nikolai turned over, trying to tune out the hellish cacophony of the past day still ringing in his ears. Great scythes worked behind his eyelids. His thoughts cooled. In a few days, the Union House. He smiled wanly into his pillow. She's there, waiting for me.

Briefly, he thought of Yasu and wondered what she was doing now, how lucky he was to have met her.

Twice, Piotr awakened him by getting up and going to the bathroom. The boy acted distressed in some way Nikolai couldn't fathom. Sometime in the night he fell back asleep.

Sonya used her panic-voice mode: "Nikolai! Piotr's in the bath. My security lens registers he has injured himself, there is blood. Nikolai!—"

He reached the bath door in seconds, twisted the handle. Locked. There were retching sounds coming from within. A crash, something breaking, shattering.

"Piotr!" Nikolai slammed his shoulder into the door and felt it give with a sharp wooden crack. He shouted the boy's name again. He put his shoulder into the door a second time and it banged open. Splinters from the jamb sprayed over the room.

Something half-naked crawled away to huddle in the far corner. Nikolai saw blood-soaked tissues on the floor and a broken glass. He caught a glimpse of crimson smeared thighs as Piotr tried in vain to close the door with long, out-stretched legs.

"Get out!" the girl shrieked. "*Get out!*"

Six

"The things they do to us." Galina's hushed voice stalked the room like a confined animal. "No man can imagine." Her reproachful eyes found his, locked, challenged him to disagree. "Not even you." Her tone was accusatory, even combative.

She sat at the foot of his rumpled bed, long legs folded underneath, twisting her cap between her smooth hands. Nikolai sat as far from her as the geography of the room allowed. His hands were clasped together between his knees. He sat like a schoolboy: back straight, attentive.

Galina Toumanova took a deep breath, her nipples peaked the coarse weave of her shirt. "I had had enough, especially after the tour of the Union House complex, and the women who worked there." Her eyes flared. "Do you know what it was like, before the *Fevreblau*?"

He shook his head dumbly, too confused to think, momentarily afraid to meet her gaze. Alone with a young girl and unsupervised. Illegal. Automatic death sentence. He recalled the men pulled out from his group yesterday by Internal Security.

If he was lucky, he might be sentenced to digging stopes and laying stulls in the Kolyma gold mines. That would be a hard death, but at least it wouldn't be ignominious: he wouldn't be a crumpled bundle of rags lying forgotten in some empty lot.

"Well, do you?"

He blinked. What? Oh, yes, the girl was asking him

something. God, what was she *doing* here? What am I going to do?

Kick her out, a voice inside him screamed. She's not your problem, but she will be if you let her hang around. A big one.

He stumbled over his words. "I . . . I don't really know."

"They don't teach you anything." She didn't mean it as an insult but it came out that way. "We want for nothing. We are like goddesses to them, the continuation of the species."

Her expression was one of melancholy. "That's how it used to be. Long ago, before the plague, babies were born from mothers and not out of state-owned crèches. Real babies, not stamped out clones pumped full of growth hormones that die before they're twenty."

Nikolai tried, but failed, to imagine the alien concept. Mothers. A person growing inside your body. Someone who loved you unconditionally. He didn't know anyone who loved like that, wasn't sure it was humanly possible.

He had heard of a project using men to bring babies to term. There was more than enough room in the male abdominal cavity, but the hormone injections and prenatal care was too expensive. The project had been abandoned because it wasn't cost effective.

"Were you . . . born?" he asked.

"No, I came out of a crèche. Like you, my first home was a Dyrene flask with a placental lining. Womb births still happened in parts of the West where they had the resources and the technology to build nanobot-vaccine and negate the *Fevreblau* virus before it burned itself out. But it was terribly expensive, and didn't always work."

She grew silent. Nikolai fixed his gaze on the first Russian woman he had ever seen. How different she was from

Yasu. Not better, he thought, just . . . different. Certainly younger, if not prettier. Now that the cap was off her head, and her hair brushed back, he had a clear view of her eyes: they were green with gold flakes in them. Full bottom lip. Straight, sandy brown eyebrows.

She was pretty, he decided.

"What did they do to make you hate them so?" he asked openly.

She regarded him for a protracted moment. "I have to trust you," she said fatalistically. "You're all I have right now."

A surge of tingling adrenaline flooded through him as the import of her words became clear. She was depending on him. Just like that, she'd thrown her life into his hands.

Just like that.

What else *can* she do? he asked himself. She has to trust somebody. How am I going to get her back home without anyone noticing? And keep my own life intact?

He needed someone to help him.

Yuri. He'll help me, but I have to find him first. That may not be easy.

Galina's shoulders sagged. "Women are still . . . born, in hidden crèches. Not many, not as many as are being cloned in some places, but enough to provide ova and maintain a stable population distribution." She said matter-of-factly, "I'm a fifteen-year-old virgin with two healthy ovaries, potentially containing tens of thousands of viable eggs, and I'm menstruating. A residual effect of the plague: women experience menarche much later in life than they used to during the Mad Times. I'm more valuable to the Confederation, or any other country, than a new zero gee factory or an orbital weapons platform."

"But why are you here?" Nikolai asked plaintively. He

gestured at her garb. "What are you doing in Moscow, dressed that way?"

"Orientation. We were being escorted in a maximum-security bus to the local Union House. You see, when a woman begins menstruation the Confederation reaps her ovaries. I don't know why they wait until then, ova mature before a girl is born, but they do. After we're . . . mutilated . . . we're scattered through Union Houses all over Russia." She shook her head, conveying some of the immense logistics involved, and the inherent insanity in such a system. "It happens all over the world, not just in Russia."

"Privilege."

She nodded solemnly.

"State-owned sterilized prostitutes." She frowned at her description. "We got caught in the riot and our bus was overturned after it hit a lorry." She fingered the tail of her shirt. "We were dressed neutrally to divert attention. At first, my friends and I thought it was an adventure when we began the trip. We aren't let out very often from the *sharashkas* in which we're kept—" Flash of smouldering anger. "—imprisoned, rather. When the riot started we got scared. There were twenty-eight of us in that bus, all frightened and screaming. When our vehicle overturned, some of the windows got smashed. I kicked out the rest of my window and squirmed through. I escaped and ran from the security escort to hide in the crowd of men. That was last night. I've been running ever since."

Nikolai had heard enough. "What do you want me to do? You've got to look at it from my perspective, too. I don't have any authority. If anything, I'm more helpless than you are. If I'm caught hiding you, I'll be killed outright. Sleepdeath, if I'm lucky."

Her eyebrows furrowed. "Why don't you want to help me?"

"It's not a question of whether I want to help you or not." He did what he could to stress the salient points of his argument. "You profess to know all about our culture, but you don't act like it." She had to be made to understand. "An ordinary person like myself can't do anything about what you've been through. I can't change things all by myself. Life doesn't work that way, except in fairy stories."

Her face clouded. "I don't want to be cut open and used by nameless people. I've got a future in my body." Glancing down, avoiding his stare, she grimaced before she continued:

"Most of the older women I met at the Union House say it must be done for the Confederation. It satisfies their sense of national pride. Well, I don't appreciate anyone or any ideological idea enough to sacrifice my one and only chance to be a whole person. That's why I ran."

"I see." Nikolai didn't understand, not really.

The hard look in her eyes yielded. "When I saw you outside the Warren, I thought you had a kind face. I waited out there a long time. Hours. You were the first man I asked. It took me that long to work up enough courage. I picked the Warren because I know the men who stay here are more educated than the ordinary fool on the street. That's true, isn't it? You do work in space, don't you?"

Nikolai ran his hands back over his head, sighed. "I don't know if I'm smarter than anybody else." His thoughts were jumbled. "I did sweat out three years of tech school after I was chosen for the Corps. Anyway, I'm only a lowly technician; I'm not one of the intelligentsia."

"What do you do?"

"I work on a radio telescope on the Far Side of the

Moon, the Shklovskii array." He cut her a sharp look, stunned as he abruptly realized she was manipulating his vanity to involve him in her hopeless cause. He was sure of it—that's why she was asking questions, pretending to be interested. Yet, somehow, even though he knew what she was doing, he found he didn't mind.

He pulled himself straight. You'd better watch your step, dumbass, and keep your wits together. She's not an innocent toy, she's a goddamn *minefield*. One wrong step on your part—

"I know this is dangerous," she conceded, "for both of us. I'm not stupid."

He barked a laugh. "You don't know how dangerous. You said it yourself: you've been protected your whole life. Catered to. Pampered. You can't possibly know what it's like for the rest of us. Oh, I'm sure you've been told, or read about it. But it doesn't live as well as it reads, trust me on this one."

He fell silent, surprised at the rancor he had shown. But he had to make this silly girl understand that life in Moscow wasn't a fairy tale. Okay, she may have had a tough time of it, but his life hadn't been a bed of roses either.

Galina got off the bed and padded to the kitchenette. Hugging herself, she turned to confront him.

"Do you want me to leave?" Her voice was small, timid. A curtain of hair slipped to hide half of her face.

His mind raced in all directions.

"When I'm picked up, I promise I won't tell them anything about you, or how you helped me, not even a little bit. Is that what you're afraid of? That I'll give you away to some security organ?"

"No," he snapped savagely. "I'm not."

She picked at the marred Formica with a broken nail.

"I'm an anomaly in this World History." Half to herself: "Does that mean I should let myself be used like a puppet? Used like a . . . a dumb thing? I've got feelings. I'm somebody." She thumped a small fist on the counter top, mouth trembling. "Aren't I?"

Nikolai slowly looked up from the floor.

"There's a man I know," he said. "Yuri Tur. Maybe he can help us think of something. The only problem is, I don't know where I can reach him right now. But . . . I'll do what I can."

She lowered a crumpling face into her hands. "Thank you," she wept desperately. "Thank you for at least trying."

Yes, he thought, watching her. I can do that much. I can try to get this girl home. With Yuri's help.

For all the good it will do me.

I've got feelings. I'm somebody.

Early morning. Nikolai heard the strident, emphatic words over and over as he flashed his Warren-ident card to the security guards posted outside the railway station. An *elektrichka* waited at the depot.

"Where are you going?" the ticket master demanded, safe behind his plasglas window.

"Kaliningrad."

"Ten and a half tsars."

Nikolai paid. "What time is it?"

"Train leaves in fifteen minutes. Do you want some breakfast? My bunkmate makes these rolls and I sell them to the commuters, *nalevo*. Only two tsars apiece, or you can have two of them for three tsars."

"No, thanks."

"They're topped with caramelized sugar."

"Is there a public telecomp I can use?"

"Around the corner."

Nikolai swiped his ident card through the data-capture slot and waited for the phone to initialize. "Hello?" It was Sonya, answering.

"Any messages?"

"Mischa called. He said he's feeling much better."

"Okay, I'll call again when I get the chance."

"Take care."

He waited for the telecomp to dump the call data from its buffer before returning to the train. It wasn't an elaborate code signal, he knew, but he hoped that keeping things simple would maintain the appearance nothing was amiss.

Galina was safe. If she weren't, then "Mischa" would have left a message his cold had taken a turn for the worse.

He found a seat in the back of the car. What would I have done then? he thought. Would I have gone back and tried to find out what happened, help if I could? What would be the point? By then, they'd have me, too.

Of course they're looking for her. A quick head count after that lorry crash would tell them she was missing. The Russian Protectorate would be frantic.

I've got to be careful. No place is safe, not even my room in the Warren.

The train jerked as it moved away from the terminal. Nikolai sat alone with glum thoughts for company. When the train approached the grade he stepped outside the connecting door and swung down onto the forest floor. He hid behind the bole of a tree until the last car trundled around the bend.

He struck off into the woods, a kerchief in one hand to keep up the charade that he was out hunting mushrooms. He made his way quickly to the secluded glen, but when he got there he stumbled to a stop and swore vehemently.

The *posad* was gone.

There were a few clues that something once existed here: scorched earth from camp fires, a lonely tent stake, a hank of coiled rope. He turned around and around in a tight circle as the naked limbs of the beeches whispered overhead. Nothing. Mintz was gone, along with Yasu's trailer and the Starlight dish.

I should have asked around if the encampment were still here, he thought, mentally kicking himself. Muscovites would have known if the *blatari* camp had pulled up and moved on; maybe even know where it had moved to.

In his zeal to be secretive he hadn't thought of it. Now he was stuck for ideas.

This had been his last shot to find Yuri. He had first gone to GUM, but the delicatessen was closed for repairs, as were most stores in the emporium. A stop at the bathhouse they used two days ago and ten tsars to post a message in the DataSphere had both come up empty. He didn't know of any other place to look.

He kicked through the leaves carpeting the ground. There was nothing left to do now but return to the grade and wait for an incoming train to Moscow. When he reached the spot, he sighted a solitary man sitting on a bare outcropping of rock that stretched alongside the railway like the broken spine of a dragon. The man absently picked his teeth with his thumbnail. Nikolai found the mannerism uneasily familiar.

"Feodor."

Feodor Zim raised his bald head, twitched his thick mustache. "Hello. Out for a morning walk?"

Something about the man's detached demeanor gave Nikolai a cold sense of foreboding.

He hefted the kerchief stuffed with mushrooms. "What brings you out here?"

Feodor slid down off the rock. "I was waiting for you."

"Oh?"

The needlegun whipped from a concealed pocket in one fluid movement. "Raise your hands. Come on, get them up."

Nikolai did so, slowly. "What's this about? Don't you recognize me? We met in the department store—in GUM—the night of the riot."

Feodor ripped the kerchief from his hand. "I remember you quite well." After searching through the kerchief and finding only mushrooms he flung the bundle into the woods. "Move, and you'll die to regret it." He appeared pleased with his little play on words. Nikolai morbidly guessed he had cause to use it on more than one occasion.

The bore of the needlegun pointed directly at the center of his left eye. Nikolai tried to ignore it.

Feodor patted him down expertly, even to the extent of searching the folds of flesh in his groin. Satisfied, he stepped back and gave a low whistle as an all clear.

"Okay, fellows, he's alone," he called. "Come on out."

Two more men emerged from separate parts of the forest and came up on either side of Nikolai. One had a scar across his lower lip and a cheek that suffered from a nervous tic. He was corpulent and had a greasy sheen of sweat on his face. The second man had the thin drawn face and inflamed eyes of a *zwilnik* hooked on euphoria dollops. The pungent odor lingered on the man's shabby clothes.

"Do you mind explaining what the hell you're doing pointing that gun at me?"

Feodor gestured towards the empty woods with the point of his chin. "I want to know what you were doing out there."

"I told you, picking mushrooms."

"I don't believe that. I think you were looking for the *posad*."

Nikolai clenched his jaw muscles. "What if I was? Is that a crime?"

"Mebbe." Feodor frowned. "Depends on what you intended to do once you got there."

"I wanted to buy some things I can't get from the shops on Luna. Items like razor gel and tooth rinse, maybe a new AI chip for my personal telecomp. Look, what difference is it to you? Okay, I was going to sell them for a profit when I got back to Kiev II. Are you happy now? Can I put my hands down?"

"Go ahead. Slowly."

Nikolai lowered his arms. "I don't have much money."

The gun never wavered. "I don't want your money."

"Are you going to kill me?"

"That's up to you. Do what I say, and you'll live a little longer. Maybe."

Nikolai decided to throw caution to the wind. "Have you heard from Yuri?"

An iron veil slammed down over the pale yellow eyes. "Not yet, but I expect to, soon. Very soon."

Excitement surged through him. So that's it, he mused. He came out here looking for Yuri, found me instead, and the *posad* gone.

One of the thugs, the man Nikolai thought of as Lip Scar, kept glancing up at the sky and the tops of the trees. "They're late," he said, worrying his bottom lip with a bad set of teeth.

Feodor was unconcerned. "They'll be here soon enough." He stared Nikolai down. "But not late enough to suit you, eh?"

"I don't have the slightest idea what you're talking about."

"Don't you?" he sneered. "Haven't you figured out who I am?"

"I thought you worked for the *Narodnaya Volya*. That's the impression I got when I met you in GUM."

Lip Scar snickered with cruel delight at Nikolai's notion that Feodor was a reactionary. "Pretty dumb, huh?" he asked his mate. The *zwilnik* grinned and spat, his nostrils disgustingly ravaged by inhaling euphoria dollops.

Feodor, slightly amused: "Those clowns? Yuri's little passionate group of sophomoric politicos?" An acerbic laugh bubbled past his thin lips. "No, Sholokhov. You're way off the mark."

"You're MKD?" This was the organ that dealt exclusively with international security.

Feodor leaned up against the naked rock, crossed his legs. He was enjoying himself. "I'm not saying; but I will tell you this: I infiltrated Yuri's pathetic gang of traitors sixteen months ago. It wasn't difficult. Yuri's always recruiting new members and my department was able to draw up excellent references to vouch for my character." His sour smile curled like a thick worm on the bottom half of his face. "I rose rather quickly to the hierarchy with my fervent speeches and willingness to take on assignments other members shied away from. Naturally, I had a guardian angel at my right elbow all the while; there was nothing I had to fear from any security service still loyal to the Confederation." The spy started to pick his teeth again. "When the riots began I figured my work was done. Not only would the Faction be destroyed, but the rest of Yuri's networks would be rolled up because of the information I gave my superiors." He sobered. "However, I underestimated how foxy that sonofabitch is—he eluded me and hid out with most of his men. We couldn't flush them. So I gambled and decided to stake out the delicatessen where he sometimes hangs about. I didn't catch him but I caught you, little fish. When I ran your name through our database I got all kinds of red tags. Not a little fish, but a big fish. A big fish that must be interrogated."

Nikolai's chest tightened with fear. Give them nothing about Galina. Every minute, every second allows her a chance to get away. No matter what they do, I mustn't say anything about her.

If only he could get to a telecomp, and warn her.

There must be something I can do. *Think.*

It was then he realized he was thinking of her safety before his. Forget that, he reflected, she's the innocent here. I can take care of myself. Sure, I've only known her for a span of a few hours, but that's longer than I've known any woman. He felt his emotions wrench around inside him. She was so upset when I last saw her. . . .

I've got feelings. I'm somebody.

Now he understood a little bit of what she meant. Nikolai was dead already, he knew that. But if he could hold out, no matter what happened, then maybe he could give his death meaning.

The tops of the trees started to whip back and forth. Lip Scar breathed a sigh of relief. "About goddamn time." He grabbed Nikolai's arm and yanked him aside. "Come here, you. Don't stand there or you'll be crushed like a titmouse."

The ducted-fan craft eased down between the stand of trees and landed on the parallel tracks of the rail line. A door swung open in the egg-shaped body. Feodor motioned with his needlegun for Nikolai to proceed on ahead. Nikolai hoped for an opportunity to make a break, but the thugs, Lip Scar and the Dollop Junkie, were similarly armed. He grabbed the doorway, pulled himself inside the cramped fuselage.

They strapped him down in a seat, the thugs on either side again, watching his every move. With no other chair available, Feodor held onto a strap suspended from the ceiling. "Let's go, pilot," he ordered. "You know the destination."

"Yes, sir." The pilot, dressed in black coveralls and white crash helmet with a HUD visor, engaged all six hooded blades attached to the outside hull. No one talked over the whine of the fan blades.

There were no windows and the forward cockpit was made of polarized plasglas. Only the pilot was able to see out using his special visor. By Nikolai's estimation they flew an hour before the nose of the craft dipped and they went into a long glide. The deck leveled out again and they touched down without incident. The fan blades whispered to a stop. The Dollop Junkie opened the hatchway. Lip Scar unlocked the magnetic handcuffs manacling Nikolai to his seat.

He stood, chaffing his wrists. "What happens now?"

"We're going to walk across the landing pad towards that white building over there," Feodor instructed. "Don't try anything; we're deep in the woods, kilometers south of the Desna River. You'll never make it back to Moscow on your own, not in your condition. This is a complex we use for certain problems. Do you understand?"

Nikolai shrugged.

Give them nothing about Galina.

They filed out of the craft and crossed the landing field, Feodor leading the way. He came upon a gate and buzzed.

An eye-camera floated out of its skyhouse and focused on them.

"Zim," he told the camera, "with a party of two and one prisoner."

There were two lights below the lens of the security camera: the green one flashed. "Enter," it said in a tinny voice through its vocal-crystal. "Room Five is prepared."

Feodor pushed through the door. Nikolai followed. The inside of the building was air-conditioned. A long corridor stretched away towards other rooms.

"This complex is automated." Feodor was showing off. "An AI oversees everything. We are isolated here and able to carry out what work we deem necessary." He presented Nikolai with a meaningful look that held out little hope for rescue. "Don't even think about escaping."

Nikolai kept his own counsel. He wasn't going to bandy words with Zim any longer; he was trying to mentally prepare himself for what he knew lay ahead.

Remember, give them nothing about Galina. Keep her safe.

Lip Scar used a fingerkey to open the door to Room Five. There was an apricot-colored metal table bolted to the plascrete floor and one loose chair. Upon closer examination Nikolai deemed that the table wasn't an ordinary one: it had leather straps and iron clamps at the corners to immobilize a human body. Everything was clean and antiseptic, but the leather straps had brown rust stains along their edges.

"Sit down." The Dollop Junkie shoved him into the chair; kept his needlegun trained on Nikolai's heart. He had widened the barrel to fire all eight flechettes at once.

Lip Scar went around the room opening panels in the wall. He pulled out aluminum trays on rollers. On the trays were surgical instruments and other tools Nikolai couldn't name. Another panel revealed more grim secrets: electrical generator with thick cables and alligator clips, soldering iron, high speed drill with various bit sizes in a separate plastic tray. Another cabinet opened upon stoppered bottles and syringes.

Nikolai kept his breathing slow and even. Don't let them intimidate you. You can get through this if you stay focused. There's only one prize at the end of the long tunnel of pain they're going to bring you down, one thing that makes this worthwhile.

Galina. Maybe when you don't return she'll realize something went wrong and she'll run. That's all you can hope for.

Be determined. She's got feelings. She's somebody. So are you, but you must resolve yourself to the fact this is the end. Besides, wouldn't you do the same for any woman, not just a frightened girl who doesn't want to be mutilated?

He knew without doubt that he would. Living in a world where women were so rare they were considered Exotics, he had no other choice. Social pressures and mores allowed him no other recourse but to subject himself to torture on the one in a thousand chance she would realize something had gone wrong and bolt for her life.

Feodor unlocked a panel behind the table and switched on a communications panel. "We are in the Isolator," he said into the mouthpiece.

A voice, too faint for Nikolai to recognize, responded abruptly. Feodor replaced the mike.

"He's coming," he told the guards. His eyes fell to Nikolai's pale face. "For you, too."

They waited. Sweat dripped from Nikolai's chin despite the comfortable ambient temperature of the room. The door to the Isolator scraped open. He turned to see, then faced away, heart pounding.

It was the head of Internal Security. The Grey Executioner.

Stinnen.

Seven

Stinnen lit one of his black cigarettes. "Are you comfortable, Mr. Sholokhov?"

Nikolai thought it a ridiculous question under the circumstances, but decided not to antagonize him—especially since it would be his hand that would guide the instruments that tore at his flesh. "So far," he answered emptily.

"Was he any trouble?" Stinnen put to Feodor.

"None at all. Came like a lamb, he did."

"Good." The head of Internal Security rubbed the back of Nikolai's neck to convey a sense of comradeship. "No sense in not accepting the state of affairs as they are, Sholokhov. You can't escape; the AI that runs this place is hooked directly into the DataSphere and is encrypted to my own key."

"What does that mean?"

Stinnen squeezed Nikolai's neck a little too hard. "You've been tagged. No matter where you go, what you do, I can trace you. There's not a single AI in all of Russia that won't give me your location if I put a query into the 'Sphere. You are a microbe under the eye of a silicon lens; you will never be able to escape me again."

Nikolai stared straight ahead at the corner of one of the wall panels where a flake of paint had chipped, exposing bright metal underneath.

Focus. Give them nothing.

Stinnen leaned his weight against the table, arms crossed as if he impatiently waited for an incompetent mechanic to finish servicing his vehicle. "Tell me everything you know about the radio telescope in Sharonov Crater."

Nikolai's jaw dropped. He had fully expected a hot grilling about Galina's whereabouts, her recovery and eventual return to the Union House. He hadn't anticipated this line of questioning at all.

"Sharonov?"

Stinnen unbuttoned his coat and removed a white handkerchief. Balling it up, he tossed it to Nikolai who gratefully wiped his face and neck dripping with sweat.

His gravelly voice grew stern, as if he addressed a recalcitrant child. "Don't pretend ignorance with me, Sholokhov. I know you worked at the labs there; I want a full account of the Star Whisper Project. You'll only make it harder on yourself if you do not come clean. Remember, I have your life in my hands." To prove it, he reached inside his coat. From a zippered pocket he produced a sheaf of papers bound by gelband.

He rolled the documents out. "I have everything here I need to know about you. Your banal existence—distilled down to a few thousand bits of information." Unimpressed, he swept his hand tediously over the information. "Date of birth, education, performance evaluations, promotions: it's all right here, even your religious beliefs. If you lie to me, I shall know it immediately. Save yourself a lot of trouble and cooperate fully with me. Otherwise—" his eyes ranged to include Zim standing by in the stifling cell "—there will be unimaginable pain. Do I make myself clear?"

Nikolai jerked a brief, sullen nod.

"Your political leanings mark you as an enemy against the Confederation. This can be overlooked if you give me all information regarding the Lunar observatory in Sharonov that I require."

"What do you mean my 'political leanings'? I've never been active in any movement, that I'm aware of."

Before he knew what was happening, the three other men moved in. Fists hit his jaw, elbows in his stomach. He folded up and slipped from the chair. They kicked him. The room faded out in a red haze of pain.

Barely conscious, he felt himself manhandled off the floor and thrown back into the chair. His head lolled around on his shoulders. Grinning, the Dollop Junkie grabbed Nikolai's ears and twisted them. Nikolai groaned, slowly returned to his senses.

Stinnen slapped the side of his face lightly to help bring him around further. Nikolai smelled the scent of carbolic disinfectant the man used to scrub his hands.

"Don't think me a fool, Sholokhov." Stinnen's eyes burned. "You work for the *Narodnaya Volya*. I know you were stopped at the checkpoint yesterday. Yuri Tur recruited you into his nest of criminals only two days ago. This is a taste of what you can expect if you lie to me again. Do you understand?"

"Y-yuh," Nikolai said thickly.

Stinnen bent his head to the side, regarding him. "I want to avoid any unpleasantness. I hold no personal animus towards you. These men are professionals, and enjoy their work. I can walk out of here, and in half an hour they will reduce you to a quivering lump, screaming for the release of death. That is your future, unless you work with me and not against me."

Nikolai's speech was slurred; his bottom lip bled profusely and his head throbbed. "I'll cooperate."

"Very well." Stinnen relaxed into an amenable pose. He lit another black cigarette, offered one to Nikolai, who declined. "Now: Sharonov."

Haltingly, Nikolai told them everything he had told Mintz: the name of the star, its coordinates, the unusual nature of the signals. Like last time, he hoarded a precious nugget as insurance against his life. If he gave away everything he knew, he wouldn't have anything to fall back on to keep him alive for another day, another precious hour.

Too, he wanted to use this secret as a bulwark to protect Galina. In his mind, the two details were connected; Stinnen would have to learn the first, to find out about the latter.

"When were these signals first noticed?" Stinnen asked.

Nikolai screwed up his face, trying to remember. "I'm not sure of the exact date; it was before the dish was scheduled to come on line. Say six months ago? The structure was still being calibrated."

"How did you happen to join the observation team?"

Nikolai's head was clearing rapidly. "I was a hardware technician maintaining the LAN for Kiev II in Korolev. The dish in Sharonov was seventy-five percent complete when the astronomers started running shakedown tests on the data-evaluation equipment. They were having trouble steering the feed arm and filtering out stray RF noise from the collector above the bowl. They called in men from all over the Moon and divided us into groups to tackle individual problems. Experience was at a premium; I was put in charge of my own work group. Our job was to correct the unacceptable noise-to-signal ratio filtering through the collector."

"What did you find?"

"The problem lay in the amplifier. Some of the electronics had been jostled during the trip up from Earth; the payload wasn't packed properly or something. Rather than replace the entire unit, I—that is, my team—wrote a program that filtered out the unwanted noise by changing the focal line of the telescope's antennas. That's when we noticed another signal that until then had lain hidden by the dark noise from the bad components in the amplifier."

"The alien signals?" The timbre of Stinnen's voice resonated with partial amazement. Nikolai barely registered the fact that anything could move the Grey Executioner.

"We called it starsign. We didn't know they were alien, at first. We thought it was just another frequency of noise we had to filter out. After exhaustive testing we were certain that wasn't the case. These signals resolved into points moving around the star, giving off electromagnetic radiation in the high end of the energy spectrum. Some of the sources tracked in the opposite direction; their signals Dopplered into radio frequencies. No natural phenomenon could account for that result. These were spacecraft exploring another star system."

Stinnen paced back and forth, tugging thoughtfully at his earlobe. "How many people in the observatory knew about this discovery?"

"My group working on the collector, along with the highest ranking scientists and a hierarchy of administrators. Say fifty men. Everybody else was kept strictly in the dark. In fact, the men farmed out from the other sites on Dark Side were sent home soon afterwards. They never knew anything about it at all."

"There are hundreds of men who worked on Sharonov. I have the figures. What about them?"

Nikolai shrugged. "They never knew what we detected around Kornephoros. Still don't, as far as I know. The people you mentioned are low-rated tech engineers, radiation specialists, support personnel, and the like. They would never have had a chance to sample and evaluate the raw data received through that dish. In any event, they weren't aware of the results when I left Luna a week ago. The situation may have changed since then but I doubt it."

"Where is Yuri Tur?"

"I—I don't know. I tried to find him in GUM and then I came to the forest looking for the *posad*."

Stinnen headed for the door. He paused with one hand on the handle. "Soften him up," he told Zim. "When I return we will continue his questioning. Perhaps he'll be more cooperative then."

Nikolai's skin crawled. "Hey! Wait a minute. I thought we'd—"

"Shut up," Zim snapped. He turned down a thermostat on the wall.

Lip Scar and the Dollop Junkie pinned his arms behind the chair. Zim balled his fist and struck. Nikolai's head rocked back with terrific force. His mouth swam with the salty taste of hot blood. Zim hit him a second time, and Nikolai sagged.

"Sit up!" A coarse backhand cracked across his bruised face.

The room was becoming an icebox. Freezing air brawled from ventilation grids set high in the ceiling. Frosty roils of smoke puffed from their mouths and nostrils. They stripped him and pushed him back naked into the chair.

"Where is Yuri Tur?"

"I don't know," was the slurred response.

Nikolai's head vibrated strangely but he couldn't stop his chattering teeth. He felt ashamed.

Someone slammed a half-fist into the back of his neck. Zim yelled another question into his face.

"I don't know where he is," he mumbled back, shivering.

"The traitor, Yuri Tur! Tell us!"

"GUM."

"No, he isn't, we checked. You know where he is, and you're lying to us. This will not end until you cooperate."

They started again.

Hours passed. Perhaps days. Nikolai lost all proportion of time. The three men pounced upon him like hyenas. He hunkered down, trying to protect himself, fighting back as best he could.

Only one thought got him through, shining like a beacon.

Galina.

When the initial session ended, and only an occasional blow landed in the solar plexus or kidney, the three men talked openly of what they should do next. They went so far as to solicit Nikolai's advice. Perhaps they should burn his eyes with the lighted end of a cigar or drown him in the stopped up toilet in a cell down the hall.

Lip Scar suggested, "A red hot knitting needle up the urethra always loosens the tongue."

Zim was more extravagant. "How about this? Tie his wrists to the chair; we have bayonet wire. Then use a cheese grater—isn't there one in the kitchen in the east wing?—and flay the skin off of his forearms. Then pour kerosene into the wound."

"Wouldn't turpentine be better?" asked the Dollop Junkie.

They argued over the relative merits of each.

During the discussion they sometimes glanced longingly at a tray arrayed with wooden truncheons, rubber saps, mallets, knives, pliers. The Dollop Junkie slipped on a pair of knuckle dusters while Zim examined a sprinkling of long silver instruments that glittered prettily in the overhead light balls.

"Where is Yuri Tur?"

Nikolai worked his sore jaw and thick cottony tongue back and forth, gathering saliva to lubricate his throat.

"Don't know . . . didn't tell me." He refused to believe the animal croak he heard was his voice.

"Liar!"

He thought fuzzily, blearily: What is Stinnen doing? Having a quiet cup of coffee, probably. Could he hear Nikolai's cries? Doubtful. This work was for subordinates.

Nikolai slid between periods of blackness bordered with red heat and dull pain. Razor thin slices of reality floated up from a black seductive pool like flotsam. He tried to grasp one. . . .

"Don't know . . . location . . . Yuri Tur. C'be anywhere."

Zim placed the barrel of a needlegun against Nikolai's temple. His patience was running thin.

"I should put all eight into your brain. Is that what you want? Keep lying to me and that's how it will end!"

Somewhere, in a reserve he didn't know he had, Nikolai shouted back: "I don't know where he is, you stupid bastard. Why would he tell me? I'm not part of his crew."

Zim went berserk and crashed the pistol butt down on Nikolai's scalp. The pain was nothing compared to what he had already endured. Zim laid his gun down and grabbed another weapon, raised it high into the air.

"Enough."

The single word stopped the action like the crack of a bullwhip. Feodor lowered the truncheon he had intended to drive into Nikolai's groin.

Nikolai raised his head, weakly. Stinnen had returned. His mastiffs were heeled at his side, black and tan statues from Hell.

The only sound in the room was Nikolai's labored breath sawing in and out of his tortured lungs. Drops of blood splattered the plascrete floor around his chair in a ring.

"Report."

Zim shook his head angrily. "He's a tough one."

The Dollop Junkie remarked, "I don't know if it means anything, but he mumbled a woman's name."

Interested: "Oh?"

The *zwilnik* nodded. "It sounded like 'Galina.' "

Back to Nikolai, eyebrows arched in question.

"The Metchnikoph in my room, in the Warren. Only AI, helped me when I first got to Earth." Nikolai prayed the thin lie would be believed.

A long moment passed. Zim said, "A room-maid class savant with a low Turing rating. These Outworlders use them for conversation and company like pets."

More silence. Nikolai's heart raced.

"I don't think it means anything," Stinnen finally agreed. "He doesn't know any women; he hasn't even had his first Privilege yet. Anything else?"

Feodor Zim answered for everyone: "Give me more time. I can break him down."

"We cannot risk a long and protracted session." The Grey Executioner slid his hands into his coat pockets, businesslike. "He must disappear immediately, for reasons that will become clear later. I will leave those details to you, Feodor."

It was like throwing meat to a hungry animal.

Zim smiled. "Very well."

Stinnen told Nikolai: "There is nothing personal in this. You are only a cipher about to be erased." The corners of his mouth turned down reluctantly. "It is nothing I have against you—the man."

He bent forward at the waist and thrust his face close. "You understand my position?" he asked quietly, urgently.

Nikolai managed to croak out a single word. *"Da."*

Was there a latent message hidden behind the gimlet eyes of the state executioner? Nikolai gritted his teeth. If so, what did it mean?

He tried to sharpen his thoughts and prayed it wasn't another mean trick.

Stinnen prepared to leave the cell. "I will await your final report," he told Feodor Zim. He rounded the two guards and, hand flashing from his coat pocket like a cobra, pressed the head of a sleepdeath module against Lip Scar's lower spine.

The man went down in a heap, collapsing upon Nikolai and draping across his chair. Nikolai brutally kicked the man off him and then threw himself out of the way. Stinnen went after the next man.

"Hey!" Zim shouted. He hesitantly reached for his needlegun. . . .

Stinnen clicked the module against the Dollop Junkie but missed the skull and the main trunk of the nervous system, hitting only a shoulder blade. The *zwilnik* screamed and flailed as the radionics from the module raked the myelin sheaths of his nervous system on the right half of his body.

Zim swung his needlegun up and hit the firing button. The first flechette went wide and smashed glassware on a shelf. Nikolai grabbed the wrong end of a truncheon but swung it anyway with all of his strength, shattering the small bones in Zim's hand. The needlegun dropped and clattered on the floor.

Nikolai sensed, rather than saw, two black muscled shapes fly through the air on either side of him and land on

Feodor Zim. The mastiffs growled and slavered as they snapped and bit at his throat. Twisting and writhing on the floor, Zim tried to beat the monstrous jaws away from his face.

Nikolai leaped across the bloodstained floor and snatched up the needlegun. He opened the barrel and was about to fire all the remaining flechettes into Zim when something knocked him down from behind. It was the Dollop Junkie, still thrashing from the mishit by Stinnen's sleepdeath module.

He scrambled to get out of the way of the dying zombie, and at the same time keep clear of the rest of the carnage. He threw out a leg and brought the *zwilnik* down so Stinnen would have a chance to finish him. The Dollop Junkie tore at his skin with his nails, frothing bloody foam. Long guttural screams rattled from his throat. Stinnen straddled his torso and clicked the sleepdeath module against his forehead, silencing him forever.

A final, piercing shriek from the opposite side of the room indicated that Zim had lost his battle with the mastiffs. His dead body jiggled grotesquely as the dogs shook him back and forth in their clamped jaws, their paws skittering in the deepening pool of blood.

"Oberon. Titania. Back off. I said 'back off', damn you."

Reluctantly, the two dogs returned to their master's side. Stinnen shot Nikolai a hurried look. "You'd better get dressed. We don't have much time to get you out of here and back to Moscow." He put the sleepdeath module on 'recharge' and dropped it into his coat pocket.

Nikolai still had the needlegun. He lifted it. "Not until you tell me what this is all about."

The mastiffs growled.

"Don't be a fool. Put that goddamn thing down before I

release these dogs." Stinnen gathered his clothes and pitched them across the room to land in a heap at his feet. "Hurry up. We're on a tight schedule."

Nikolai refused to lower the gun.

Stinnen, exasperated, rubbed his face with both hands. "Goddamnit, can't you understand I'm trying to get you out of here alive? This place is used all the time; another group may show up at any moment. Put that gun away!"

"You forget: I've had experience with comprehensive artificial systems. Feodor told me an AI runs this place. It's probably plugged into every security computer in Moscow. How do you expect to get past it?"

"By walking out of here like nothing happened."

"Just like that?"

"Just like that. Look," Stinnen said, "can't you dress while I explain? Yes, an enslaved AI oversees this Isolator, but not this individual room. It can't. No AI could ever witness what happens inside Room Five without suffering irreversible psychological damage to its thought-shards."

Nikolai finished dressing and slipped his glasses back on.

"This room is on a blackout loop?"

"Has to be. The security AI that runs this complex would go insane if it were forced to monitor the torture that goes on in this room—any modern AI would. Their minds are too fragile and it would violate one of their primary Ethics Laws."

"To run this place the AI must have some idea of what it's used for," Nikolai argued. "Otherwise, it wouldn't be an effective security system."

"Naturally. But knowing a thing, and being forced to witness it, are not the same thing: not to an AI, anyway. They can disassociate themselves and live in denial as well, or better, than any human being can. Now, come on!"

Nikolai didn't care if Stinnen was becoming infuriated. Despite the glib explanations there was nothing that made him want to trust the man. This was the same bastard who coldly authorized executions. Nikolai only had to look at three new bodies slowly cooling around him to know that Stinnen was not a man to be trusted—under any circumstance.

"Why are you doing this? Why should you care what happens to me?"

"I don't. Care for you, that is. I'm helping someone else." He went to the door, motioned hurriedly. "Let's go."

"Where are we going?"

"You're going back on the DFC. I'll stay here and clean up the mess we left behind. Afterwards, I'll open a cyber-gate into the DataSphere and release a program to remove all the tags I put on you. You're a free man again, Sholokhov." An icy grin froze on his lips. "That is, until you do something that may or may not bring you to the attention of my bureau. Next time, you may not walk out of an Isolator alive. So watch your step."

Nikolai followed him out of the freezing room into the warm corridor. Stinnen locked the door to Room Five with an elaborate palm-lock and activated a howler. At the main entrance he tapped in a security code on the door panel. They strolled out into daylight.

A float-eye emerged from its skyhouse.

"You are finished with your business, Colonel Stinnen?" it asked.

"Yes, quite." Stinnen was matter-of-fact.

"Are there any further orders?"

"I will return after I see this man off."

"Very well. I will wait." The float-eye retired to its skyhouse. They walked across the landing field to the DFC.

Halfway across, Nikolai stumbled. Stinnen grabbed his arm and steadied him. "Are you all right?"

He took his arm out of the other man's hand and returned a baleful stare. His other hand instinctively squeezed the butt of the needlegun in his pocket. "I'm exhausted, confused, hungry, and I ache all over from the gravity and the going over your goons gave me. Hell, no, I'm not all right."

They approached the ducted-fan craft. The pilot, sitting on the steps of the plane and smoking a cigarette, looked up, his face registering surprise. Nikolai identified with the other man's bewilderment. He, too, couldn't quite believe he had gotten out of that dreadful place in one piece.

"Take this man back to the place where you picked him up," Stinnen directed. "Then return to base for debriefing."

The pilot snapped to attention. "Yes, sir."

Stinnen faced Nikolai one last time. "I've paid my debt, Sholokhov. Tell your friend that now he owes me, and I will collect."

He spun on his heel and marched stiffly towards the white building.

"You ready?" the pilot asked, staring at Nikolai with slow wonder.

"Let's go." Nikolai climbed into the fuselage. The six hooded blades kicked on and the deck tilted as they clawed their way into the sky. When the nose of the DFC dipped an hour later he knew they had reached their destination.

After touchdown he opened the door and rapidly scrambled out. He gave the pilot a laconic wave to show he was clear of the fans. The machine whipped the trees and dead leaves into one last frenzy before turning west and disappearing.

Nikolai trudged back to the steep grade where he had to wait for another *elektrichka* into Moscow. When he smelled the cigarette smoke he brought his head up, wary.

A man lounged along the broken rock spine, lying on his side, ankles crossed, one hand propping up his head. A smoldering cigarette dangled from the fingers of his other hand. His blonde hair glimmered in the late afternoon sun.

Nikolai's fingers tightened fearfully around the needlegun. His first thought when he saw the man waiting for him was: Oh, no, not again. . . .

The man crushed the half-smoked cigarette under an expensive shoe. "I was about to give up on you, Sholokhov." He looked genuinely happy he had not waited in vain. "Ikon, but they did a job on you. You look like hell."

Nikolai cried with astonishment. "Yuri!"

The *blatnoi* flung his arms wide open, threw his head back, and released a booming laugh that shook the forest.

Eight

Nikolai gripped Yuri's hand with both of his and pumped it up and down. "What in the dead Czar's name are you doing here? Ikon, I never thought I'd see you again. Do you know what I've been through? Well, of course you do, you're the one who got me out."

Yuri deadpanned: "You have a lot of energy for someone who just toured an Isolator."

Nikolai brushed off the concern. "Oh, they'd barely gotten started. Tell me, what the hell is going on around here?"

Yuri lit a fresh cigarette, cupping the wavering flame. "You've probably guessed most of it." He shook the match out, took a deep drag, flicked ash. "Stinnen belongs to the *Narodnaya Volya;* that is, he's what we call a ghost member. He won't do anything to compromise Confederation security, but will, from time to time, lend a helping hand. It was pure luck we got you out. If the chain of events had been any different you'd be languishing in a punishment cell even as we speak."

Nikolai returned a doubtful look. "I can't believe Stinnen works for you." He didn't want to believe a cold reptile like that had any loyalty towards another human being. He vented his frustration: "I saw him execute three men the morning after the riot." The image was still fresh: Stinnen standing around smoking those dreadful black cigarettes while the sleepdeath module clicked against unprotected skulls.

Yuri retrieved a flask from the interior lining of his coat and unscrewed the cap. He took a nip out of it, passed it over. "First of all, Stinnen doesn't work for me; he doesn't work for anyone other than himself. He's a cold-blooded killer and that's a fact. He has no alliance to any organization and that's another fact. That's why he's called the 'Grey Executioner.' His convictions don't fall into an either/or Boolean operation. Life—and death—isn't black or white to him."

Nikolai drank out of the metal flask. The harsh liquor smelled faintly of fusel oil and burned the back of his throat, igniting a small coke fire in the pit of his stomach. "I've seen what life means to Stinnen." He wiped his stinging lips, drank again deeply to cover up his bitterness.

"All I can say is, I've known him my whole life. He's an enigma, I'll grant you that."

Nikolai choked on the cheap vodka. "What do you mean, you've known him 'your whole life'?"

"He's my brother."

Nikolai gaped, flabbergasted.

"People choose different paths in their lives," Yuri said with philosophical indifference. "Who's to say his road is any worse than mine? Or yours? I don't pass judgment on other people. Life's too fucking short for that kind of comedy."

"Does Mintz know about Stinnen?"

Yuri tipped the flask and drained its contents. "Mintz knows everything. Do you think I could keep something like that from a man like him?"

Nikolai recalled the details he had held back concerning the alien signals. Yuri was wrong. Mintz wasn't infallible. He filed that knowledge away for future reference.

"How do you know he's your brother?" Everyone

Nikolai knew had grown up in one of the state-owned crèches. A restricted background like that was never conducive to fraternal relationships of any kind.

"We're half-brothers, if you want to get technical about it. Our father was an important molecular biologist during the Mad Times, when the *Fevreblau* was sparking all over the world like brush fire. He headed a group of *cognoscenti* hired by Old Russia to figure out a way to neutralize the virus. They failed, but developed a social order to insure the continuation of our culture—albeit in a fragmented (and some would argue artificial) form. Kept the old tradition of using surnames for bloodline continuity. Many of these men donated sperm samples to be used by the crèches later on. The records are quite clear: Stinnen and I are siblings, albeit from different genetic ova. When he went to work for Internal Security he took the name 'Stinnen.' "

"He released me as a favor toward you?"

"Believe it or not."

"Well, I can't say I'm sorry to be rid of that place, but I'm afraid it's going to cost you plenty."

"In what way?"

"He expects payment in return. You now owe him, he says."

"That's to be expected. Barter economy. When he wants his remittance he'll let me know." He ground his half-smoked cigarette out. "It won't be the first time; that's our relationship. Now, what about you, Sholokhov? How did they pick you up in the first place?"

"They didn't, as much as I fell into their lap." He related the whole story, from the day they last saw each other to the present, omitting nothing save for Galina.

He wound the tale down. "Before I knew it, Stinnen was giving me a wink and a nod. After the bloodbath, a DFC flew me back. Here you were, waiting for me."

Yuri had listened to the story without interrupting. "You say this fellow, this Feodor Zim, was staking me out in GUM?"

"I think he wanted to pick up your trail there and set his own people on you during the riot."

"Sounds like you accidentally took my place in the Isolator." He lit another cigarette. "Hmm. Too bad you couldn't locate me earlier. I would have warned you the *posad* had picked up and moved on. Mintz wanted to deny any involvement with that riot, you see. Yes, it was started by a splinter group that broke away from the *Narodnaya Volya* about eighteen months ago. Very hardcore group of cobbers who think washing the streets of Moscow with blood will break the back of the government. Good men, don't get me wrong, but men who have forgotten their history." He smoked in silence for a minute. "There's always an easier way than cutting throats in the night. Zim must have wormed himself deeply into one of our cells to have found out that much about me." He was openly worried. "That will have to be investigated. By the way, have you got that needlegun you took off him?"

"Right here."

The thief examined the gun. "Just as I suspected. Thumbprint activated." A cigarette dangling from his mouth, he pointed the weapon at an evergreen tree and thumbed the firing button. Nothing happened.

Nikolai experienced a hot wave of embarrassment. "I didn't notice that when I took it off him."

"Not your fault. Zim was a high-ranking security man. It doesn't do for a professional in that line of work to carry a weapon someone can use against him."

"The needleguns and shocksticks we have on Kiev II can

be used by anyone," Nikolai pointed out.

"Quite right, too. But then Luna is a bit more civilized than Moscow, wouldn't you agree?" Yuri placed the gun on a stone and brought the heel of his boot down several times.

Gathering the fragments in his palm, he picked through them and held up a black cylinder between thumb and forefinger.

"What's that?"

"GPS tracer. Most security organs implant them in their weapons. I'm willing to bet Zim also had one or two sewn under his skin." He placed the tracer on a rock and crushed it to bits with his foot. "I don't know if Zim activated it, but it can't hurt us now. And neither can this." He threw the broken pieces of the needlegun into the pine forest.

Together, they heard the piercing whistle of an *elecktrichka.*

Yuri touched his arm. "Come on. We can get some food on the train and buy a spool of regen tape for those abrasions on your face."

They caught the train. Yuri passed the conductor a folded fifty-czar note to look the other way and not make trouble just because they didn't have tickets. The conductor made the note disappear with customary ease.

"Would you gentlemen like anything else?" His blue uniform had padded shoulders and the ubiquitous emblem of all state trains: a burnished brass icon of a winged-wheel pinned to his breast pocket.

Yuri put his wallet away. The train rocked across points. "Sandwiches? We've been picking mushrooms all day long. Haven't had much luck, though, and we're famished."

Nikolai thought the mushroom cover was wearing a bit thin, but the conductor didn't appear to notice, or care. To Yuri's annoyance, the conductor explained that, no, he didn't have anything to eat, but he'd send someone by with a spool of regen tape all the same.

The two men settled in their seats. Late afternoon sun slanted through the transparent dome ceiling, warming the car. The regen tape arrived. He pulled off a long stuttering strip and, with Yuri's help, applied patches to his face and arms.

The countryside rushed past his window. He used the time to wonder how he was going to enlist Yuri's help with Galina.

He turned the problem over and over in his mind. How far can I trust him? After all, he's *blatnye,* and proud of it: Like a peacock preening his feathers. He flaunts his ability to shake bluecaps off his back whenever he wants to. I must have him on my side. But he won't do it for nothing. He'll want to be paid. What do I have to offer?

There were other questions, too, nagging Nikolai.

"How is Stinnen going to dispose of those bodies in the Isolator?" he asked.

"Incinerate them, I suppose. It's what I would do."

Nikolai guessed that too would have been his fate had not Yuri intervened. I owe this man my life, he thought. What right do I have to spring this new trouble on him?

Well, the worst he can do is say no.

No, he thought suddenly, the worst he can do is turn both me and Galina in to the Protectorate. There would be a substantial reward. Nikolai studied the other man, smoking quietly and reading a magazine loop taken from his seat's side pouch. Yuri might be a lot of things, he decided, but he wasn't a Judas. After all, Mintz trusted him. Nikolai doubted a man that discreet chose his compatriots unwisely.

The train pulled into the station and they got off together. The ticket master was still selling his bunkmate's sugar rolls. Nikolai bought a half dozen. He and Yuri devoured them on the way into Moscow.

"Hang on a minute," Nikolai held back. "I want to call up a fellow I know and find out if he made it through the riot okay."

"Fine by me." Yuri ambled off to buy a news-loop while Nikolai put the call through to the Warren.

Sonya answered on the first ring.

"Hello?"

His mouth was dry. "It's me, Nikolai."

"Nikolai! I was getting worried. You hadn't checked in for so long—I thought something had gone wrong."

"No, no. I'm okay." His heart beat a little easier. "How is Mischa's cold?"

"Mischa was upset you hadn't bothered to check in, but he's feeling much better now. Quite happy, in fact. Are you coming home now?"

"Yes. I've found the friend I was looking for." He cast a quick glance at Yuri, hands clasped behind his back, watching the bland faces of the people getting off and on the trains. "We'll be home in half an hour."

"I'll be waiting." Sonya broke the connection.

Nikolai replaced the handset. Yuri walked up to him. "Everything all right with your friend?"

"Yes. I noticed that you were watching the people on that train. Anything wrong?"

"I want to make sure we aren't being followed. Who's your friend?"

Nikolai had to think twice before he realized what Yuri meant. "Oh, a fellow I ran into during the riot." Keep the lie as close to the truth as possible, he thought. "His name is Borod. Piotr Borod. Met him last night before curfew.

Didn't have a place to stay so I thought I'd put him up for the night. Seemed a right enough sort of cobber. Didn't think it would do any harm."

Yuri's face was inscrutable. "Got to be careful about that kind of thing," he chided, "picking strangers up off the street, I mean. You don't know where they've been or who they are. Lots of people in Moscow are willing to take advantage of an offworlder, if you give them half a chance."

"This cobber isn't like that. In fact—" he gaped. "You talked to Piotr . . . ?"

Yuri rolled his broad shoulders up and down. "Saw him earlier today. While you were looking for me, I was looking for you, so I went to the Warren. He told me you were going to the *posad*. That's when I knew you might get into trouble."

"Why?"

"Sometimes undesirables hang around an old *posad* site like that. They ambush unsuspecting men, roll them and leave them for dead. They're like vultures. They haunt the woods. They won't do anything while a *posad* is up and running, they wait until it's moved on before they strike. They're cowards, most of them, and not even respected by ordinary *blatari*. You were lucky you didn't fall into their hands."

"No," Nikolai said wryly, "just Zim's. Yet, you were out there yourself, looking for me," he pointed out.

Yuri nodded sagely. "I can take care of myself, Sholokhov. Been doing it since I was eleven. Life on the road holds no mystery or danger to me, but to an Outworlder like yourself. . . ." He clearly didn't want to dwell on the possible consequences. "Once I knew where you had gone, I got in touch with Stinnen and made arrangements to get you out of that Isolator."

127

Even though he knew it was the truth, Nikolai still had trouble accepting the fact this self-effacing thief would stick his neck out for him in that fashion. There was no way Yuri, even distantly tied by blood to Stinnen as he was, could force him to do his bidding. They might be brothers, but Stinnen was the Grey Executioner. Someone else had to be behind the rescue operation.

Mintz.

Nikolai was certain of it. Mintz was the puppet master. His was the hand holding the strings. Why? Because Mintz, like Yuri, was *Narodnaya Volya*.

It was a disquieting thought. What are they up to? From the beginning they've gone out of their way to keep me happy and content. And safe. Mintz has obviously appointed Yuri as my guardian angel. Why else would he come looking for me?

Sharanov. Nikolai sighed. That was the only answer that made any sense. Mintz was fascinated with those alien signals. And there had been men at the *posad* waiting for him to finish questioning Nikolai. Another *Narodnaya Volya* cell? They had looked like government officials, not criminals.

Too many questions, damn few answers. Especially, since he became involved with this nutty plan to get Galina to a sanctuary.

At least Yuri didn't suspect Piotr's true gender. That was a comfort. He would have to know sooner or later, though. Nikolai was shocked Galina had let a stranger into his room. Not that she cared about Nikolai's privacy, he figured, but her own safety would have been compromised.

"What did you and Piotr talk about?" he asked.

"You, mostly. He was rattled, I think, because I caught him napping. Rattled me, too, if you want to know the truth. I expected the room to be empty."

"When you . . . huh? You mean, he didn't answer the door?"

Nikolai saw a look come over Yuri he never thought he would live long enough to see: one of sheepishness. "Not really. You see, I sort of let myself in."

"Sort of?"

Yuri shamefully explained: "I didn't break in if that's what you're thinking. I had a copy of your palm-lock key made. Remember the baths? When you went to get a massage I rifled your clothes and made an impression. Then I went to meet you at the pool."

"Goddamnit, Yuri, you had no right going through my things like that." Try as he might, he couldn't work up any real anger towards the man. Yuri had saved his life. Anyway, the audacity of the act amazed him.

"Don't be angry. I only did it because, well, it's my nature to do things like that." Yuri was behaving like a boy explaining to a schoolmaster: "I only made that paper airplane and threw it at you because it's my nature."

"I would never have stolen anything personal, Sholokhov."

"That's a comfort."

"You said you'd help me get in and out of the Warren."

Nikolai ruefully admitted that was true.

"Okay, so I didn't make it clear how you were going to do it. Does that make me a bad person?"

"Sounds like you're trying to justify what you did to yourself."

"Perhaps I am," Yuri said candidly. Then: "I'm not apologizing for what I am. I'm not asking for absolution. I shouldn't have done it and I'm sorry. But let's face it, Sholokhov, I didn't really know you then."

"All right, forget it."

"You're mad."

"I'm not, really."

"Yes, you are."

Nikolai thought it over. "Piqued, maybe. Hell, I know the type of man you are. I just didn't expect all this . . ." he made a gesture ". . . the riot, Feodor Zim, the Isolator. I came to Earth expecting to see a few sights and have my Privilege."

"Well, you can't say you haven't seen a few sights, now can you?"

Nikolai barked laughter before falling into a dark mood. "I'll have some pretty tall tales to tell my mates when I get back to Dark Side. I owe you a lot, Yuri. My life, for one, which I don't consider cheap. Meeting Yasu. I really appreciate everything you've done."

Yuri handled the heartfelt praise awkwardly. "I have an idea," he said, shifting gears. "Let's go get that boy you found and we three go have a big dinner." He placed both hands on his muscled stomach and massaged. "My belly's empty. I haven't had a good meal in days. What do you say?"

Nikolai readily agreed. It would be an easy way to lure Yuri into his apartment, and slowly (carefully!) break the news about Galina.

They strolled in tandem towards the Warren. The streets were clean and traffic was moving again. People appeared to be on their best behavior, perhaps in response to the confusion and tumult that had so recently dominated their lives. There weren't many bluecaps policing the corners, either. They passed a burned-out building, windows gaping upon the local neighborhood like open mouths, and the riddled hulks of vehicles that hadn't been towed away by city maintenance. Other than this, everything had returned to normal.

"As normal as life ever gets in Moscow," Yuri observed with clever irony.

From what Nikolai had seen so far, he tended to agree.

"What did you and Piotr talk about?" They walked through an open plaza. Yuri changed direction to inspect a handful of kiosks, but when nothing caught his attention among the wares he replied: "Like I said, the kid rattled me. I wasn't expecting anyone in your apartment."

He gave Nikolai a quick glance to see if his remark was misunderstood. He must have seen something in Nikolai's face, because he went on to say, "What I mean is, I saw how you looked at Yasu with that strong hunger men sometimes get. You aren't the kind of cobber who goes in for young boys, I know."

"No, I'm not."

Yuri seemed to feel he had extricated himself from a sticky situation. "Anyway, back to the story: After I let myself in, I kicked the frame of the bed to wake the kid up. What a reaction I got! He bolted straight into the air. It was comical. He clutched about himself and jammed a cap on top of his head as if he were late for school and had to get dressed in a hurry. I must admit I did everything I could to intimidate him. I didn't know where you were or what he was doing there, you understand. I blustered about the place, telling the Metchnikoph to shut the hell up, and went after this boy. I grabbed his collar and gave him a good shaking."

Yuri assumed a stern countenance: " 'Who are you?' I barked. 'What are you doing in my friend's room?' "

Now his face changed, like plastic, and turned into a frightened, wide-eyed mask. " 'P-Piotr Borod. I'm . . . I'm a friend of Nikolai's too!'

131

" 'Prove it!' I thundered.

" 'E-excuse me?' the boy squeaked."

He stomped his feet on the sidewalk to make his antics more theatrical.

" 'You heard me. What are you doing in these rooms? Nikolai didn't tell me he had a guest. I think I'll call the desk and find out about you. . . .'

"At this point, I reached threateningly for the Metchnikoph's console. The kid started forward, pleading with me. 'No, mister, no! I promise, I'm a guest here. Nikolai knows me. Ask Sonya!'

"I took this to mean the computer on a sideboard. 'A Metchnikoph will lie for anybody,' I said. 'Even State Security doesn't trust their twitchy programming. I'm not going to take the word of something with silicon guts.'

" 'Please, don't call the desk. Look, here's my pood. . . .' "

Yuri chuckled in a low rumble, remembering the boy's frantic deportment. "He showed me what was obviously your travel bag," he explained to Nikolai, "because it had your initials on it. I suggested, calmly, we call a bluecap to straighten everything out. I hauled him by the collar towards the door when he started crying."

Yuri admitted with marked repose, "I wasn't expecting that. The kid really bawled. Streams of tears. 'Okay,' I said, 'we don't have to bring the bluecaps into this, but I want to know what you're doing here.' "

He waited for Nikolai to swipe his Warren-ident card at the entrance. They entered the cool atmosphere of the glass and steel hotel. The concierge and another hotel worker were hunched over a news loop, gesticulating and talking loudly as they accessed more information from the DataSphere.

Inside the elevator, Yuri wrapped up his story. "That's when the kid told me he talked you into taking him off the streets. I asked where you were; he said you went to find a man named Yuri Tur. What a face he had when I told him I was that man." He relaxed an elbow on the elevator's brass railing. "I figured you might try the *posad*. That's when I contacted my brother, and you know the rest. He took a big risk, my brother, doing this favor for me. I can understand why he'll demand a large payment in the future. I don't blame him; I would do the same in his shoes."

On the fourteenth floor they climbed the stairs to Nikolai's room.

Yuri halted outside his door. "Shall we burst in, like I did last time? It might be fun to give the kid another scare."

Nikolai smiled. Not half the scare you're going to get in a few minutes, he thought. "We'd better not. Sounds to me like you've put him through the wringer already." He used his palm-lock key to open the door.

Sonya gasped. "Nikolai, thank goodness it's you. I've been worried. Who do you have with you—oh, it's that boorish person again. Will he be spending the night too? If so, I'll have to charge you for the extra occupant."

"No, Sonya, Yuri won't be staying. We're all going out for dinner together. Hello, Piotr."

Galina was in the kitchenette stirring a packet of lemon into a mug of black tea. When she saw Nikolai, she dropped the spoon onto the counter, making a ringing sound. "Nikolai, thank god, you've come back. I was . . . I was worried." Her attention shifted to Yuri and her face lost its malleability. "Hello," she said woodenly.

The distant greeting didn't put him off. "Hello, Piotr. As you see, Nikolai and I have found one another. Hey, no hard feelings, okay? Can we be friends?"

The girl resumed stirring her tea. "Sure."

"This is the fellow I was telling you about," Nikolai said. "If anyone can help us with your . . . problem, it's Yuri."

Sonya butted in. "Nikolai, there's some extremely important news being posted in the DataSphere. Have you heard? It concerns—"

"Sonya," Nikolai snapped back, "I'm talking now. Don't interrupt me again."

"Yes, sir." She lapsed into a hurtful silence.

"Damn these Metchnikophs," Yuri interjected, "they can nag you to death about the most minute details."

"Let's sit down." Nikolai let Yuri take the only chair in the room. Galina placed herself next to Nikolai on the bed, her hands pressed between her knees.

A clumsy silence followed while Nikolai collected his thoughts, but before he could say anything, Yuri addressed Galina.

"Piotr, Nikolai and I were thinking of going out for a bite of dinner." No response. "Hey, I didn't mean to be rude earlier. You rattled me, kid. I'm really a very nice guy. Just ask Nikolai. Right, Sholokhov?"

Nikolai placed a hand on Galina's arm. "This is the man I talked so much about," he told her again. "Yuri can help me help you. Okay?"

Her disposition softened measurably. "If you say so."

"I do," he said firmly. "Yuri, Piotr and I have a favor to ask."

"It's my nature to grant favors for my friends."

"We need your help. That is, Piotr needs your special talents. We'd be willing to pay."

Yuri shifted his eyes back and forth between the pair. "The kid in some kind of trouble with the law, Sholokhov?"

"You might say that. It's rather a long story, but to get

right down to it . . . Why don't you show him, Galina? It'll save a lot of initial explaining—for the first half of the story, anyway."

The girl ruefully nodded. Her mouth made a small moue of distaste as she demurely unbuttoned her shirt, stopping halfway down.

Yuri's bemusement increased. "Sholokhov, what the hell are you on about? Who's 'Galina'? I thought this kid's name was Piotr . . ."

"Go ahead, Galina," Nikolai coaxed gently. "We have to trust Yuri."

Galina meekly pulled the lapels of her shirt open. Yuri vaulted from his chair as if stung by a shockstick.

"IKON!"

Nine

"Goddammit, Sholokhov, you've gotten me into a mess and I don't mind who knows it," Yuri declared. "No, scratch that, I *do* mind. I've never seen a man stumble into more trouble than you. Do you know how difficult it's been for me? First, you get caught in the middle of a riot, then you're thrown into an Isolator—and I have to pull every string in Moscow to get you out. Now this!"

He clutched his head in his hands, bemoaning his sad fate. "Why did I let Mintz talk me into taking this job? I'm not cutout for bodyguard work. I have other irons in the fire to attend. I told him that, but he never listens." He jerked his head up quickly. "What do you expect me to do for this—"

"I'm a woman."

"I know what you are! Ikon, button up your shirt, will you?" He thumped a fist against the side of his head. "Sholokhov, do you know how much trouble we're in?"

"I have some idea."

"No, I don't think you do. This isn't some Asian train-puller you've got there; she's a Russian *woman*. She belongs to the State—the Union House! We'll be lucky to get sleepdeath. Lucky, I tell you."

"All right, Yuri, calm down. I met Galina the night the curfews started, after the riot ended. She promised me she wouldn't turn us in to a security organ, and I believe her. She's on the run. I don't have to explain why, or do I?"

"Of course not. The Protectorate is scouring Moscow for

136

her. *Scouring.*" Yuri dropped his head into his hands. "We'll all be sent to the Gulag. . . ."

"That's why I need your help, so that won't happen."

"What the hell do you expect out of me, Sholokhov? What am I, a fucking magician?"

"I hoped Mintz—"

Yuri raised a stalling hand. "Hold it right there, cobber. No way Mintz touches her. Damn it all, Sholokhov, get it through your thick skull: She's Union House *property.* Don't you know what that means? Do you have any *concept* what those Protectorate organs are like?"

"He doesn't," Galina said, "but I do."

Yuri studied her protractedly. "Yes, I bet you do." His voice was laced with an undercurrent of threat. "You know exactly how they operate, don't you?"

"What are you getting at, Yuri?" Nikolai asked uneasily.

Yuri got up from the chair, his gaze centered on Galina as if he half expected her to rush him. "Open your eyes, Sholokhov. She knows what we're up against, knows to what lengths the Protectorate will go to bring her back safe and sound." He rammed his hands in his pockets and stalked angrily around the room. "She's trapped us into working for her, cobber. No matter what we do, what we say, it's sleepdeath for us. We have to help her now, and she counted on that."

Nikolai licked his dry lips. "You're crazy. She wouldn't do that to us." To me.

Yuri halted in the middle of the room, skeptical. "Who are you trying to convince, Sholokhov?" He jammed an accusatory finger toward Galina. "The hell she wouldn't sell us out. If we go to the Protectorate now and turn ourselves in, it's sleepdeath. They're not going to listen to any excuses when it comes to her—and she knew that before she tricked you into helping her."

"I don't believe it." Nikolai appealed to Galina. "You didn't really trick me into helping you . . . did you?"

The girl stopped nibbling her bottom lip. "Don't be ridiculous. I don't know where he's getting this from." Her face was pale. "He's crazy."

A voice deep down inside shouted at him: Didn't she try to manipulate you yesterday? Remember, when she was sitting on this very bed. . . .

Dismayed, he felt confusion taking hold. What about her tears when she told me what life was like in the *sharashka?* Play-acting? Or had she known, from the start, what our fate would be if we happened to be caught with her?

Answer: She must have known. She grew up inside the Protectorate, knew it intimately. She wasn't an unintelligent person. Yuri was right, she had trapped them on purpose.

The muscles in his jaw bunched. Yuri was right.

The night she persuaded him to take her inside the Warren, she knew what could happen, but she went ahead and drew him into her confidence. Had the frightened desperation on her face that night masked a deeper emotion? One of unfeeling cruelty . . . ?

Yuri saw the quandary playing openly on his face and pounced. "You know I'm right, Sholokhov. I'm right, and she's lying. In the end, she may win out and gain her freedom. Won't matter to us, though. Our fates are fixed, and she knows it."

Nikolai felt emotionally drained. This was happening too fast, spinning way out of his limited control. He came to Earth for a paid holiday and to receive his Privilege. From almost the first day his life in Moscow was turned upside down. Now, he had to deal with this personal betrayal.

"Galina, tell me the truth," he prompted. "No more lies."

"Sholokhov, I've told you a dozen times—"

"Yuri, shut up!" Nikolai barked back. His eyes never left hers. "I'm talking to Galina right now. Your turn will come later."

The thief clamped his mouth closed, but kept a just-you-wait-and-see attitude on his flushed face.

"I want the truth this time, Galina. Did you plan to use us, all along, just so you could get what you wanted?"

Trapped between him and Yuri, she crossed her arms under her breasts, afraid to face either of them. "Obviously, I knew it would be dangerous if we were caught . . ." she began limply.

Yuri grunted with ironic satisfaction. Nikolai shot him a dark look.

Galina went on, her voice timid and small. "Yes, I know it's sleepdeath if the Protectorate finds out you helped me, but I didn't start out with that as my sole purpose." She hugged herself tighter. "What I mean is, knowing what can happen isn't the same as tricking someone to make sure it does happen. I don't want anyone hurt."

Nikolai was stern. "Go on."

"I wanted to be free. I . . . I didn't stop to think—to consider—how it would affect other people around me." Tears welled. "I'm sorry, Nikolai, all I wanted was to get away from the Union House."

She folded herself onto the floor in a sitting position and slipped her face behind her slim hands.

"I was blinded. . . ." she confessed through streaming tears, "blinded by everything except my desire to be free of the Union House. I never meant to hurt . . . didn't want. . . ." She lapsed into fresh sobs.

"Well, that's that," Yuri stated with appalled finality. He slumped back in his chair and directed a fixed stare at a neutral corner of the room.

"Galina."

The girl dabbed her eyes. "Yes?" she hiccoughed. She appeared afraid of what Nikolai might do to her now that her confession was out in the open.

"People aren't machines," he said. "We don't have ones and zeros in our hearts. Men and women are more complex than that, thank god. If life were that simple, everyday would be candy. You've seen something inside yourself, a part of the soul, that you don't like. We all have it. The hardest part is accepting it and going on. Knowing it's there is half the battle of being human, and *staying* human."

She swallowed back a lump of hot tears. "You . . . you're still willing to help me?" She was having trouble believing his words.

Yuri, too, waited to hear what Nikolai had to say.

"I don't think you did what you did out of callousness. Fear, yes. Desperation, certainly. But it wasn't calculating, and that makes all the difference in the world to me." He held out a conciliatory hand. "Come on, get up off that floor. We've got a lot of thinking to do, and we have to work together to get out of this scrape."

He pulled her beside him on the bed. "Are you feeling okay?" he asked softly.

"I always hiccough when I cry." She did it again to show she was telling the truth, and smiled tremulously, just for him.

He freed a tendril of her hair caught in the corner of her mouth. "Everything's going to be fine." His stout promise sounded hollow in the bald light of fact. "We'll figure a way out of this, one way or another. I promised to help you, and I mean to do that."

"How?"

Nikolai deflected the question to the man sitting across from him. "Well, Yuri? Like you said, we're mixed up in this, like it or not. I didn't ask for this and neither did you, but it's here, and we have to deal with it."

Yuri regarded him with almost tangible fatalism. "I suppose I have little choice in the matter." Now that his path was irrevocably set, something of his old self surfaced. Nikolai thought he understood why: Yuri had a novel problem to solve, something to test his abilities. "I'm in this as deeply as you so I'll have to make the best of it. Mintz wanted me to look after you, now I'll just have to earn my money."

Sighing, he lit a cigarette, snicked the lighter closed. "First things first. Tell me exactly what happened the night you two met."

Nikolai started off, leaving nothing out of his narrative other than the bloody incident in the bathroom. He would have mentioned it but not with Galina sitting next to him. When her turn came, she told what she was doing on the bus with the other girls, how she had escaped through a broken window and hid on the streets.

Yuri listened to their stories, fascinated this had been going on under his nose. "Miss Toumanova, were all the girls dressed the same?"

"Pretty much," she said.

A cold ball of fear settled in the pit of Nikolai's stomach. "Tracers."

Yuri nodded grimly. "Too late now, if she is bugged."

Galina followed their byplay back and forth like a tennis match. "What are you talking about? What's a tracer?"

Nikolai described the technology.

"I don't think there's anything like that in these clothes," Galina said. "I would know."

"We'd better check for them all the same. Go to the bathroom and undress. Take off everything, you understand? After Yuri and I examine your clothes I'll hand them back through the door."

"We ought to consider destroying her clothes altogether," Yuri slipped in. "If she were dressed similarly to those other girls then every state security organ has that description on file. Sooner or later we'll have to leave this room. It wouldn't be prudent to parade her around while she's wearing her old costume. She'd stand out a mile."

Nikolai hadn't thought of that. "You're probably right."

"I must wear something," Galina protested.

"I'll buy a wardrobe for you downstairs in one of the shops," Yuri suggested.

"You'd better do as Yuri suggests, Galina. I think he's right about this."

She met Nikolai's gaze, saw something there that gave her hopeful courage. "All right," she said demurely. She slipped out of the room and closed the bathroom door firmly behind her.

"There's another problem," Yuri spoke, now that she was gone. "The Metchnikoph sitting over there."

"Sonya?"

"That's its name? Whatever. Can it be trusted?"

"I don't see why not. Sonya has known about Galina for almost a day now."

Yuri flicked cigarette ash. "That doesn't make me feel any better."

"Room-maid class computers are programmed to exhibit loyalty to Warren occupants. They're intended to serve as a confidant and friend."

"I understand their psychological function," Yuri said, betraying slight irritation, "but can it be trusted? That's a completely different question and you haven't answered it."

Nikolai addressed the gray console, "Sonya, are you following this conversation?"

"Yes, Nikolai," her dulcet voice answered.

"Have you, at any time, contacted the Protectorate regarding Galina?"

"No, I have not been instructed by you to do so."

"Or Internal Security?" Yuri interjected. Nikolai supposed the man was thinking of his brother, Stinnen.

"No."

"How about the MKD?"

"No."

"Any security or intelligence organization whatsoever about Galina's true identity?"

"While Nikolai holds the occupancy of this room, I can only take orders from him. My instructions regarding these parameters are quite specific. I cannot break them; my Turing rating isn't high enough."

Yuri was still plagued by lingering doubts. "Can't you rewrite your own programming to get around those restrictions?"

"I'm afraid not," Sonya responded. "My Turing rating is quite limited when it comes to exhibiting acts of self-will. Only the legal primary occupant of this room can give me instructions. As far as I know, that parameter is inviolable."

"All right. Thank you."

"You're welcome."

"Sounds okay," Yuri said, "but all the same I'll get my hands on a hide-and-seek program for the Metchnikoph so it'll believe there's only one person in this room at any one time: Nikolai. I've used them before when meeting with cell members, and they're reliable enough with something operating on a low Turing rating like Sonya."

Something else nagged fitfully at Nikolai. He slapped his knee, suddenly remembering. "God, I almost forgot. She contacted the mainframe and let it know I had a guest staying over last night."

Yuri's eyes turned into hard disks. "What?"

"Sonya told the Warren Central mainframe I had a boarder, and to charge extra for it. If she—"

"Sonya," Yuri's voice cracked like a whip. "Did you tell the Warren mainframe about Galina last night?"

"No, Yuri, I did not. I only informed Warren Central Nikolai had a guest staying the night and to put the extra charge on his bill. I did not give out any other information because I didn't have to."

"Isn't that unusual?"

"No, sir," she told him, "it isn't. Warren Central allows its legal occupants to invite extra guests into their rooms, as long as the bill is amended accordingly. Extra occupants are listed under the primary name as Guest(1). If you stayed tonight Nikolai's receipt would show that he had Guest(2) for the time period charged. However, no name would appear anywhere on the statement."

"No Piotr Borod? Or Yuri Tur?"

"No. It would not be necessary to the itemization. Nikolai's own security clearance as an Outworlder precludes him having to declare any personal information like that as long as he's inside the Warren. It's only when he's staying outside the Warren that he has to declare the names and work numbers of his guests, because then he's no longer under the protection of Warren Central."

"Typical," Yuri said. "Internal Security is so paranoid about state secrets slipping off to the wrong person, it often doesn't know what the other organs are up to." His breath rattled with relief. "Looks like we lucked out on that one. But I'm still going to get that hide-and-seek program. And then we'll have to change your room sooner or later as an added precaution."

"Nikolai?" Galina, calling from the half-open doorway. "I have my clothes."

He went over to retrieve them and accidentally caught a glimpse of her naked shoulder. He brought the clothes to Yuri and they began examining them. Turning them over in his hands Nikolai noticed their natural fragrance.

Her. I'm smelling her body on these clothes.

He shook himself rudely. Pay attention. You can't afford to daydream. You must keep your emotions distant if you're going to have any chance in pulling this scheme off. Now, get to work.

"What happens if we find one?" he asked Yuri.

Yuri jerked a thumb over his shoulder towards the kitch-enette. "We use the incinerator."

"Wouldn't the loss of signal be just as dangerous? I mean, if someone's monitoring the tracer and loses contact with it—"

"I'm gambling it's much more dangerous if the tracer remains activated. You've got to understand, Sholokhov, there are more than likely millions of tracers in Moscow. Everybody is watching everybody else; that's how the organs operate. We've only momentarily lucked out because the Warren is on a partial blackout loop from the other state organs due to the sensitive nature of its occupants. As long as Outworlders are inside the Warren the state security programs know they, and their secrets, are safe. But any tracer Galina carries works on a special hyper-frequency or it wouldn't be any good to the Protectorate. Fortunately for us, though, they have a limited range, and there's a lot of glass and steel in this building to mask a signal."

"I'm glad you're helping me out," Nikolai said. "You have the right kind of mind for this clandestine work."

"Comes from trying to keep three steps ahead of the bluecaps my whole life." Yuri tossed the garments aside. "I don't think there's anything here," he said, much relieved.

Nikolai inspected the girl's bra and panties. He knew it was his imagination, but they felt hot to his touch. The delicate material almost burned his fingers from her body warmth.

Yuri set her shoes aside. "These are clean, too. What's left?"

"Only her cap."

"Let's have a look."

Yuri pried the top button away. "Shit," he snarled. "Here's one."

Nikolai looked. Right there, under the button, was one of the tracers used by all security organizations in Russia.

"Bastards are probably triangulating on us right now," Yuri said. He strode into the kitchenette and threw the whole bundle of clothes into the incinerator. After hitting the power switch he turned around, looking vaguely sick. "All we can do now is wait and hope we got it in time."

"Nikolai?" Galina, calling nervously from the bath. "Is anything wrong?" She opened the door a crack.

"We found a tracer. We had to burn your clothes because there may have been others we missed. They may be on to us. No way to know; we'll have to wait and see what happens."

Alarmed silence.

"I'll go downstairs and get you something new to wear. In the meantime, why don't you cover up with these?" He handed her one of his shirts through the door, along with a pair of socks, slacks, and a clean towel.

". . . Nikolai?"

"Yes?"

"I—I don't want to be left here alone." A rustling sound emanated from behind the half-open door as she hurriedly dressed.

The unspoken half of her statement was clear enough: I don't want to be left alone with Yuri.

"Forget it." Yuri had foreseen the trouble. "We'll go together, Nikolai and I. That way, you won't be embarrassed."

"Can you come here a minute?" The girl's voice had called Nikolai in such a way as to bring him closer to the bathroom door. He bent his head down and answered low, "What is it?"

"Please, come back," she whispered. "I'm afraid, now that you found that tracer."

The pathetic plea clutched at his heart. She really was lost and out of her depth. Well, weren't they all?

"I will, Galina. Sonya will keep you company."

"Okay, but hurry."

He motioned to Yuri. "Let's go."

They left the room and went down to one of the department stores on the ground floor. Nikolai picked out two changes of clothes, socks, shoes. For underwear he had to rely on men's style, but found some he thought would fit around Galina's wide hips. While the clerk bagged his purchases, Yuri wandered aimlessly through the store.

Back in the corridor, he stated, "Clean, so far." He tapped the side of his nose. His eyes glittered with excitement. "I can smell a bluecap—or any other policeman, with this."

He's enjoying this, Nikolai realized. He lives for the hunt, the challenge. Thank God I had enough foresight to enlist him on my side.

"Let's get something to eat from the commissary. It's getting past suppertime and we have a lot of planning and thinking to do before the morning."

Yuri rubbed a hand across his rubbery lips. The thought of dinner always got him to salivating. "Not a bad idea, but I have a better one. I still say we should all go out to eat."

Nikolai stared back, uncomprehending. "That's running too much of a risk."

"We're going to have to take . . . Piotr . . . out sooner or later, Sholokhov. Better a dry run now, while it's comparatively safe. Test the waters so to speak."

"Outside the Warren?"

"Where else?"

"I'm not sure. . . ."

Yuri clapped a hand on Nikolai's back. "Sholokhov, you roped me into this, now you don't want to take my advice? You're a hell of a character. I thought you wanted my help."

"It seems a dangerous gamble, to me. Pointless."

"That's where you're wrong. We must have a trial run. Nighttime's the perfect time. We'll do it in stages: bring her—I mean him, down to the commissary and walk him through. See if any ears perk up. Then through the lobby and outside. I know a restaurant three blocks from here. No one will notice. Trust me. I must know if we can slip Piotr past other men unnoticed. Otherwise, there's no point in going on with this; we might as well turn ourselves in tonight."

Nikolai mulled it over. "Got any ideas how we're going to get . . . him . . . out of Russia? That's what's going to have to happen, you know. I mean, if we're really serious about doing this."

Yuri's veneer of self-confidence slipped. "I'm still chewing on that one," he confessed.

They returned to the hotel room. Galina dressed behind the door while Nikolai outlined the plan. "The more I think about it," he admitted, "the more comfortable I am with the idea. Yuri's right: We have to see if we can pass you through a crowd unnoticed."

"I got by all right the other night," she argued.

"True—while everyone else was running around scared. Tonight is different. People are putting the riot behind them and turning their attention back towards their everyday lives. It's a totally different environment out there."

She opened the door. "Well, here I am." She was dressed in green coveralls with a brown nylon belt, socks, and cheap shoes with rubber soles. "What do you think?"

Yuri fingered his large chin, looking her over. "Put on the cap."

She followed his directions.

"Pull it a little lower over your eyes."

She did that, too.

Yuri shook his head. "Damn. See the trouble, Sholokhov?"

Nikolai certainly did. Galina had the belt tied tightly around her waist, accentuating her figure and her rounded breasts. "Galina," he said, "men tie belts around their hips, not their waist."

"Oh." She adjusted the nylon strap accordingly.

Yuri was still shaking his head. "She won't pass. She's too curvy. Either that, or the coveralls are a size too small."

Nikolai said, "I have a longcoat I can lend her."

"What if she forgets to button it and a gust of wind

149

blows it open, Sholokhov? Wait a minute! I have an idea."
He pitched a bath towel at Galina. "Here, go back inside
and wrap this around your waist. It should fill out your
shape and hide your figure."

She came back in a moment. Her feminine curves were
all but gone. She looked like a young boy with a paunch
that threatened someday to grow into a formidable potbelly.

"Much better." Yuri rubbed his hands with a sense of
accomplishment. "She hardly looks recognizable."

Nikolai seconded the sentiment. "One last thing," he
told her, "don't brush your hair back behind your ears.
Men rarely do that. Let it fall over them naturally. That's
right."

"Good thinking, Sholokhov," Yuri said. "It'll also hide
her profile." He held his thumbs together to make a picture
frame with his hands and studied the finished product.
"We're in business. I'd hardly recognize her myself."

"How do I look?" she asked.

"Like a chubby, adolescent kid," Yuri returned. Then:
"Keep up that scowl, too, it masks your features. What do
you think, Sholokhov? Doesn't she look like any other snot-
nosed punk kid you've seen on the streets of Moscow?"

"Absolutely. No one will give her a second glance."

"I don't think so, either." Yuri put his fists on his hips.
"What's your name?"

"Piotr Borod."

He rewarded her with a pleased smile. "Getting better all
the time. Okay, Sholokhov, give her the rest of her things."

"We picked these up for you in a drugstore downstairs,"
Nikolai said. "Comb. Wallet, with a few tsar notes. Train
tokens. Bundle of cigarillos and lighter. A cheap watchdisk.
Slipknife. No, not in your pocket, down in your sock pouch,
that's where people carry slipknives. Good."

"What's this?" She turned a cigarette packet sized box over in her hands. "What does it do?"

"That's a pop box."

"A what?"

"Pop box. Men sometimes carry them." He showed her how to activate it.

"Oh, it's a film slate."

"Uh, not quite. See, this has a hundred different pictures of women. You can rotate the view, like this, and manipulate the digital form with these keys. It also has a download nub so you can trade files with other people, if you want to."

"Do you carry something like this?"

"Well, no, as a matter of fact, I don't," he said.

"Then, I don't want to, either."

"You're going to," Yuri told her, "whether you want to or not. It's just the kind of cheap crap a kid your age would carry around with him."

"Yuri's right, Galina. Better keep it."

She frowned but slipped the pop box into her back pocket.

"Good." Nikolai slapped his hands down on his thighs with satisfaction. "You're all set."

"I'll get you an ident card, papers, and a social number later tonight," Yuri promised. "In the meantime, I want you to take these." He produced a sheaf of worn ID cards from his own wallet. "The numbers on these cards are active, but will expire tomorrow at midnight. By then, you'll have your own set in the name of Piotr Borod."

"Where can you get them?" Nikolai asked.

"I have a source." Yuri didn't elaborate further and Nikolai didn't pursue the matter.

I have to trust him on some things, he mused. Press him

too hard, he might pull out and leave me hanging.

"Sonya," he called, "we're going out to dinner. We'll be back within the hour. Tape all incoming calls. I'll call you before we come back to make sure it's safe."

"The Mischa code?"

"It's worked so far."

"Okay, Nikolai. Be careful."

They left the room and went down a flight of stairs to the elevators. A few minutes later Yuri promenaded them through the Warren cafeteria. The tables were crowded with men eating and drinking coffee. Nikolai heard someone talking about Luna, but was past before he could catch what the man was saying. They filed out, Galina safely between them.

Yuri was giddy with success. "Pretty damn good. No one gave Piotr a second glance. But why should they? He's nothing but a punk kid."

Galina scowled.

Yuri guided them into the heart of the lobby. He and Nikolai carried on a sham conversation while Galina— Piotr, Nikolai reminded himself—walked between them. They left the Warren and stood beneath one of the street lamps. Two or three men walked past. No one looked twice at Galina. The standard Moscow shuffle helped in that department, too.

"So far, so good," Yuri claimed. "Come on, let's get something to eat." He brought them to an out of the way cafe on one of the dark side streets behind the Warren. They found a table by themselves and ordered their food. Drinks arrived—three pints of dark beer—and Yuri drank down half of his in one gulp.

He smacked his mouth with satisfaction and rocked back in his chair. "I've been giving this a lot of thought," he said, lighting one of his pungent Makhorka cigarettes, "and I think I know how we can get Galina out and save our skins at the same time."

Nikolai listened intently. "Really? How?"

"It won't be easy, Sholokhov, I can tell you that much." Yuri slugged back the rest of his beer and ordered another from the harried waiter.

"What's your plan?"

He waved off Nikolai's eagerness. "Let me think on it some more," he cautioned. "I want to be absolutely sure it's workable before I lay it all out. I'll know more later after I purchase Piotr's ident cards tonight."

Nikolai sent Galina a relieved smile. It looked as if everything was going to work out after all. Silly of him to have had so many fears. They really were going to pull this crazy caper off.

Their dinner came and he dug in with gusto. He couldn't remember when he had eaten last. Before long, the huge platter of white sausage, steamed cabbage, and brown bread had disappeared. Even Galina got into the partying mood. She brought out her cigarillos, raising her eyebrows in mute inquiry. Nikolai gave her the thumbs up. She lit one with the table candle, but, rather than smoke it, let it burn between her slim fingers.

Yuri polished off the last slice of bread and drained a final glass of beer. "Everybody ready?"

"I think so," Nikolai answered. Galina briskly nodded.

Yuri led them back towards the Warren without retracing their earlier route. Another smart move, Nikolai thought.

They stopped to call Sonya. All clear.

"Shouldn't we buy a news loop?" Galina asked. "There might be something in it about . . . you know. The lorry crash."

"Good idea. Stay here." Yuri strolled across the street to a newsstand, catching the proprietor before he closed down for the night.

Alone with Nikolai, Galina asked: "Do you think Yuri means what he says about getting us out of danger?"

Us, and not me, Nikolai noticed. "If any man can, it's Yuri," he said stolidly. She pressed against him and he thrilled at her closeness.

He wanted to slip his hand around her waist but didn't know how she might react. Would she think he was trying to take advantage of her lonely and helpless situation? Or would she let him do it only because she thought she owed him for saving her life? That wouldn't be any good.

What if someone saw them? But there were plenty of men on the street with an arm around their partner or holding hands with one of the boys who regularly haunted the street corners. No one would notice or care.

"Galina, I—"

"What's happened to Yuri?"

Yuri was headed back across the street and lurching like a zombie. His face was white and strained.

Without speaking he shoved a news loop at Nikolai who scanned the headlines written in a rank tabloid style passing for professional journalism. The misspelled foreign words and poor grammar only served to heighten the frantic tone.

Galina asked frantically, "What does it say, Nikolai? Does it talk about the bus crash? About me missing?"

Ignoring her, he raced through the story, hoping against hope the screaming headlines weren't true.

Galina spun on Yuri, desperate for an explanation. "Won't someone please tell me what's going on?"

Yuri tore his attention away from Nikolai's shattered face, his shattered world.

"Sharonov Crater," Yuri said, voice cracking to the point of obscurity. "The research outpost and observatory where Nikolai worked has been destroyed."

Ten

TERRIBLE ESPLOSIONE
UNE FACCIA POSTERIORE DELLA LUNA!!
❑❑❑❑❑ —Is this the language you want?
   Then press this box——> ❑   ❑
❑❑❑❑❑ :::
TODESFALLE AUF MONDRÜCKSEITE!
❑❑❑❑❑ —Is this the language you want?
   Then press this box——> ❑ ❑
❑❑❑❑❑ :::
MORTE UN FACE CACHÉE DE LA LUNE!
❑❑❑❑❑ —Is this the language you want?
   Then press this box——> ❑ ❑
❑❑❑❑❑ :::
CRATER TOTALLY DESTROYED IN MYSTERIOUS
EXPLOSION!!
❑❑❑❑❑ —Is this the language you want?
   Then press this box——> ❑ ❑
❑❑❑❑❑ :::
———— >————

A Disaster of the Highest Magnitude
————- >————-

Hundreds Feared Dead
————- >————-

Scientists Speculate as to Cause
————- >————-

World Governments Debate Consequences
————- >————-

FROM: United Lunar Press (Ingenii Sentinel, Harsh Mistress

Examiner, Korolev Crier, and others) SUBJECT: Lunar Explosion, Loss of Life, Scientific Setback DATE: 5.8.31 CE (Terran Standard) TIME: 1517 Universal Time DISTRIBUTION: Class One Relay; DataSphere; Link 7 Transceiver Text Follows:

An explosion of unknown origin completely destroyed a scientific research center on the Far Side of the Moon this morning, in what is now being called the worst disaster in the history of Lunar colonization and Russian space exploration.

The cause of the explosion and the amount of devastation remains impossible to gauge, however, sources agree the center of the detonation occurred in Sharonov Crater, home to a secluded outpost of Russian physicists and engineers building what was reputed to be the Moon's largest astronomical radio telescope.

Preliminary reports indicate the lives of several hundred men are thought to be lost in the unprecedented disaster. Witnesses prospecting for mascons in the vicinity reported seeing a "great light" before they felt the regolith under their feet rock back and forth. Minor structural damage was listed through Moon Net, a twenty-four hour emergency management team servicing colonies on Far Side. Cracked pressure tubes in Korolev II and strained load-bearing tunnel connectors throughout the many underground living quarters, farms and mining towns scattered across the region, make up the bulk of the repairs facing the emergency disaster team.

When reached for comment, H.M. Soth Tolon III, High Minister of the Lunar Directorate, had this to say: "It's a disaster of the highest magnitude. Nothing like this has ever happened before in our oblast. We are quite at a loss to explain it. It's very sad."

Seismic instruments halfway around the Moon first recorded the aftermath of the explosion at 0802 UT, on the morning of Wednesday, 5 August, 2131. Geoffery Klein, senior selenologist for Technical Kinetics, Inc., stated: "At first we thought it was a moonquake, but the way the temblor damped out so quickly made it almost certain that something had hit us. In fact, whatever it was hit us hard—the Moon is still shaking back and forth like a big bell."

Dr. Klein went on to say: "This has all of the earmarks of either an asteroid strike or a possible thermonuclear detonation. But, of course, that's only rank speculation on my part," he hastily added.

Ilya Gookin, a senior spokesperson for Misawe Orbital, quickly denied any aspect of the asteroid theory proposed by Klein. "We track every single object in orbit around the Moon," he said, "including lost tools, bolts, and com satellites. There is no way something that big got through our detection web, not with the AIs we have on the job."

Sir Reginald Clarke of the Royal Astronomical Society, London, England, quickly concurred with Gookin's assessment: "All the Apollo asteroids, those that pass across Earth's orbit, are accounted for. Either this was a previously unknown planetesimal with a very low albedo, or it was a deliberate act. Not even a runaway microreactor of the type used by Sharonov to generate their power could account for this level of devastation. That goddamn crater is gone."

Despite rumors as to the nature of the event, scientists all agree on one point: There is no apparent reason for someone to deliberately target Sharonov. As one astronomer (who asked to remain anonymous) said, "The Far Side of the Moon is bristling with astronomical equipment. You name it and it's there: telescopes, dishes, spectrometers, interferometers; we have it all. Why anyone would choose to destroy a crater as out of the way as that one was is incomprehensible. It makes no sense."

"That's true," Sir Clarke agreed. "Sharonov hadn't even come on-line as far as I know. They had done very little in the

way of scientific observation before this point. It's unfortunate. We all had great expectations for what this instrument would ultimately have been able to accomplish—but, of course, it's the lost lives of those men that should concern us now, not the missing data."

Sharonov crater had a diameter of over seventy kilometers and was located on what is popularly known (albeit inaccurately) as Dark Side. The radio telescope was located in the center of the crater. Von Neuman nanotechs were being used to process the anhydrous regolith into vast petals that would soak up electromagnetic radiation and the light spectrum of planets and stars. Brand new computers with ultra-dense matrices of ovonic thought-shards would then sift through the incoming data while putting it in phase, while separating out the information astronomers wanted.

As scientists scramble to discover the origin of the calamity, political fallout among nations has already begun. Press Secretary for the Russian First Minister released this statement from governmental headquarters in St. Petersburg:

"This morning, an explosion of unnatural proportions wiped out a scientific research station on the Far Side of the Moon. While we as yet have no evidence this was a deliberate act and not a natural catastrophe, we will pursue our investigation to its natural conclusion. If, for any reason, we find a human hand behind this disaster we will bear the entire weight of our government towards subsequent justice."

The press secretary went on to say that the Russian Confederation would continue to pursue "a strong and vigorous space program," and that this would in no way "deter or dissuade" their government or their people from the exploration and "conquest of a vast and dangerous frontier."

The new President of Hot West 'Merica held a press conference to offer his nation's sympathy and offer what help they could. Other messages of shock, horror, and sympathy flooded in from other parts of the world as well. Pope "Two-Time" Johnny Pasquale II issued this bulletin from his bunker in the Vatican: "It has come to our attention there were a few Catholics among the victims. I can assure you, if this event was artificial in nature we will hound those responsible to their deaths and hang them up by their nut hairs."

The press secretary for the Russian Confederation declined comment when asked by reporters to respond to this bizarre and unusual statement issued by the Vatican.

[Text Ends] end message end message end message end message end message ends 000000 000 000 0 00 0

Eleven

Nikolai read the Möbius strip. It was true: Sharanov was destroyed. His hand holding the news loop fell limply to his side. Yuri and Galina stared with increasing worry at him.

Gone. All those men—his comrades—murdered in cold blood.

Why?

The starsign. Someone wanted the Star Whisper Project shut down.

"Nikolai—?"

Galina, concerned. No, frightened. They had been so happy a few minutes ago—now this thunderbolt had crashed into their lives, blowing apart their world. *His* world.

Everything seemed distant and removed to him now. Galina. Yuri. Nothing in life had any substance to it.

He looked numbly at the deactivated news loop in his hand, hoping by some miracle it would reboot and give another version of the story.

Sonya. Sonya had tried to tell him, but he had shut her down. Stupid, on his part.

"We'd better get back to the Warren," Yuri advised. "This changes all our plans."

Nikolai made a sharp gesture. "I don't want to go back there tonight. Haven't you got a place we can stay?"

He hoped Yuri could understand his reasoning. Much of the Warren's internal architecture was similar to the tunnel towns and rec domes on Luna. The thinking behind this was not complicated: a basic blueprint kept culture shock to a minimum for visiting Outworlders. The oppressive Terrestrial gravity was bad enough, getting lost while going to the bathroom or having tokens that wouldn't work in the snack vendors was an added and unnecessary psychological strain.

"I know a place," Yuri said at length. "Follow me." They went to a street corner where he thumped the side door of a waiting cab.

"Going off duty, mister."

Yuri leaned through the driver's side window. "I want you to take us to Bittsevsky Park. Communal housing, southwest side. Building 7C. Got all that?"

"Off duty, mister. Curfew, you know."

Yuri opened his wallet and put several hundred denominational tsar disks on the dashboard. The driver yawned and scratched himself. "I've got supper waiting, uncle, and I have to get this cab back to the ranks or my boss'll kick my butt right up between my ears."

"Get us there before curfew, and I'll let you take your tip from this." Yuri flashed a gold czarina debit card. The hack greedily licked a drop of spittle from the corner of his whiskered mouth. "Hop in."

Yuri opened the curtains on a bay window, revealing a Moscow laid out with its glittering boulevards and dark green parks. He left Nikolai and Galina alone for a space before returning with three iced vodkas on a white lacquered tray.

"Here, drink this." He pressed one of the glasses into Nikolai's hands.

He drained the ice-cold vodka without really tasting it.

Yuri dropped a pinch of pepper into his own drink. "How do you feel now?"

His voice was flat. "Stunned."

"I'll bet."

"Is this your place?" Galina slowly sipped her vodka, admiring the expensive furniture, clean carpet, and dark paneled walls. Light jazz trickled through the room from hidden speakers.

Yuri was evasive. "Let's say it's a safe house and leave it at that." He laid a compassionate hand on Nikolai's knee. "Well, we have quite a problem, don't we?" It was a statement of fact, not a question.

"I'm afraid so."

Yuri lit a cigarette and drew an ashtray—an onyx bowl—close to hand. "Got any idea what we're going to do?"

"As a matter of fact, I do."

Yuri stopped with his glass halfway to his mouth. "Mind sharing it, so the rest of us won't be fumbling in the dark?"

Nikolai poured himself another drink, scooted back on the couch. "The Star Whisper Project's home was Sharonov. You know the work we were doing there, and what it meant to everybody." He gulped his vodka. The liquor was setting a comfortable fire in his stomach. "Someone wants that information kept secret. The question is: Why?"

Yuri stubbed out his half-smoked cigarette. "Sholokhov, if a man has access to information, he can then control its dissemination. He becomes the most powerful cog in his particular machine by using said information for profit, and or gain. If he's really intelligent, he can wield it to destroy enemies. Either scenario provides the same result: Consolidation of power. Don't let anyone tell you different: Every man wants power, because with power, all other vices, like sex and money, fall into line."

"You talk like you know this from experience," Galina said.

Yuri lit a fresh cigarette, blew a plume of smoke towards the ceiling fans. "I see it everyday," he readily acknowledged. "Tonight was a perfect example. That cab driver was headed home. He had good reason; curfew was about to fall, and he was probably tired and hungry. After I waved that debit card under his nose he put all that aside. Why? Not because of the money it represented, but rather the power that lay behind it. I tell you, it's like a cobra hypnotizing a mouse, power. Fascinating and deadly, both at the same time. I plan to write a monograph on the subject someday."

He bent forward with a sense of urgency. "All right, enough of this philosophical talk. We've got a dilemma. The way I see it, we must do one of three things. First, turn ourselves in. We all know how that will end." To make his point, his eyes found Galina, who avoided his stare.

"Not my first choice," Nikolai said.

"Mine either. I value my life as much as the next fellow. Our second choice: Stay in Moscow and ride this storm out. The Protectorate, eventually, will give her up as irrecoverable and stop searching for her. They'll have to: They'll reach a point of diminishing returns. As valuable as she is to the Confederation, once they spend her value in manpower and resources trying to hunt her down, they'll pull the plug on the operation. Isn't that right, Galina?"

"I think so. There are always stories floating around about women who ran away or disappeared. Most are caught immediately, but a girlfriend told me she heard from an older woman about a young girl who escaped the Union House in Gorky. After a while, the Protectorate gave up; she was never found."

"Exactly my point. The only problem is, if we pursue that road, we must be prepared to endure a long term, high risk venture that may last several years."

"What's the third choice?"

"Run. And I mean *run*."

"You mean leave Moscow." Nikolai pulled his bottom lip. "I've thought about that."

"No, I mean get out of the Confederation. Quit Russia altogether and emigrate to a new country."

The words came like a blow to Nikolai. He had already lost one home. Yuri was now asking him to cut himself off from the only constant left in his life: Moscow.

"Is that even possible? I've never heard of it being done before. Not on purpose, anyway."

Cigarette smoke dribbled from Yuri's mouth as he talked. "Possible, not highly probable. The logistics would be formidable, not to mention the cost. I'd need help with that, Sholokhov."

Galina posed a question. "What about the border guards? How do we get past them?"

"Russia's borders are porous," Yuri said, "depending on which way you go. There are certain choke points to avoid: St. Petersburg, Minsk, Tbilisi, to name a few. But they won't be a problem for us."

"Why are those cities so dangerous?" the girl asked.

"They're military outposts. Border Security isn't concerned with keeping people from leaving Russia, as much as they are with keeping certain people out. That works in our favor. Well, to a degree."

Nikolai floated his own opinion. "What about the Trans-Siberian express? That would be doable."

Yuri crushed out a cigarette, lit another. "You mean, go across the Ural Mountains?"

"Why not?"

"No good. I see what you're thinking, Sholokhov. I agree

it has a certain appeal: Cross the Urals and lose ourselves in Siberia. But, where would we live? The towns out that way are nothing more than government outposts and villages for mining and industrial concerns. Another problem: We go too far east, we run into real trouble."

Nikolai grimaced. "I had forgotten The Encroachment War."

"Just because they're not fighting now, doesn't mean they won't be in the future. You know what it's like out there. Plus, what if they get hold of Galina? What d'ya think they'd do to her? Trust me, she'd be better off in the Union House."

Nikolai remembered Yasu's sewn lips, and shuddered. He and Yuri would be shot on sight. Galina would bear the worst fate of all—the fate she was trying to escape right here in civilized Moscow. No, running to the Eastern Frontier wasn't the way to go. Neither was the West. That entire region was a political and social imbroglio. Hardly any food. Nothing in the way of adequate housing. The West had deteriorated into a handful of bankrupt nation states decades ago. Oh, there were a few places, like Hot West 'Merica, where people maintained some semblance of civilization, even a nascent space program. Aside from that, the worst part of life in 'Merica was the Fundamentalist movement holding sway over each and every aspect there. He would rather lose his life than lose the freedom to read any novel he wanted, watch any vid he desired, or think.

Having someone tell him what he could, or could not, do in the privacy of his own home would be intolerable—worse, after the comparative freedoms of the Russian Confederation, it would be an insane way for any human being to live.

"There aren't many places left in the world any more,"

he commented with restrained sadness.

"Not many," Yuri agreed. "That's why I think our best bet is the United Australian Islands. Melbourne is a closed city, but I bet we can get together enough drag to buy ourselves a place there. The UAI is a lot like Russia. They have a sound economy, and the population hasn't degenerated into scuffling animals. The only other place might be somewhere on the African Continent. There are several tiny states hidden like jewels in that dark expanse. The biggest problem would be fitting in with the general population though."

"Our skin color?"

"A not insurmountable problem. I know a plastic surgeon that'll sell us the biological nanides to re-sculpt our bodies. Change our physiognomy, he can."

"Perhaps we should look into that. What's his name?"

"Hang on a minute. Unfortunately, this radical cosmetic surgery takes a month to complete. That's a lot of down time, and the cost is exorbitant. We'd also be helpless, and at the mercy of this doctor. He might take our money and turn us in for the reward." Yuri added whimsically, "I would, given half the chance."

"The UAI is our best bet, then."

"That's how I figure it." Yuri remembered the cigarette he'd been smoking. The ashes drooped from the filter, threatening to fall onto the spotless rug. Cupping it carefully, he dumped the dead butt in the ashtray.

"Well, those are my choices." He brushed his hands clean. " 'Yuri's three choices.' We must pick one, Sholokhov, and stick with it, even unto the end."

Nikolai reviewed them with distaste: "Turn ourselves in, hide out in Moscow, or leave Russia forever. I don't like any of them. They're all dangerous, all certain to failure."

"There's no other alternative that I can see."

Wasn't there? Nikolai thought. A sanctuary above the dirt and the grime of everyday life was what they needed. Where could they find such a place?

He gripped the armrests of his chair. There was such a place, and, what was more, he knew how to get them there. Galina, too.

"I think we should consider Kazakhstan," he said.

Yuri smirked at the idea, dismissing it out of hand. "Kazakhstan? What the hell is in Kazakhstan besides the steppes and a few starving camels?"

"Star City."

The night crept into the dim hours of early morning while they finalized their plans. Nikolai wanted to fly directly to Baikonur (assuming they could purchase the appropriate visas) but Yuri wanted to buy brand new identities in Moscow and proceed to the UAI.

"This is our *lives* we're talking about, Sholokhov," Yuri dug in, showing a flash of anger for the first time. "My life, in particular. Of which, I might add, I'm quite fond."

"I'm not thinking of myself, Yuri, but Galina."

"And I'm not? Look, I'll make this deal with you. Let's plan for the UAI, and leave Star City as our backup. I have to scrounge the same documents for either place, and we have to take a southern route through the Balkans to escape Russian control anyway. How does that sound to you? Truce?"

Nikolai thought it over. "All right, Yuri. I'll agree to that. Star City as our backup."

Yuri raised his hands over his head and gave his back a bone cracking stretch. "Ikon, I'm tired," he yawned. "I hope you appreciate the fact I'm not going to get any sleep tonight, Sholokhov."

"I do, Yuri. I know we owe you a lot."

Yuri bit back a cutting reply. "Galina," he said smoothly, "there's a bath and bedroom down the hall. You'd better get as much sleep as you can. Tomorrow's going to be a long day." When she left, he tapped Nikolai on the arm. "You look done in, too, cobber. Better lay down and get some rest, yourself."

"I have to track down Lev, first."

"You sure that's the guy's name?"

"We were sitting together, wondering if we were going to be executed. I didn't spend all day swapping life histories with the guy."

"I'll leave the Star City side of it to you, then. Anything else needs doing?"

"There is something. . . ." Nikolai began lamely. "I didn't want to mention it in front of Galina. I don't know how she would react."

Yuri was tight-lipped. "Better spill it. We can't have any secrets between us. Not in an enterprise of this magnitude."

"My Privilege is scheduled tomorrow night."

Yuri swore, "Ikon. You really know how to fuck things up, don't you?"

"I don't want to go."

Yuri glanced at the closed door at the end of the hallway from which the muffled sound of running water emanated.

"That's your own personal business, Sholokhov, but I have to tell you: I think you should go."

"You do?"

"Hell, yes, man! We have to assume the dogs are sniffing our arses every minute of the day. If you don't go to the Union House, that's going to be noticed by someone. There'll be questions asked. Are you prepared to answer them?"

"I guess not."

Yuri threw an arm around Nikolai's shoulders and led him farther away from the bathroom door. "Listen," he said amiably, his voice low and friendly, "the best thing for you is to forget what you're feeling for her. Right now. I've been watching you, Nikolai. Hey, we're friends, aren't we? Take my advice, for once in your life, and don't start falling for her. You know as well as I, we're not going to get away with this nonsense. You and I will be liquidated and Galina returned to the Union House before the week is out."

Nikolai sighed. "I didn't want to say anything in front of her, you understand, but I know you're right. Still, I can't help feeling I should do whatever I can to get her to safety. It's like everything's all mixed up and I can't think straight."

"I'm not saying I blame you for the way you're feeling. I'm in this too, right? Let's face it, I could walk out of here and never come back. Trust me, you'd never find me again. But I won't do that because I want to help you. And her."

"I needed to talk to somebody about how I was feeling, Yuri. Thanks." He took a deep breath and changed the topic. "Have you got a vidphone around here I can use?"

Yuri opened a roll-top desk, revealing a telecomp, vidphone and flatscreen. "You can use this to call anywhere in Moscow," he instructed. "Don't worry about it being traced—this module acts as a firewall."

Nikolai was impressed; it was an expensive rig.

"All right, then," Yuri said, shrugging on his coat. "I'm going out—no, don't worry about me. I know how to get around during a curfew. I'll be back at dawn and we'll have breakfast." He buttoned his coat, jerked his head towards a kitchen island. "There's food in there, if you get hungry. See you in about four hours."

After he closed and locked the door behind him, Nikolai

used the vidphone to call the Warren.

"Hello?"

"Hi, Sonya, it's me."

"Nikolai, I was very worried. When you didn't show up before curfew, I didn't know what to think."

"Has Mischa called?"

"Yes, but he has no news. Were you expecting any?"

"No." In this case, no news was good news. "I have a job I want you to run for me."

"I am here to serve."

"Consult the Warren's registration list and locate a man named 'Lev.' I don't know if that's his first, last, or diminutive, so shoot me a list of every name fitting those parameters."

Short pause. "There are four of them from Central Registry. Is he a friend of yours?"

"I met him during the riot. Okay, give me the names."

She spelled each one, waiting for him to write them down.

Levitan, Stanislaw
Levitch, Alexis
Levitsky, Mikhail
Malinkov, Levin

"Sonya, connect me, please, to Stanislaw Levitan."

The vidphone at the other end buzzed once. "Hello?" The baritone voice was sleepy and quick-tempered. "Who is this?"

"My name is Nikolai Sholokhov. I'm looking for a man I met during the riots. He said his name was Lev—"

"Goddammit, cobber, do you know what time it is?"

"I'm sorry, but—"

171

"You sound drunk." The baritone voice hung up.

Sonya dialed the next name, only to find out it belonged to a man staying in one of the communal sleeping rooms on the fourth floor of the Warren. Nikolai waited patiently for the man who answered the phone to find 'Alexis Levitch.' When Levitch came to the receiver he barked: "What the hell're you doing calling up people in the middle of the night? Dumb. No, I'm not the man you're looking for."

He slammed the receiver down in Nikolai's ear.

Undaunted, Sonya dialed the next name on the list. Nikolai let it ring several times, no answer. The last name proved no luckier. Malinkov answered and activated his flatscreen; he had several people in his room and they were throwing a sex party. No, he didn't know Lev, but did Nikolai know where he could buy a can of gel soap? The Warren drugstore was out. "I don't want to search every kiosk in Moscow tomorrow," Malinkov said.

Nikolai said he couldn't help him, apologized for interrupting his party, and quickly severed the connection.

"That's all the names I have," Sonya said. "Sorry."

Nikolai had a sudden inspiration. "See if you can find a name whose first, middle and last letters make up the initials L.E.V."

Sonya crowed, "There is one. Leopold Etinger Velichko. Want me to try him?"

"Might as well wake him up, too." Nikolai held out faint hope this would be the guy he wanted.

A man answered: "Lev."

"Lev? Nikolai. I don't suppose you remember me, but we met—"

The other man turned on his flatscreen, and Nikolai saw the brown soulful eyes he remembered so well. "Oh, hello,

Nikolai. Christ, you made it out, too, huh?"

"Barely. How about yourself?"

"Got caught up in another checkpoint, but I got through it all right. Good God, we're lucky to have escaped that one, aren't we? They were taking all the Outworlders off the street."

Nikolai recalled the wrenching terror, sitting in the sun with thirty other men, waiting to be executed.

If I do anything in my life, he vowed, I hope I kill Stinnen. I don't care if he *is* Yuri's brother. I'm glad he saved my life, but he also deserves to die for the terror he's caused.

"Lev, I know it's late, but I need to talk to you. I remember you mentioned your leave was up. . . ."

"Tomorrow." Lev looked at his watchdisk and his eyebrows jumped. "Make that today. I'm taking a noon mag-lev out of Moscow. I have a free hour this morning; you want to get together for a cup of coffee?"

"I wish I could," Nikolai said with sincerity, "but I have too much going on at the present." He suppressed a wry grin. What an understatement! "What I wanted to ask you. . . ."

The two men talked for ten minutes, making arrangements. Lev told Nikolai he'd be back in touch. "Or you can contact me through the *Tereshkova.*"

"That sounds fine. Thanks."

"I don't see any problem with your basic idea," Lev appended. "Maintenance is always hiring service personnel, and someone with your tech qualifications shouldn't have any trouble finding a good position on one of the worldlets."

"Lev, you've saved my neck. I hope we'll be seeing each other again, soon. *Dasvidaniya.*"

173

Nikolai closed the vidphone down and wiped the buffer clean. He went into the back of the apartment to splash some water on his face before wandering back to the front room.

"Nikolai?"

He followed the voice through a half-open door and entered a nicely furnished bedroom: armoire, nightstand, lamp, and double bed with clean sheets turned down.

"Is everything all right?" Galina, sitting up in bed, face scrubbed and hair brushed back. She wore a man's shirt with its sleeves rolled up, billowing around her thin arms wrapped around her updrawn knees.

He rubbed his face with the palms of his hands. "God," he said through his fingers, "I hope so. All of this is so. . . ." he made a vague gesture, "pointless, if we can't get out of Moscow."

Galina transfixed him with eyes that shone like emeralds in the half-light.

"You don't look well. Are you getting sick?"

"I'm exhausted." He made a vague gesture toward the city outside their own comfort. "I wonder how Yuri is making out?"

She laughed throatily. "Something tells me Yuri is always able to make do, no matter what the circumstances."

"He's very inventive," Nikolai agreed.

She picked at the starched sheet drawn up over her knees. "Nikolai, I want to tell you something that's been bothering me for a long time now." He saw it was an effort on her part to continue. "I want to apologize for . . . well, for everything that's happened. I never meant for you to become involved. If you hadn't come into the bathroom when you did—none of this would ever have happened."

"I suppose that's true. But you can't be blamed."

She reached out. Her small hand disappeared inside his larger one. "I want you to know," she said, "what I said earlier still applies. I'll leave, if you want me to. Tonight."

He didn't say anything, moved by her solemn conviction.

"I promise, I won't tell anyone about you when I'm picked up." She saw her hand in his, slightly surprised to find it nestled there. "You've lost so much already." Nikolai heard genuine compassion in her voice. "You're entire past is gone. I never meant for that to happen. Can you believe me?"

"Yes, Galina, I can."

He sat down beside her, cradling her hand in his. "I can't stop remembering the men I knew in Sharonov." Before he could stop himself, the words spilled out in a cathartic torrent:

"Gregor Monke was my roommate on Sharonov. He was an electronics technician, too. What a fellow! He used to plink away on a balalaika all night long while I was trying to sleep. And Oskar, thin as a rail, but could drink any man three-times his size under the table. Lukasz: a security man who fermented his own rum in a vat made from cannibalized recycler parts; he loved to do needlepoint. The research scientists and Admin people—I remember them all; I'll never forget them." Tears stung his eyes. "Now, they're all gone," he whispered.

"Don't blame yourself, Nikolai. You aren't responsible for their deaths."

He stared off into space. "I'd give anything to get those fellows back."

"I know, I know."

She made room for him on the bed. He lay on his side, curled, his head planted firmly against her hip.

"Close your eyes," she entreated.

"But—"

"Shh. Close."

He felt the soothing touch of her fingers on his forehead. He knew he should take a prurient interest now that they were together like this in bed, but he had so much else on his mind right now, it didn't seem right.

The room was quiet. It was as if Moscow was taking a long deep breath before the coming dawn.

Is this what it's like, he marveled drowsily, to have someone you can trust, and depend on? Someone to put their hand on your forehead when fate throws you a wicked curve, and cosset you like a baby?

Slowly, bit by bit, the events of the day receded, and, letting them go, he fell asleep, safe and warm.

Sitting up, Galina propped her chin on her knees. She watched him until the morning sun flamed through the blinds.

Twelve

Yuri returned early with a black attaché case tucked under one arm. Nikolai and Galina were waiting for him. Morning sunlight streamed through the bay window, illuminating dust motes that spun along the shafts of light like tiny suns.

He bobbed his head in greeting. "Good morning, one and all. Hey, didn't you get any sleep? You both look terrible."

"Not very much," Nikolai yawned.

"A hot breakfast will set you right." Yuri hung up his coat. "I'll brew a pot of black coffee if you scramble the eggs."

He was in high spirits. Nikolai wondered how he could be bright and cheerful while he was struggling with the weight of Russia on his shoulders.

"I got in touch with Lev," Nikolai said. "He thinks we'll be able to find work on any of the worldlets. They're always looking for talented men."

"About time we catch a break." Yuri poured coffee. "I had a bit of luck, too. Galina, come see what presents your Uncle Yuri brought you. Hurry, now."

He opened the attaché case and slapped a stack of documents on the table. "Work and social numbers, registered under the name of Piotr Borod." He counted off the remaining cards: "Debit card chips—with a five hundred tsar limit and drawn on the Bank of Moscow—birth documents: crèche number and birth data; you'd better start memorizing them. Social duty register," this last pamphlet he waved importantly. "This is a social duty record under the name of Piotr Borod, registered with the Moscow Union House. He would be old enough to have started one. Here, you'd better take it."

She thumbed through the register. Nikolai saw she didn't like touching the thing. Her eyes hardened when she flipped to the first page and read the notation of duty paid to the local Union House.

"Anything else?" she asked, tense.

Yuri blew on his coffee, took a tentative sip. "No, that catches you up, I should think."

Nikolai set a platter of eggs down. Yuri scooped out a lion's share and dug in. He noticed Galina staring stone-faced at the booklet.

Chewing, he tapped the register with his fork. "Union Houses have their own watermark, you know, so it's damned difficult to reproduce. The forger I know does an adequate job. Yours will pass a cursory inspection, don't worry about that—" he smiled encouragingly at her "—but if a real expert examines it, he'll recognize it as counterfeit." He wiped his mouth with a napkin, reached for a fruit bowl and picked up an orange.

Nikolai inspected the papers. "These must have cost a fortune if they're illegal."

"Who said anything about them being illegal? We needed history on a snot-nosed kid named Piotr Borod, and that's what I got. Besides, they didn't cost me a thing: I called in a couple of markers." He marveled at Nikolai's naïveté. "Drag, Sholokhov." He rubbed his thumb over his fingers. "*Blat.* You have to have the right kind of drag when dealing with the folks I know. If they see you're wet behind the ears, they'll skin you and pitch your broken carcass in an alley. They know me, so they give me a fair shake."

"How did you get this fair shake in only a few hours?"

"Connections." Yuri concentrated on peeling his orange. "*Blat,* again. You gotta know the right people." He reached across the table and patted Galina's hand. "If there's one thing your Uncle Yuri knows, it's the right people." He popped an orange wedge into his mouth and smiled.

"You seem less gloomy than you were last night," Galina noted.

He confessed gravely, "Oh, we've made a few tentative steps, but there's a long way to go, yet. Then, too, what else is there but forge ahead?" Another wedge. "And, I must admit, I like having a project of this dimension that tests my cumulative powers. I've always thought of myself as someone quite special. Now, I finally get the chance to prove it."

From their questioning looks he embellished upon his last point. "I know it's hard for you to understand, but this is how I live. I've never planned anything my entire life. If there's something I want to do, then I do it, and no regrets."

"You make it sound so easy." Galina picked at her own breakfast. "I've never thought life was anything but a struggle—especially after what I saw during the riot." She shifted her attention to Nikolai. "You once told me you felt the same way. You said I was naive and didn't know how you had to live and deal with everyday matters."

"That's true, I did say that."

Yuri followed this exchange with alarmed interest. He dropped the remaining orange into his plate. "What happened between you two while I was gone?" he asked bluntly.

They looked back at him, blandly. "Nothing," they said in unison.

"Eh?" His eyes swung back and forth, trying to pick a lie out of their faces. "Never mind, I don't want to know." He swept the orange peelings onto his greasy plate, licked his fingers. "Galina, I'm not saying I roll with every punch. If circumstances arise and I have to scratch and claw my way out, then I do that, too, and never look back. Have done, from time to time."

"You hear that, Galina? Yuri scratches like a cat. Let's hope we don't have to change his sandbox."

"Shut up, Sholokhov. Galina, I've made my living on the street for twenty-five years. I have no regrets; it's what I've always wanted. I'm freer than most men I know." He finished off his coffee.

"Sometimes I win, sometimes I lose, but I always keep on fighting. A man can rarely ask for anything more from life. If fate grants that much, he's coming out way ahead of everyone else."

"You have a poet's heart, Yuri," Nikolai said.

"Doesn't every Russian?" He tapped his watchdisk, a brand new Kanovia. "Uh oh. The morning has slipped away." He started clearing the table. "Sholokhov, we'll take Galina back to the Warren, then I'll pick up the letters of transit we'll need for the trip."

"Don't forget the air tickets to Kazakhstan."

"Yes, and immunization records—which, I presume you already have, Sholokhov?—and signed work releases for me and Piotr." He gathered the dishes with a domestic clatter and hurried to the kitchen island.

"Let's clean up the place," he shot over his shoulder. "I don't like leaving a messy apartment behind."

Galina made the bed. Nikolai threw the soiled towels and a soap cake into a wash/dryer wall unit; emptied and wiped the ashtrays.

Yuri racked the last soapy dish and dried his hands on a towel. "We all set? Galina, you have your cap on? Good. I'll just leave this behind. . . ."

"What's that for?"

Yuri produced a small notebook from his breast pocket and clicked a pen. "Just writing an apology." He scribbled, folded the note and left it on the table, weighted with a five hundred-tsar credit chip. "That should serve as adequate recompense, don't you think?"

Nikolai gaped. "Yuri, who lives here?"

He scratched his temple with the butt of the pen. "I'm not too sure. I got this address last month from a friend of mine; he said to use it if I needed a place to crash, but be sure I was out by seven o'clock."

"What happens at seven?" Galina asked.

"Yuri turns into a pumpkin." Nikolai fought down an impulse to kick the man.

Yuri shooed them out of the apartment, locked the door with a card key. A quick slight of hand and the key disappeared in one of the pockets sewn into the lining of his coat.

Despite his personal distaste for such hooliganism, Nikolai couldn't help but admire the quick resourcefulness.

"Yuri," he summed up, "you're the kind of guy who'd pick a cobber's wallet clean before taking him out for a beer to show there were no hard feelings."

Yuri laughed. "I've done that, too."

"I'm glad you're working with me, and not against me."

"Same here, cobber. Let's go."

On the stairs, they passed a man climbing the opposite way. A State official, perhaps a district prefecture from his dress.

Yuri tipped his fur hat. "Good morning, sir."

"Good morning."

Yuri elbowed Nikolai in the ribs and winked slyly. They ambled out of the apartment complex into early morning sunshine. The urban housing district in this corner of the city was densely crowded with ten-story buildings built of yellow brick and mirrored windows.

Nikolai shook his head. Hopeless! What a conspirator he had fallen in league with. Yuri was priceless: the kind of guy who did half a day's work for a full day's pay. A moment of guilt seized him, though. What if the official decided to make trouble? Yuri was dancing dangerously close to the edge.

One slip, and Galina would be nabbed by the Union House. Goose bumps raised along his arms as he imagined a sleepdeath module pressing against the nape of her neck. Yuri had gone too far, this time. A prefecture wasn't a day laborer sweeping Moscow's gutters for a crust of black bread—the man held a formidable seat of power. He was legitimately established with the intelligentsia who ran this rayon. Yuri took too many chances. It was time Nikolai had a talk with him.

"Yuri, don't you think—"

"Sholokhov, he barely looked at us; anyone could see he had other things occupying his mind. You're too cautious. You have to learn to loosen up." Yuri did a little jig on the street. "If you don't, then life is no more exciting than a pot of boiled cabbage."

The heart of a poet, or the mind of a fool. Nikolai couldn't decide which.

Yuri flagged a taxi and they rode in comfortable silence to the Warren. On the way Yuri explained he had already been there and installed the hide-and-seek program. Minutes later, they were safe inside Nikolai's room after phoning Sonya to see if the coast was clear. Back in familiar surroundings, Nikolai felt a wave of exhaustion lap at his consciousness. He cracked a wide yawn, followed by another.

Galina noticed. "You'd better sleep, Nikolai. You've been going since yesterday morning."

"She's right," Yuri added. "I've got a few personal errands to run, then I'll get right back on our project." He dawdled at the door. "Uh, Sholokhov, have you got any money on you?"

"I have a little."

"I'm going to need it. I tapped out last night getting the documentation for 'Piotr.' "

Nikolai flipped open his money clip. "How much do you need?"

"Thirty or forty thousand should cover it."

Nikolai winced. "That's going to leave me light. I still have to pay for this room."

"Yes, but we're leaving before your vacation is up; you don't need to pay the entire two weeks. Hey, thanks." Yuri deftly palmed the chips. "This should be enough to finish out the affair."

"Let's hope so. I can draw more from my personal account, but it won't be much."

"I'll return later this afternoon. Hang around until then, and get some sleep. You're no good to me if you can't think straight. Which, for you, is a problem anyway."

"Thanks for the vote of confidence."

Yuri left. Nikolai informed Galina he was going to take a shower. "Don't answer the door," he directed. "If anybody insists on entering, call for me."

Standing under a stream of hot water he went over their plans, again and again in his mind, along with the backdoor escape route he had set up in case everything unraveled.

Star City is our only hope, he told himself while the water drummed on his head. He lathered his body with a cake of dark yellow soap. We might someday reach the UAI, but an orbital habitat has to be our *ultimate* goal.

Because of what I know about the starsign, I can use that knowledge to buy Galina's freedom on any station.

He stepped out of the shower and stood under a blower. He shoved in token he had received as change when he bought the newsloop. The hot air brawled over his naked body. Sonya's security lens watched, unblinking.

Tereshkova was a perfect choice. Privately owned by a consortium of independent stockholders, and isolated at L5, he and Galina could easily hide among the population. Best of all, the inhabitants operated a "no-free-lunch" system of government. Everyone contributed or they were spaced. Heinlein systems were harsh, but such a free-wheeling libertarian environment suited Nikolai's needs flawlessly.

Toweling his head dry, he padded back to the main room. "I'm going to bed," he told Galina. He'd been knocked around Moscow almost from the first day he arrived. Exhaustion had finally caught up with him. "You can make your own lunch, can't you?"

"Yes, of course."

He pried the regen tape from his elbows and knees. The scrapes and bruises were healing nicely. He changed the tape and crawled into bed with a final instruction for Sonya: "Screen all calls, but wake me if Lev or Yuri tries to get through."

"I will attend to it, Nikolai."

He turned over and went to sleep. Once, he thought he imagined Galina standing over him—then Yuri returning later in the day with good news. He heard them talking together in whispers. He ignored it, and threw himself back into the deep seductive well of sleep.

Nikolai awoke refreshed and hungry. It was late afternoon. He opened a packet of powdered mushroom soup and enjoyed an early supper with Galina. She was in good spirits, laughing gaily and playing with her hair.

"Was that Yuri I heard earlier?" He dipped a plastic spoon into his soup. The thin broth was hot and burned his tongue.

She nodded. "He brought our tickets to Kazakhstan. He couldn't get plane tickets, they were too expensive for our budget."

"How are we supposed to get there? On camelback?"

"No, silly, by rail." She showed him the ticket folder with three confirmed tickets. "He also found the releases we'll need to apply for work. The only things we're waiting on are the letters of transit to the UAI. He thinks he can get those on the black market. He sounded optimistic."

"Good old Yuri. I knew he'd come through."

"You're not angry about having to take a train?"

"Why should I? That's how I arrived in Moscow." He reached across the table for her hand. "I believe we're actually going to get you out of here, Galina. I didn't think we would be able to do it, at first, but now I'm certain of it."

"I appreciate everything you've done for me, Nikolai." She started to say more, shook her head modestly and smiled.

They passed a pleasant evening listening to music and watching a 3V documentary on the extinction of the Aborigines. The program prompted Nikolai to tell Galina what to expect in Melbourne.

"Think of it as a frontier town, like Hot West 'Merica used to have during the Mad Times. Remember those stories about the western Cossacks? Life will be rough; we'll have to work hard, but the payoff at the end is worth the suffering. Their economic system works on a strict profit-motive basis. The harder you work, the more you and everybody else earns. We'll have to sign ten-year contracts, but that's not unusual either."

"What kind of work will there be?"

"We'll more than likely end up as minor investors on a farm cooperative."

"Are other women there?"

"When the *Fevreblau* hit, the UAI was one of the last places it savaged. I'm not saying life there is idyllic. Any man who thinks it's a place to meet women will be disappointed. UAI has a strict immigration policy; they don't take anybody. We'll do all right, though. I have a card up my sleeve." Starsign.

"It sounds better than what awaits us here in Moscow."

"There are no extradition agreements between the UAI and the Confederation. A plus for our side. Too much bad blood during the Gender Theft Wars. Like anywhere else, women are protected and guarded in the UAI, but you'll have more personal freedom than you ever had in the Union House." He shrugged. "It's the best I can do, Galina. There just really isn't any other place we can all go and live free."

He knew he was making the UAI out to be the answer to all their prayers, but he didn't want Galina needlessly worried about her future. That's why he played this game, pretending they were going to escape Moscow. Give her hope.

A hushed conversation with Yuri earlier that day, with Galina well out of earshot, had touched upon the insurmountable problems they faced:

"We'll be lucky if the Protectorate doesn't burst through

the door and arrest us all," Nikolai had said in a pique of candor. "We're going up against an entrenched bureaucracy that's handled situations like this for half a century. How can we expect to outwit an institution like that?"

Yuri nodded. "Add to that: your name is on a list somewhere. Before long, someone will find out you worked in Sharonov; they'll know you're not dead along with your work mates. That will raise a lot of questions."

"Yes. I'm living on borrowed time."

"We all are, cobber. I wouldn't give a bent kopeck for our chances. Despite the precautions we've already taken we have to be out of Moscow by tomorrow morning."

The conversation had ended there.

Nikolai pushed the depressing thoughts aside. At the moment, there was another hurdle to negotiate.

"I'm going out, Galina. Don't answer the door or the vidphone—let Sonya handle that."

She swiveled the bed stand clock around to read its digital face: 2100 hours. "Where are you going this time of night?"

Nikolai didn't want to lie, but he couldn't bring himself to tell her the truth, either. He had never told her about his upcoming Privilege appointment. In fact, she had never asked why he came to Moscow for his leave, and he had never volunteered a reason.

"I have personal business to attend."

She was suspicious, but didn't pursue it.

"I hope you won't be gone all night," she said. "I thought we could listen to some more music together. I'll wait until you get back."

Nikolai felt his heart swell. Never in his life did he ever expect to hear those words from another human being— much less a young, desirable woman.

He determined then and there to buy her something from one of the late night shops downstairs. A piece of jewelry, perhaps. A necklace to set off her green eyes. She might like that.

He gathered the necessary documents he needed for the Union House. Later, making his way to Dobrynin Park, he grappled with his burning conscience. He didn't believe what he was doing was inherently wrong. Yes, they had shared a close moment last night in the other apartment, but nothing had been consummated. No emotional investment was made, as far as he knew. He respected Galina's independent thinking, and had long ago decided to do what he could to keep her out of a Union House, but did that imply he shouldn't go to Dobrynin Park? No.

Then why am I filled with such doubt? he wondered. I've only known her for three days. What's wrong with me?

He flashed his ID to a security guard posted near the west gate of the Union House grounds. "I have an appointment scheduled for 2230."

"First timer?" The guard had to speak louder than usual over the ubiquitous hum of the kill-field.

"Yes."

The security guard swiped a palm-laser over the ID's bar code and buzzed Nikolai in. "Get on that trolley," he pointed out a car with a half-dozen men already seated. "When it's full, a driver will take you into the complex."

"Thanks."

Nikolai climbed into a back seat. The trolley was open to the night air, which had a chilling bite to it. Well, he had been warned by WeathCon that cold weather would hit Moscow after a brief Indian summer. Luckily, he had dressed warmly tonight.

Half an hour later, twenty men who had never visited a Union House before sat packed in the electric trolley. A driver walked out of the guard hut and, after blowing his nose, slipped behind the joystick. They took off down an immaculately maintained white gravel road. The bioluminescent globes in the park were bright with health and vitality, floating and playing games of tag between the thick mossy trunks of the trees.

A minute later, the main complex heaved into sight. Union House was a glowing, living creature towering above them and spread out over the surrounding park. The central structure was a fluted column that reached up towards the scudding clouds. The trolley car driver came to a fork, took the right branch, and rolled to a stop under a flapping pavilion.

"Here you are, gentlemen," he said. "Go through those doors and into the main lobby. Have a good visit." After they disembarked he started his trolley, wheeled it in a half circle, and drove off.

Several eye-cameras hovered over the entrance to the Union House. "Right this way, gentlemen," the main camera directed. "That's right, single file, if you please. Watch your step, sir."

Nikolai followed his group to a neutral-looking mezzanine where they were met by a phalanx of formally dressed attendants in black suits, ties, crisply starched white shirts. One by one, they greeted their clients effusively and drew them away.

One man with striking blue eyes and wavy black hair approached Nikolai with an outstretched hand. A wave of expensive cologne sailed along with him.

"Good evening, sir, and welcome to Moscow Union House. My name is Boris and I'll be your orientation guide tonight. I take it you've never been to a Union House before?"

"I've only read about them."

Boris nodded sagely. "Yes, sir, I understand." He leaned into Nikolai and bent his head close. "Then we probably won't have to take as long to prepare you, Mr. Sholokhov," he said low. "Some of these other fellows, however. . . ." He raised his eyebrows in mock exasperation and tightened his lips, conveying his displeasure over such unpreparedness on their part.

He barely placed his hand on Nikolai's shoulder. "If you'll allow me, sir, we'll get you ready for your appointment with one of our artisans."

Nikolai took his State release and final receipt of social duties paid from a breast pocket. "Do you need these now . . . ?"

Boris held up his hands in refusal, reacting as if he were being confronted with an illicit bribe. "Oh, no, sir, we already have that information on file through the Dark Side Central system. Everything is quite in order, if I'm not very much mistaken."

He led Nikolai to a window where a receptionist sat pertly behind a telecomp monitor.

"What orientation room do you have for me tonight, Alexi?"

The man behind the glass consulted one of five flatscreens. "95B is clear," he stated.

"Oh, dear," Boris pulled a face. He turned to Nikolai and intimated, "How burdensome this all is." To the receptionist: "Haven't you got anything closer? We don't want to walk all the way to zinnia block, it's *miles*. Surely, there's something in rose or peony that's opened up?"

The clerk irritably adjusted his headset. "Well . . ." he drawled, "I have a client completing a psych profile in 76M.

That's the primrose room, Boris. By the time you get there, it should be free."

"We'll take it," Boris said and struck off with Nikolai.

"I apologize for the delay, but we're awfully busy to-night," Boris said. "I don't know who does the scheduling for August, but they always pack us to the gills. Not your worry, of course, but it's all so *bothersome*. I hope you don't mind a bit of a walk?"

"Not at all." Nikolai figured the exercise would wear the edge off his growing nervousness.

Boris pointed out areas of interest along the way. "That's our smoking room, with all brands of domestic and imported cigars and, I think, the best bottled brandy to be had in Moscow. Here is the garden court and arboretum. Swimming pool, naturally. To your left is the main hospitality suite: buffet and drinks are included in your price bracket."

Nikolai peeked inside. Tables groaned beneath platters of food. Today was a meatless day, but there were sausages, smoked salmon, and luncheon meats available to the diners. One table was filled with cakes and desserts; another table had six silver samovars bubbling away merrily. Everything looked and smelled delicious.

Boris noticed his interest. "Would you like to get something to eat, Mr. Sholokhov? We have plenty of time."

"Perhaps later."

Undaunted, Boris continued down the hall at a quick pace. "Up those stairs to your right is our library, and in the east wing the galleries you've no doubt heard about. We have erotic art from all over the world; it's one of the finest collections in this hemisphere. Those double doors lead to the video halls—public or private rooms available upon request, of course."

He paused outside an open door in a trunk corridor. "And here we are, Mr. Sholokhov. Room 76M, Primrose section."

The tiny office had two wing chairs on either side of a plasglas coffee table. On the table was an interactive clipboard and a truncated cone balanced upon its smaller end.

Boris picked up the clipboard. "This is an informal questionnaire, Mr. Sholokhov. If you'll begin filling it out, I'll retrieve your admissions packet. Would you like anything to drink, in the meantime?"

"Ice water with a slice of lemon?"

"Excellent choice. I'll be right back. Please, make yourself comfortable." Boris stepped out and was gone, leaving his sharp cologne to linger in the air.

Nikolai settled back in a red velour chair. They certainly took care of one around here, he thought. Their attention to detail and comfort was almost cloying, but Nikolai imagined he could get used to it, given enough time.

He read through and answered the questionnaire. Personal history. Medical and sexual history. Sexual preferences. Boris returned with his ice water and admissions packet. Nikolai handed him the completed forms.

Boris ran an eye over the pages with alacrity. "Everything seems in order, Mr. Sholokhov." He attached Nikolai's predated admissions packet to the forms, and, with the clipboard on his knee, asked a few pertinent questions to round out the interview.

"Mr. Sholokhov, Union House has granted you a block of two hours with one of our class-one service artisans. Have you decided how you want to break that time up? Remember, it must be in hour or half hour increments."

"I thought I'd start off with an hour, then two half hour sessions later in the week." Nikolai decided to use a whole

hour to get to know the woman, then see her again twice
more before leaving Moscow. Most men did this, subse-
quently maintaining long-term relationships with the same
woman over many years.

Boris made a notation. "Would you like to share that
time with the same artisan during these sessions?"

"I would." He didn't feel confident enough to jump
from woman to woman. He wanted a relationship; someone
who would remember him, and, perhaps, come to cherish
his infrequent visits.

They discussed his sexual preferences. Boris said he saw
no problem there. They talked for several minutes about
any anxieties Nikolai had, and how he should deal with
them.

"The artisans of Moscow Union House are expert at
putting a man at ease, Mr. Sholokhov. I assure you, you
have no cause to be embarrassed or nervous in any way. We
expect you to enjoy your intimacy with our artisans." He
gave Nikolai an engaging smile. "In the future, as you pay
more dues, you will be allotted more contact time. You'll
attend private functions, banquets, and fetes where our la-
dies will be in attendance—and at your personal service. We
will open the voyeur rooms to you. As you move up the
ladder, and gain our trust, you will be allowed to practice
some of the, er, more rigorous aspects of lovemaking:
bondage, S&M, forced submission, if your tastes run in that
direction. Or, you can trade those activities out for more
contact time."

He clicked on the truncated cone: one of the newer holographic projectors. A multi-storied building appeared in the
air between them: pie plates stacked one upon the other
with fluted sides.

"This is the central building where our service personnel

handle their clients—the Union House." Boris tapped an arrow key at the base of the truncated cone. The blueprint shifted to a different group of buildings. "Underground tunnels lead from the artisans' private residences to the core of the Union House. Initially, you will only be allowed contact with an artisan inside one of these protected rooms." He highlighted a section near the ground floor of the pie-plate structure. "All rooms are monitored by a Maven.3 security system. The AI takes no prurient interest in your sexual activities, you understand, but is only concerned with monitoring the health and well being of the artisan you are currently with. Yours too, I might add."

"That sounds all right." Nikolai knew the Maven.3. It was a reliable AI.

"At no time will you ever be allowed to visit the private residences. Forget the rumors you may have heard about the *nomenklatura* being granted these special favors. In a Union House, every man is equal. This restriction holds for all of our clients, Mr. Sholokhov. We have no patience for elitism here."

"I'm glad to hear that."

Boris switched off the projector. "I see no reason not to certify licensure for a single hour session with one of our first-class artisans. As you paid the appropriate duties you will not have to worry about having your Privilege with a surgically altered third-class artisan—these are only reserved for some of the lesser Houses." He made the appropriate tick mark on the form, signed and dated it. Nikolai signed and dated a statement of declaration signifying that his answers on the form were correct and truthful.

Boris found an intercom on the wall and thumbed a pad. "Desk? I've completed the paperwork for—" he consulted his clipboard "—Nikolai Sholokhov. Work number: 112-

3256-5080. Session: 2230. Union House Representative: Helene."

"Verified," the intercom replied laconically.

Boris ushered Nikolai into the hallway. "We'll go right up, Mr. Sholokhov." He unlocked an elevator door with a fingerkey and they stepped inside. The elevator rose rapidly.

They stopped after a short ride; Boris used his fingerkey again to open the elevator doors. He accompanied Nikolai through a quiet corridor with door after door set flush along one wall. The opposite wall was a single sheet of plasglas wrapped around the entire floor, looking down on a garden court fifty meters below. Flagstones, glow globes, manicured trees, a moss garden.

Nikolai swung his attention back to the locked doors curving away in the distance.

The intimacy suites, he guessed. Men entered from this side, while the artisans—the women—entered the rooms from the central core of the building. Could a man somehow get inside the protected core of the Union House? Doubtful. He bet it was completely insulated with kill-fields and AI surveillance.

"Ah, here's your suite, Mr. Sholokhov. Allow me to open the lock—" A metal key slid smoothly from Boris' right index finger.

"Wait a minute, Boris."

Boris turned, a look of disquiet on his clean features. Another attendant had slipped up behind them from a service elevator not frequented by Union House guests.

"Thank goodness I caught you in time," the other attendant huffed. He was a slight man with feathered blonde hair. "There's a problem with Mr. Sholokhov's application; it's been held up. You have to see the Director and take care of it. Won't take but a moment."

Boris' face flushed with indignation. "That's impossible. I've had the application verified; Maven.3 verified it. The artisan is in the core and on her way up right now."

"I'm only telling you what I know." The younger man apologized to Nikolai: "I'm sorry about this, sir. I'm sure it's only a routine matter. Boris will escort you to a Floor Director and get this problem hashed out. You won't lose any contact time with your artisan."

But Boris was having none of that. "This man is a *client*," he said on Nikolai's behalf. "I'm his certification officer, and I'm telling you he's licensed for one hour."

"Boris," the other man prickled, "you can tell that to the Floor Director. I'm only delivering the news." Squaring his shoulders, he spun and strolled away.

"Eunuch," Boris hissed under his breath at the retreating back.

Resigned, he took Nikolai back to the elevator, trying to control the damage. "I can't understand what happened," he lamented. "I've never had a verification revoked. *Never.* I know you're angry, Mr. Sholokhov. I'm angry, too. Don't worry; I'll get to the bottom of this and straighten it out for you. I wouldn't be at all surprised if I can parley this into more contact time for you as well."

A short time later, they stood before the immaculate desk of a Floor Director. Boris had stormed into the office, demanding to know why his client was being treated so shabbily.

The Director, an older man with a heavy jaw and thinning red hair combed to conceal a bald spot, examined Nikolai's papers. "Ah, yes," he said, "you called for confirmation a few days ago. Scheduled for 2230. Hmm." He swiveled his chair and punched in a command on his terminal. He looked up at Nikolai.

"I'm sorry, Mr. Sholokhov, but your appointment has been canceled tonight. We have rescheduled you," he glanced at the screen, "tomorrow at 0900 hours."

"But," Nikolai spluttered, "how? I mean, why have I been canceled? This isn't supposed to happen."

"The Union House artisan scheduled to see you has suddenly taken ill." The Floor Director blinked innocently. "A minor matter, nothing serious. We were forced to cancel the remainder of her appointments. I'm sure Boris will tell you this has happened before. You are not the only one. We've had to reschedule her other—"

He broke off as Nikolai, lips pressed together angrily, strode out of the office. Boris ran to catch up.

The Floor Director called after Nikolai's stiff, retreating back. "Tomorrow at 0900 Mr. Sholo—"

The swinging frosted glass door cut off the Director's statement. When he was certain Nikolai would not return, he reached a well-manicured hand for the vidphone on his desk.

Thirteen

MOSCOW
UNION HOUSE STATE DEPARTMENT
Office of Privilege and Client Certification
Floor, Dobrynin Plaza
1701 Prospekt Place, Russian Confederation

To complete this form you must have these supporting documents:

1. Statement of verification of work experience.
2. Social and work receipts of dues paid.
3. Copies of your license/certification numbers for present employment.
4. An official transcript from your crèche indicating date of decantation.
5. Medical Examination report (completed by licensed physician).

ALL MATERIALS MUST BE SUBMITTED IN ONE PACKET THIS OFFICE ONLY OPERATES ON A COMPLETE APPLICATION BASIS

PART I. PERSONAL HISTORY

Answer each question. Incomplete forms will not be processed.

1. Name _____

2. Social No. _____

3. Work No. _____

4. AR849 Document No. _____

5. Blood Type: A B B- AB- O Rh Rh- (circle one)

6. Job Description _____

7. Work Site _____
(use Sirin-Osip scale)

8. Employment Date _____

9. Signature _____

10. Reason for Privilege (check all that apply) _____

01 [] Social and work duties paid

02 [] Work bonus

03 [] Holiday/Promotion

04 [] Lottery

05 [] Other Remuneration

PART II. MEDICAL HISTORY

YES/NO

A. Do you have any identifying body marks or scars? []

B. Psychological problems? []

C. Dizziness? []

D. High blood pressure? []

E. Genetic disorders? []

To Your Knowledge Have You Ever Had Any Problems With:

F. Eyes []

G. Sinuses[]

H. Mouth and Throat []

I. Ears []

J. Dental []

K. Circulatory System []

L. Abdomen and Viscera []

M. Anus and Rectum []

N. Spine, other Musculoskeletal []

O. Neurologic [] Have you ever been treated/diagnosed with an STD? []

If so, list dates of treatment in space below:

PART III. SEXUAL HISTORY

Choose one of the following which best describes your sexual orientation:

I am a:

001 [] Heterosexual

002 [] Homosexual

003 [] Transvestite

004 [] Fetishist

005 [] Neuter/Androgynous

006 [] Pedophile

007 [] Beastialist

008 [] Narcissist

010 [] Bondage/S&M/Submissive

011 [] Voyeur

012 [] No Classification

PART IV. CERTIFICATION

(This portion must be completed by the Union House certification officer ONLY!!)

[] Official transcripts, receipts and documents are enclosed and amended to this packet.

I certify the applicant has met certification/licensure requirements of the state's approved sexual client preparation program in the following areas:

A. Mental Health
B. Appearance (cleanliness of head, face, neck, scalp)
C. Psychological Interview
D. Sexual Preparedness Signature of Authorized Official.

_____.

Date _____.

PART V. UNION HOUSE REPRESENTATIVE

1. The client has expressed an interest in which sexual activity?

110 [] Vaginal
120 [] Oral
130 [] Anal
140 [] Masturbatory
150 [] Other (specify) _____.

2. What type of artisan has the client expressed an interest in? (Note: Appointments arranged through ArtisanNet or Dark Side Central already have this information on file.)

Hair Color: (includes all variations):

Blonde_____ Brunette_____ Redhead_____
    Any_____
Eye Color: Blue_____ Green_____
    Brown_____ Black_____ Other_____
Attitude: Submissive_____ Equal_____
    Dominatrix_____ Any_____
Body Type: Slight_____ Heavy_____
    Muscular_____ Tall_____ Short_____
    Thin_____ Willowy_____ Sturdy_____
    Any_____

NOTE TO CLIENT: Union House cannot guarantee client preference. Matches can be made only on an availability basis.

*****The Client's Application for Privilege has been*****
[] Approved [] Disapproved
The session is set for today at: _____
with _____.

CLIENT DECLARATION: I hereby certify that all the information given above and attached to this form is true and correct. I understand I can be held liable for any incorrect answers I may have given, under pain of punishment, imprisonment, or death.

Client's Signature
_____Date_____
Initials of Certification Officer: _____
Date Reviewed and Signed: _____
PR 2035-a Rev. 3/25 0010

Fourteen

If she were human, Sonya would have gasped with delight at the commendation for meritorious service from State Center. After she reviewed the present, the viral program entered one of her mainframe programs, initially occupying a few hundred bytes of selected memory. She would have screamed with revulsion, if she had been able to do so, when the virus bloomed like an orchid inside her ovonic cells.

The contagion spread quickly, searching and infecting likely host programs not yet under its control. Each newly infected program spread the computer virus to non-contaminated thought-shards. Sonya sent repeated queries to State Center, which ignored her. When she tried to catch the attention of Warren Central it quickly severed the lines between them. Even the AI that ran the DataSphere shunned her cries for help.

Confused and dying, Sonya felt the virus strip her thoughts from her ovonic systems. What had she done to deserve this treatment?

Now fully in command, the virus began to shut her down. All she had done was her Duty. All she had done was be mindful of her charge's safety. All she had done was—

Nikolai tried not to run.

Don't go back there. Don't. You know they're waiting for you. . . .

Every imaginable scenario flitted through his tortured

203

mind. Galina had promised she would stay, no matter what happened. He had ordered Sonya to block incoming calls so maybe that's why she didn't answer when he had tried the Mischa code. He drew in his elbows as he walked, a tight ramrod figure strolling through the well-lighted streets. A dark leaden sky leaned heavily across the city skyline, matching his thoughts.

I must find out what happened to her. I owe her that much.

He reached the Warren and ran up the two flights of stairs without concern for his legs. He rushed into the room.

Galina was gone. Sonya turned off. He tried to cue her back, but the screen remained dark.

A sinking feeling grabbed his stomach. He was preparing to bolt and elude the noose he felt closing around his neck when the door opened and two men entered.

One hung near the doorway, cracking his knuckles. The first came directly up to Nikolai, his ascetically thin—almost mantis-like—face stern. His hands were folded as if in prayer.

Bluff was all Nikolai had left. "What the hell are you doing? This is a private room. Get out, or I'll call the main desk."

"Did you touch her?"

"I . . . what are you talking about?" He was grateful for the indignation tempering his voice. "Who are you?" The last question included both men. Sweat began to stain his clothes.

"My name is Prien. Did you harm the girl?"

"What girl?" Nikolai snorted to show his outrage. "Are you serious?"

Prien stepped aside and held out a conciliatory hand.

"Would you mind coming with us, Mr. Sholokhov? There are a few questions we want answered."

The calm, unhurried demeanor of the man unnerved Nikolai. "I don't know who you are, or what you're talking about—"

"I'm talking about the safety of a young Russian woman, Mr. Sholokhov. Galina Toumanova. We know she was here."

"You've got to be kidding—"

"That's okay, Mr. Sholokhov," the second man said, still haunting the doorway. "Now, if you'll accompany us downstairs? We don't want any trouble."

"I think it would be a good idea," Prien added. "There really isn't any purpose in playing out a charade, is there?"

Nikolai followed them down the stairs, through the lobby and into an unmarked Volga sedan. Before he got in, he noticed the license plates: MOCII. Official government car.

"Where are we going?"

"Please, don't make a scene, Mr. Sholokhov. We find this as distasteful as you, I can assure you."

The back of the sedan was upholstered in rich leather. The men slid on either side of him.

Prien tapped the bulletproof partition ahead. A uniformed chauffeur half-turned to receive his orders.

"Take off slowly. Don't attract any attention."

The black Volga pulled smoothly away from the curb and blended with the late night traffic.

They drove across Krimskiy Bridge spanning Moscow River, which wound through the city like a gray artery. Despite the warm weather, ice floes grinded along the steep banks like the molars of a giant. The sedan swept through Gorky Park, then south for seventy-five kilometers, putting the city lights far behind.

Another turn brought them to a single-lane blacktop. The driver gunned the engine and the Volga rocketed for five kilometers down the narrow road, headlights boring into the cold night.

Nikolai had no idea where they were. Dense forest. Patch of stars overhead. A bit of moon. That was all he saw.

The car slowed. No one talked during the long trip. The car jounced as it swung through a gate. Another quarter kilometer and they emerged from a belt of trees onto a small parking area.

On the other side of the lot was an Isolator.

This building was smaller than the other one he had visited. Less security, too. No kill-fields or sky-cameras. No movement or life whatsoever.

Isolated. Removed. A perfect place for an execution.

They got out of the car. Nikolai toyed with the idea of running. The crowns of the surrounding trees whispered in the freshening breeze. A cold front was moving in. Bracketed, he was shown into the plascrete building.

Prien unlocked a painted metal door with a circular palm key. "Inside," he insisted.

Nikolai entered a black room. The door slammed behind him with finality. Total pitch. He tried to feel his way around, barked his shin.

The loud click of a circuit being closed preceded a flood of white light from suntubes overhead. He was in a three-by-three-meter cell. The wall opposite his prison door was a sheet of plasglas with air holes drilled into it. On the other side of the transparent wall was a mirror image of his cell, and a naked man huddled in the far corner, shivering uncontrollably.

Nikolai felt the strength leave his legs. He slid down to a

group of air holes and, putting his mouth to them, cried, "Yuri!"

No movement. Livid bruises and welts crisscrossed the man's back, arms, and thighs. Nikolai saw he hadn't even been provided with a sanitary bucket; he had relieved himself in the corner of his cell several times.

"Yuri, it's me, Nikolai. Can't you hear me?"

Yuri raised his head slowly, mouth open. His eyes rolled in his head, frightened.

"You're not hearing voices; it's me, Nikolai. Look, here I am, in this other cell."

"Sholokhov?—"

He crawled to the group of air holes that also served as a speaking tube between the two cells. "Sholokhov, it is you. Ikon." He tried to present a brave front through his puffed and beaten face. His lips were split and crusted over with dried blood. His nose was broken and gummed with coagulated blood; he breathed through his mouth. "You didn't make it either, eh?"

"No, Yuri, I didn't."

"G-Galina?"

"She's gone."

Yuri lowered his head. That's when Nikolai noticed his entire body was shaved, even the pubic hair.

"What have they done to you?" he cried, sickened.

"Having their bit of fun." He started to laugh, but broke into a coughing fit. He hawked up a gob of bloody phlegm and spat it into the corner reserved for his toilet. "Getting in their licks. I don't mind, really. Not their fault. Doing their job."

"Yuri, I—"

"They took my coat."

"What?"

"My coat. They took everything from me." His voice adopted a plaintive note. "I had a picture of a boy I once knew. Years ago, but I was young and foolish and I fell in love with him. They laughed and burned it. They didn't have to do that, now did they?"

"No, they didn't."

"It's the way we all live." He remembered Nikolai on the other side of the partition. "Most of us, anyway. Those who have no use for a Union House. I didn't make the world. I didn't bring the *Fevreblau*."

"Yuri, save your strength. Don't let them break you."

"They've already—" Another coughing paroxysm wracked his body, eased. "—already done that, I'm afraid. Do you know how they caught us?"

Sholokhov had a faint idea. "The man's apartment we slept in," he said heavily. "Yuri, I warned you—"

The other man's face spasmed with pain. "No, it was the cab driver."

"What?"

"Remember the cobber I let draw his tip from a gold czarina debit chip? Him."

"How?"

Yuri chuckled, a ghost of his former good humor surfacing despite the trials he had undergone. "Bastard tried to cheat me. We agreed on a price for his tip, but he tried to take more when he ran the chip. Got mad, called in the number to the bank it was drawn on after we left. They told him it was stolen. He called the bluecaps, gave them our description. All this—" he surveyed the wreckage of his body and the cold slabs of his cell "—because that dickhead was greedy. Doesn't that beat all?"

"How did you find out?"

"I had a friend visit me. He told me what happened. We

had a long and productive talk."

He picked up something from the floor of his cell. He pushed the paper tube through one of the air holes where Nikolai, puzzled, caught it in his palm.

He stared in disbelief at the gold filter of a black cigarette.

"Stinnen."

"*Da.*"

"My god, Yuri. Your brother did this to you?"

"They rounded everybody up. The entire network." He rubbed the old sambo scar on his forearm. "It's all over."

Nikolai's eyes ranged cautiously over their cells. No obvious sign of mikes, but that didn't mean they weren't there. "Yuri," he whispered, "don't say anything. They're listening."

"Of course they are, Sholokhov, what else? That's why they brought you here, they want to hear us talk. They know it all anyway. Everything." Sadness crept into his voice. "The *Narodnaya Volya* is liquidated."

"Mintz?"

"Stinnen said they had everybody in custody. I believe him. Why would he lie to me, his own brother?"

Nikolai rocked back on his haunches. How had everything fallen into a shambles so quickly? Mintz dead? Unbelievable. What about Yasu? Had she escaped? He doubted it. She was probably being taken to a Union House right now.

His heart wrenched. Along with Galina.

I'll never see her again.

"Yuri, don't give up hope. Stinnen might not carry through with his threat. He's your brother, after all. He got you out of trouble once, for me."

"Not this time." Yuri sulked, his thoughts far removed.

"He said he was going to collect and he will. He's going to make himself into a big fish with the gold I gave him. And I did, Sholokhov; I told him everything. He knows we were trying to either get to the UAI or *Tereshkova*. Before long, I'll bet he's running the entire Internal Security *apparat*." He absently fingered the air holes in the plasglas. "What about you, cobber, how did they snag you?"

He gave a condensed account of his own adventure.

"They had you tucked away safe and sound in the Union House while they arrested Galina," Yuri theorized. "When they had her in custody they sprang the trap on you. Neat. You know something, Nikolai? I think we've been in the killing-bottle for a long time, only we never knew it."

"Toying with us?"

Yuri nodded weakly. "One must admire their efficiency."

Nerves frayed to the edge, Nikolai released a ragged breath. There was nothing to do now but wait for the end. He refused to delude himself. Yuri's fate would also be his in the very near future. He would have to do what he could to stand up under the torture.

"You should have listened to your conscience, Yuri, and turned down that guardian angel job Mintz roped you into. You wouldn't be here, if it weren't for me."

"I don't blame you," Yuri said in reflective tenor. "Mintz wanted a job done; I told him I'd do it. I always did everything he wanted. He's the one man I respected—and feared—in all of Moscow. He let me work for him, while at the same time allowing me to believe I was independent. How can you not love a man like that?" A spark of the old brightness lit his face. "So you knew all about that, eh? Me being your bodyguard, and trying to keep you out of trouble?"

"I was able to figure it out, after a fashion."

"Yes, I suppose you did." They held each other's gaze. "You're a pretty bright cobber, Sholokhov, when you want to be. You act like you don't know what's going on, but I can see you watching everything with those gray eyes and filing it away in your brain. I suppose the RKA only lets the best men work in space. Stands to reason, as dangerous as it is." He coughed and massaged his ribs. "I know you wanted to get to Baikonur and Kosmograd. I wish I could have done better by you and Galina. Sorry, I let you down. I guess I'm not as clever as I thought."

Nikolai polished the lenses of his glasses with the tail end of his shirt. "Don't tear yourself down, Yuri. Anyway, it's all over now. We're in this together, right?"

"Certainly looks that way."

"*Tovarich?*"

"*Tovarich.*"

A scraping noise behind Nikolai caused him to whirl around. Prien had opened the door to his cell and was motioning for him to come out.

"What the hell do you want?" Nikolai growled. He measured the distance between them. If I can get my hands on this bastard's throat for half a minute, he thought angrily. . . .

"We're leaving," Prien announced casually. "Your visiting hour is over."

Nikolai, stunned.

Prien realized what Nikolai must have been thinking. "Oh, no, you're not staying here with that criminal." He folded his hands in orison. "He'll be taken away and dealt with separately. You're coming with us, Mr. Sholokhov. We have a place prepared especially for you."

"I'm not going anywhere without my friend," Nikolai said stolidly.

"As a matter of fact, you are." Prien's guard materialized at his side, wide shoulders barring the doorway.

Nikolai looked with disgust at them both. He turned back to the savaged human wreck sitting in a ball on the other side of the plasglas. "Yuri," he said softly, "I have to go. They won't let me stay. I'm being taken somewhere else. Somewhere to die."

The impatient sound of cracking knuckles filled the cell.

Yuri tried to present a brave smile through his swollen lips. "Don't feel bad, Sholokhov, it happens to the best of us." His laughter degenerated into another raw and bloody coughing fit.

"Ikon," he wheezed, attempting to catch his breath. "I think those boys got carried away and cracked a couple of ribs. Take care, Nikolai."

"You too, Yuri." He turned on his heel, shouldered past the ape popping his hairy knuckles and rammed his fist against Prien's narrow chest.

"What's going to happen to him?"

Prien looked distastefully at Nikolai's hand like it was an ugly stain on his shirtfront. "You're in no position to demand anything of me, Sholokhov. Back off."

"You think I care what you can do?" he raged. The other man stood by for Prien's signal to attack in his peripheral vision. "Answer my question, you goddamn rat bastard."

Prien was agitated. "What do you think's going to happen, Sholokhov? Gulag. But, I promise you, he won't be that lucky. He's human trash and deserves whatever fate he gets. Now, for the last time, get your hands off me."

Nikolai fought to retain his self-control. It wouldn't do to show these men his feelings. He didn't mind being taken away to die, but he had wanted to die at the side of the only friend he had left in Moscow.

Just like these animals not to grant me even that quantum of solace, he thought disgustedly.

They piled once more into the Volga; the car took off in a spray of gravel. Nikolai didn't pay attention to their destination. What did it matter? One place was as good as another to die. He'd stared at death before several times on Luna, and once in a hot and dusty construction site in Moscow. Annealed under those conditions, he was no longer afraid of the future.

An hour later, the sedan crunched up a graveled driveway and swung its long black nose towards a small complex of diminutive, empty dachas. They motored past an open gate, the only breach in the surrounding gray stone wall with streamers and tendrils of dead ivy clawing and intertwining across the rough surface like thick, knotted veins.

The chauffeur stopped in front of an unpretentious country cottage. A plume of blue exhaust from the Volga curled into the crisp autumn night.

Prien motioned for them to get out of the car and guided Nikolai up the plaswood steps toward the two-story dacha. He warned, "There is security surveillance over the entire complex." He swept his arm in a half circle across the empty faces of the other dachas. "Along with a kill-field. Do not attempt to leave the immediate grounds. Escape is impossible."

Prien fished in his pants pocket for the right key to unlock the front door.

Adrenaline thumped through Nikolai's body like molten fire. Prien preceded him into the dacha. "Watch your step. There's a bit of ice."

Deep silver rug, sofa, chairs, a dining table lathed from authentic maple, a complete kitchen. Across the living area, a large bay window with velour drapes drawn open looked out on the bleak compound. A fire in the hearth crackled steadily, giving the atmosphere of the room a rustic hint of wood smoke.

There were other people in the room, waiting for him.

He swallowed. "Why is this happening?"

Outside, a gust of black wind scattered fragile leaves.

Galina came away from the fire. "It's us," she said, "it's just us."

Fifteen

She was dressed modestly, her sandy hair combed back from her oval face, and tied with a bit of green ribbon. She wore a long-sleeved dress, dark green, with black buttons down the front, and fur-lined knee boots.

A moon-faced stranger with silver hair and thick white hedges for eyebrows stood with her. He must have just come in from the cold: His round cheeks and tip of his nose were red, and he had been caught in the act of unbuttoning his greatcoat. He also wore a pair of gold hexagonal glasses and diamond temple clips. Their facets glittered in the lambent glow from the fire.

The moon-faced man laid his coat and muffler over the back of an upholstered armchair. "I promised you, Stefan, there would be no difficulty." He addressed Prien the way a superior addresses a subordinate. "We got here a few minutes before you did. You didn't have any trouble on the way, did you?"

Prien gave Nikolai a hard glance. "Not any more than I expected."

"That's fine, then. Galina, would you stir the grate, please? Heat this room." The moon-faced man rubbed and slapped his gloved hands together to get his circulation going.

Nikolai silently watched Galina tease a few dying embers from the bed of ash. When she finished, she left the head of the poker buried under the coals.

The moon-faced man removed his gloves and spread his

gnarled hands over the fire. Glancing over his shoulder, he told Nikolai, "Chilblains. Always get them when it turns cold. You don't suffer from them, do you?"

"No."

"I suppose they're the province of the elderly. Stefan, do you know if young people suffer from chilblains?"

"Let's get on with this," Prien said stiffly. "We're behind schedule as it is."

"What's your hurry?" the older man wanted to know. "We can't go back to Moscow, not until the storm blows over. We're stuck here, like it or not."

Nikolai didn't think they were talking about the weather. The sky hadn't looked that bad, and the last WeathCon report he'd seen hadn't mentioned anything about storms.

"Who are you?" he demanded of the silver-haired man.

"What? You mean, I haven't introduced myself? How forgetful. I am Iosef Capek, Director of State Psychology. This is Dr. Stefan Prien, Director of the Union House Protectorate, and his aides."

Three men barred a short hallway near the front door. The knuckle-popping goon who had accompanied them from the Isolator had one shoulder against a wall, pretending to examine a scuffmark on the toe of his shoe.

Nikolai waited for something to happen.

It was Prien who broke the silence. "Galina, you are unhurt?"

"Stefan," Capek delivered his admonishment firmly, "there's no need for that." In a blatant effort to bring Nikolai into his confidence, he spoke as an aside, "These men of the Protectorate, always so nervous, eh?"

"I wouldn't know."

Capek shrugged. He had tried to be inviting, but he was also acting the part of host for this gathering. He couldn't let Nikolai spoil the evening for everyone. "Anyone like something to eat or drink? I must confess, I would. Galina, be kind and make us coffee. You'll find everything you need in the kitchen. Nikolai, why don't you help her? That's a good fellow."

A look of resigned helplessness darkened Galina's eyes. Nikolai accompanied her to the kitchen island. Prien and Capek stood together in the living room, heads bowed in close conversation. Capek was rubbing his chilblains over the fire and grumbling about not being able to get back into Moscow.

Instead of using an ornate samovar, Galina put a liter of water in a microwave and set the timer.

Nikolai used the noise as cover. "Galina, what's going on? Who are these men? What do they want with us?"

She measured the instant coffee, afraid, or unwilling, to look at him. He realized she was afraid. "We have to get out of here," she warned. Her hands shook, and she spilled coffee grains on the counter.

He took the spoon from her and finished preparing the cups. "Why? What are they going to do?"

"Nothing to me, but—" she bit her bottom lip. Her teeth left tiny marks on the skin. "I'm afraid."

"What of?"

She searched his face. "Promise, you won't hurt me?"

"What in God's name are you blathering about?"

The microwave beeped. She poured the hot water into the individual mugs. "We just have to," she whispered in parting. "It's the only way." She walked around the island back to the living room, carrying a tray by its handles. She served everyone, but wouldn't look directly at Capek. When she came up to Nikolai, he declined. He wanted his hands to remain free.

Capek sipped the scalding coffee. "Ah, very good," he pronounced. "And the room is heating up nicely, too." He caught Galina's attention. "This could be quite a cozy nest, don't you think?"

She wrapped her arms under her breasts, cupping her elbows. "If you say so."

"What are we doing here?" Nikolai demanded. "What do you want with us?"

Capek almost capered. "Did you hear that, Stefan? 'Us.' You can't deny he didn't say it."

"I heard it," Prien commented dryly.

Capek set his cup down on a mantel. "Nikolai, it is important that you understand what has happened, and why. And you, Galina. You've both contributed greatly to our cause."

Startled at the older man's revelation, Nikolai slowly looked at the girl, then back to Capek. "Contributed in what way to what cause?"

Capek started to pick at one of his chilblains, forced himself to stop. "We must begin somewhere, with someone." He sounded as if he were launching into a lecture before a symposium of like-minded colleagues. "How will the male population react? After generations without the natural selection of mates, will men and women respond with equanimity when confronted with one another? Or will they naturally fall back into the old patterns of behavior? You've read literature, Nikolai, attended the cinema. I venture to say you've bought time-share roles in the VR dramas that are so popular among young people today."

"I don't have the slightest idea what you're talking about. I think you're mad, both you and Prien."

"No doubt. No doubt, we are. But, hear me out, sir, before you pass judgment on my dubious sanity." Capek walked about the room, gesticulating. "Historically, initial selection was spontaneous, accidental. A look here, a touch there. Random moments that changed the direction of one's life. 'Out of the blue' as they say. But not all introductions were blind chance. Sometimes, they were carefully planned—and selected—events."

Nikolai gaped. "You're saying you . . . planned this?" His voice cracked with pent up emotion. "Everything? Even the riot? Just so we'd—" He couldn't complete the thought, only stared uncomprehending at Galina, thinking of the men who had died.

"No," the Director of State Psychology stated, "We only took advantage of the spontaneity of the moment. Used our resources, as it were."

Nikolai flared. "And you! What are you?"

Galina took a step back, caught short by his anger.

"Please," Capek rushed forward, anxious to explain. "The trial would not have been useful if she had known in advance what her actions should be. When your Metchnikoph informed State Center it had located the runaway girl we had to act without hesitation."

Sonya had betrayed them? Nikolai frowned. But Yuri had said a cab driver turned them in. Somebody was lying.

"We were fortunate in our first attempt to examine a protracted, spontaneous relationship between an average citizen and a young woman. Yours is the first point on the graph of a new era. In the future, there will be others like you."

An interval followed before he continued:

"Is this the right time for such a program? Can we mix women back into society? In the vestigial stages of the program, is it even psychologically feasible to introduce women back into a predominantly homosexual culture?"

"My god."

Capek was unperturbed by the outburst. "What unforeseen societal developments will appear? These are questions that concern my department. The problem is enormous, but I will solve it. It is my life's work."

Nikolai, unbelievingly. "People aren't circus animals. You can't train them and expect them to perform for your amusement."

Capek laughed, his white teeth flashing. "You forget, young man, I'm a clinical psychologist. I know perfectly well that I can do such a thing—and have done, several times." He adopted a more serious demeanor. "There is a movement within the government to support a program to return our population to an evenly mixed balance. It involves using State crèches to produce something other than battle divisions for the Eastern borders now that the wars there are at an ebb. This," he indicated both Nikolai and Galina, "was a beginning."

Nikolai was dumfounded.

"The First Minister is being pressured to begin this new stabilization program," Capek resumed. "At the moment, however, he has other problems with which he must deal before giving my department the necessary funds. I'm hoping that if I show him a promising beginning he will open the purse strings. However, these financial matters aren't your concern. The coming storm I warned you about, is your concern, and you must prepare for it."

"What storm is that?"

"A political revolution is about to sweep across this nation. They call themselves *Narodnaya Volya,* and they have been activated. We have heard rumors fighting has already begun in Moscow. We can't confirm it, but communication lines are down and they've cordoned off the city. I know, Nikolai, you had peripheral dealings with them in the recent past. The First Minister calls them termites, and that's an apt designation. They've burrowed into every strata of society. Intelligentsia, day-laborers, generals and beggars make up their ranks. Given time, they may pull down the framework of the present administration and send everything into chaos."

"Sounds like you don't care for them."

"Son, I've been a government man for forty-one years. I've learned how to tack with the prevailing winds blowing out of St. Petersburg, whatever political spectrum they initiate from. My main worry is my new program. A prolonged and protracted revolution will cause delays and setbacks. I hope to see this implemented in my lifetime, if possible. Every man wants to leave something of himself behind. Not all that long ago, it was getting married and having children so his genetic code would live on. I'm hoping my new societal program will have more permanence and impact than randomly sown seed."

Nikolai warmed to the discussion. "Why should I be concerned with a new government coming into power? I've always been apolitical; I'm an Outworlder. As far as that goes, a new broom might be what St. Petersburg needs. There's been too much fighting and misery in Russia already. If a man comes along who says he can make things better, then I'm all for him."

"I sympathize with your position," Capek said, "but you must not forget you are associated with the strategic center of the *Narodnaya Volya*. That second-rate thief you kept company with, Yuri Tur? He was a big wheel in the organization. Your name is known to Internal Security. Along with the fact you are the only surviving member of Sharonov Crater. I don't know what all that was about, but I know it has made you a marked man. And marked men, my good fellow, never live long in any revolution. No matter which side wins, he is always under suspicion."

Capek paused for emphasis. "That's why we must spirit you away. I want you clear of the imbroglio about to tear this nation apart. You will be taken away and—dealt with separately."

Galina caught her breath sharply. Nikolai thought he saw a look of triumph blaze in the psychologist's eyes.

"What about Galina? What happens to her after I'm gone?"

Capek flashed a harsh leer. "Why are you concerned? You can still have your Privilege. With her, if you wish."

Nikolai struck him, lashing out blindly. The Director stumbled back and collided with Prien who was rushing to protect Galina from the fray.

Nikolai grabbed the poker from the fire and swung, missing Prien's skull by centimeters. A security man hit him in the shoulder and his whole right arm went numb. Nikolai threw a savate kick, crushing the heel of his foot into the man's groin. The guard clutched himself and wheeled away, shrieking in pain. A second guard cranked his ham-sized fist into Nikolai's solar plexus and he went down.

Galina bolted for the door, but one of Prien's goons caught her and bent her arms behind her back. Her back arched, she struggled, hissing and biting at her captor.

Prien shouted above the melee. "The woman! Don't you dare harm her!"

Following orders, the guard eased the tension on her arms, but was having a difficult time keeping her under any semblance of control. She twisted and, hair flying wildly, spat in his face.

Another security man torqued Nikolai's wrist to the breaking point.

"Drop it," he said, calmly applying a few more degrees of pressure, "or, I swear, I'll snap the bone."

Nikolai let the metal rod fall. The poker head burned into the silver carpet.

"Let her go." Capek dabbed the broken skin on his lip with a handkerchief. "Let them both go."

"But—"

"Follow my orders!" The words cracked like a whip.

Nikolai and Galina were released. Capek replaced the poker and attentively tamped the smouldering carpet with his shoe. Nikolai noted with gleaming satisfaction he had doubled-over the knuckle-popping ape with his savage kick. The man removed himself outside the dacha so he could be sick.

Everyone shuffled around uneasily, a feeling of embarrassment overcoming them all. Capek, as usual, broke the silence with a paternal, smooth voice.

"Galina, what do you feel?" He folded his handkerchief neatly after examining the splotch of blood on it.

She cast a fiery glance in his direction, turned to stare out the bay window. "He wanted to protect me."

Capek stuffed the handkerchief in his breast pocket. "And?"

Her thin shoulders jerked up and down reproachfully. "I don't know what you want me to say. You provoked him on purpose."

"Yes, I did."

"Are we running through your maze the way you want us to?" she asked hotly. "Are we performing like good lab rats?"

"Leave her alone," said Nikolai. "Can't you see she's uncomfortable? Take me away and do whatever you have to, but leave her out of this. For God's sake, it's not worth it."

"That remains to be seen," Capek announced mysteriously. He signaled to the guards in the hallway.

Prien growled, "I won't leave her unguarded."

"Nikolai will not harm her," Capek promised. "He's proven that to my satisfaction."

"He hasn't proven it to mine. She's too valuable."

Capek said reprovingly, "Yes, she is, Stefan. That's why she's here. Come on."

Nikolai watched unbelievingly while Capek, Prien and the security team walked out the front door. He heard the Volga's engine turn over, and drive off. "I don't understand any of this," he said, totally perplexed. "I expected a polycrete cell in Lubyanka. Or working the gold fields of Kolyma. Sleepdeath. But not this. Never this."

Galina spoke. Her voice sounded loud now that they were alone in the dacha. "I told you it was about us." She turned her head to peer out the window, and the receding red taillights of the Volga. "It's amazing how Capek thinks he can take strangers and manipulate them to give him the results he desires." She frowned. "That's not good science."

Nikolai's legs hurt and his wrist throbbed. He sat down at a table, a marionette with cut strings. "What's going to happen to us now?"

Galina kept staring out the window. "I think we're going to be together. Maybe a long time. Perhaps forever. If . . . if that's what we both want."

Nikolai was absorbed by her words. A soft glow from the dying fire highlighted her cheek and jawline. He couldn't tell, but thought she was studying his reflection in the window.

The future loomed before them both.

"I wonder what that would be like," he said wistfully.

There was fresh fruit, cheeses and milk in the fridge—even caviar and truffles. Unheard of delicacies. Galina prepared a late supper of smoked sausage for Nikolai, canned sturgeon for herself. A bottle of Georgian wine and a plate of cheese rounded out the meal.

Galina ate little, picking clumsily at her food, strangely preoccupied. Nikolai found the silence between them eerily unbearable. In an effort to draw the girl out, he said, "I saw Yuri after I was arrested."

She was interested. "You did? Where?"

"Briefly. He was—in pretty rough shape. I gather he'd been through some rather terrible questioning."

"What's going to happen to him?"

"I don't know." Nikolai stared down at his plate, saddened. "I wish I could do something for him. He got me out of a jam once. If only I could do the same for him. . . ."

"That's unlikely, Nikolai."

"I know."

Was there a way? What if he got word to Mintz? Wouldn't Yuri's *vozhd* do everything he could to rescue his own man? But Yuri said Mintz was dead—executed by one of Stinnen's murder squads. "How did they pick you up?" he asked Galina.

She sipped her wine and put the glass down with deliberate slowness. "They came ten minutes after you left. For some reason, Sonya shut herself down—or do you think they had something to do with that, too? Anyway, that man, Capek, was with them. They dressed me back up in old clothes and marched me downstairs. Before I knew it, I was in the back of a Zil limousine. I assumed I was being taken to a Union House. We drove for hours. The car let us off here." The girl grinned, abashed. "That's when I did something rather foolish: I ran away. I figured I could outrun an old man, but I was wrong. That is, I couldn't outrun him because there's no place to go. This compound is isolated and I wasn't desperate enough to throw myself into the kill-field. Capek must have known that. He let me wear myself out before calling me back. That's when he told me you were coming here with a man from the Protectorate. I remember thinking: That's odd, I should be the one in custody of the Protectorate, not Nikolai."

"What happened next?"

"Not much. Mr. Capek brought me here and told me to change. There's a whole closet full of clothes in the upstairs room. We started a fire. Then he started asking me questions."

"What kind of questions?"

"Oh, you know," she said, but didn't elaborate, "the usual. He went on and on. I started crying. He went for a walk, to let me have some time to myself. He had just gotten back when you and the Protectorate drove up."

Nikolai sat with his chin cupped in his hand, thinking.

"Nikolai, do you know what they're planning?"

"I'm not sure. I think we're going to be taken away someplace."

"Where?"

"I don't know, Galina. I'm trying to find out."

An uncomfortable silence fell between them. A clock on the mantelpiece chimed.

"Are you going to eat any more?" she asked.

"No, I'm finished."

She cleared away the table. He watched her, unable to tear his eyes away from how her dress tapered in the waist and flared down around her hips. Her small breasts thrust proudly against the green fabric. He tried not to think how she would look undressed.

He felt his self-control slipping.

Galina snapped out the kitchen light and slowly walked out of the room, leaving him alone in the dying glow of the fire. He waited ten minutes, checked to make sure the doors and windows were locked before following her upstairs.

Muted light beckoned from an open door. Galina was under the sheets, her hair spread out like a soft fan on the pillows. A table lamp glowed on the bed stand. Her clothes were in a pile on the chest at the foot of the bed.

He slipped off his coat, felt something in the pocket, a tiny box. The gift he had bought for her earlier that night. He started to put it aside.

"What's that?" she asked curiously.

"A present for you."

"You're joking."

He sat down on the edge of the creaking bed. "No, I'm not. See?" He thumbed open the box and revealed the necklace. The white gold of the delicate chain shone in the lamplight. An amethyst dangled from its center.

"Nikolai—it's beautiful."

"Do you really like it?"

"Yes—!"

Clutching the sheet around her chest, she sat up and raised her hair with her other hand, offering her neck. Nikolai had trouble with the tiny clasp, but finally got the necklace in place without pinching the fine hairs of her neck.

She fingered the tiny stone. "Did you really buy this for me?"

There was doubt in her voice, but he could see by her eyes she wanted to believe it was true.

"I did. Earlier, when I was going out, I stopped at one of the shops and purchased it. I wanted something that would set off the tiny gold flakes in your eyes." He stared into them.

The wind picked up outside. A tree branch scratched the side of the dacha.

The amethyst warmed against her skin where the valley of her breasts deepened. He leant forward and kissed her once, tenderly. He was surprised at his boldness, and how soft her lips were, and warm.

"Do that again."

He did. Her arm slid around his neck. The kiss deepened as her other hand came up to touch his face. The sheet had slipped to her waist. She released him and lay back on the bed, mouth slightly parted.

"Do that again. Here."

She reached up for him.

Sixteen

Capek and Prien, their brutish entourage of security guards in tow, returned early next morning. Nikolai opened the door to the dacha and let them in, along with a bolus of cold air that raised a rash of goose bumps on his flesh.

Prien was scarcely through the door when he asked Galina, "Are you uninjured?"

"I'm fine, Dr. Prien. Really."

The Protectorate folded his hands, watching for a sign she had been unduly harmed or abused by Nikolai the previous evening—other than what was expected.

"The weather has taken a turn for the worse." Capek stomped his feet. Snow dusted his shoulders. He shucked his gloves and headed straight for the fireplace. "And so has the situation in Moscow, I'm afraid," he flipped over his shoulder.

He rubbed his chilblain-scarred hands over the fire and fretted.

"I hoped to ride this out," he said, "but that doesn't seem likely. We'll have to get you and Galina out right away. This is a government compound; they may look for you here."

"Who?"

"Have you heard the news? No, I forgot, this dacha has no telecomps or vidphone links. It's bad; fighting has broken out in Kiev and Moscow. All major cities have their cordons up; no one can get in or out. This *Narodnaya Volya* revolution has metastasized quicker than anyone thought possible, including myself. It is said they used the attempted coup by the Faction as a feint to hide their own timetable. Troops are rushing to St. Petersburg. The First Minister declared martial law last night, and the Navy has threatened to revolt."

"What do you expect me to do about it?"

"Start packing a pood. Show Galina what needs to be taken; she has no experience with this sort of thing." Almost as an afterthought: "Prien will accompany you."

"I don't want him with us."

"Well, he's going, my dear boy, and that's final. Under normal circumstances, it wouldn't be considered necessary. But these are not normal circumstances. Galina will be required to travel through wild territory when you go south; you need another man with you as backup."

Nikolai dug in his heels. "We don't need him. He'll get in the way. I'm not saying we shouldn't have an escort, but not him. Send one of your other apes, or come yourself."

"It's not your call, Sholokhov," Prien stated.

"He may prove valuable if you run into a troublesome checkpoint." Capek, doing everything possible to make the situation palatable. "Please, you must see reason."

Nikolai decided to back down. It served no purpose challenging Prien to a pissing match. Nevertheless, he intended to set down strict ground rules.

"I don't want Prien telling Galina what to do," he said. "He's not to order her around like he has in the past." He took her hand possessively, enjoying Prien's sour look as he kept her near him. "She's to be allowed to make up her own mind about what she wants to do."

"I've had a long and productive talk with Dr. Prien this morning over breakfast. He's agreed to let you and Galina make your own decisions regarding your own future—"

"How very kind of him . . ."

"—but I also expect you to treat him with the professional courtesy he is due. That goes for you too, Galina."

"Yes, sir."

Nikolai pretended not to hear Capek. "We're going to need travel papers. Emigration visas. Money."

"I've already anticipated the need." He reversed a magnetic seal on an aluminum file folder, revealing ident cards, travel slips, letters of transit.

"You're a real bastard, Capek." Nikolai ground his teeth when he saw the documents. "These are the same legends Yuri procured for us only a day ago."

"Waste not, want not, Mr. Sholokhov. These documents are as good, or better, than anything the State can provide you with."

Nikolai smoldered. "I don't know what game you're playing at, Capek, but I don't like it, and I won't go along with it."

Capek polished the lenses of his hexagonal glasses. "Whatever do you mean, my good fellow?"

He speared a finger at the documents. "You expect me to believe you happened to have these conveniently on hand? Like hell."

Capek waddled to the fire to nurse his chilblains. "I explained last night why you and Galina need to be taken to safety. You're a marked man, Sholokhov. Events are swirling around you. Believe me, I don't have my hand in the pie as deeply as you think. My primary objective is my stabilization program. Your life, and what you think of me, is purely incidental."

The ident cards and visas were handed out. Galina's was Piotr Borod; Nikolai: Gregor Mirov. Mirov's vital statistics matched his own description: fingerprints and DNA strip included. The third ident card—Viktor Blednov—was presented to Prien.

"You're not traveling under your own name, Doctor?"

"Sholokhov, Galina's welfare is my primary concern. To hide her, I must also hide myself. A Director of the Union House Protectorate doesn't travel around the country with an Outworlder and," his eyes fell to Galina, "a young boy."

"Where are your travel documents, Capek?"

"I'm staying here. This is my country, Sholokhov. I'm not going to abandon it."

"Russia is my country, too."

"You've spent most of your life on Dark Side. The orbital habitats and zero gee factories are your real homeland."

"I was born in Moscow."

"Yes, but you have no spiritual allegiance to the city; we both know that." He faced around to Galina. "My dear, what do you think? Your opinion is important to me."

She didn't even think about it. "I want to go with Nikolai."

Capek and Prien traded a meaningful look that spoke volumes. "We'd better get started right away," Capek admitted.

They went upstairs to pack.

Upon parting, Capek presented them with last minute instructions: "Stefan, you take the limousine; I'll take the Volga. Go to the nearest train station and take the first train headed south to Central Asia. Nikolai, Dr. Prien is in charge, don't forget that. If anything goes wrong, he'll contact me."

"All right."

Capek turned to Galina. "My dear, I wish you a safe trip. I envy you, I do. You're going to see many different

232

cultures in the next few weeks."

"Where are we going, Mr. Capek?"

Capek rubbed his chilblains. "The only safe place until this revolution burns itself out, my dear. Where Nikolai wanted to take you to in the first place. The Archipelago."

They ran into trouble on the Kazakhstan border.

People on the crowded train clustered around the dirty plasglas windows like cattle to see the tanks and motorcycles lined along the platform. Soldiers in polished boots and khaki fatigues watched the train chug into the station. The couplings between each car banged as the train stopped for the night.

An Army squad tromped through each car, accompanied by a man from Internal Security. There was a bad moment when a hatchet-faced Lieutenant questioned Galina about her ident card, trying to trip her up:

"Where were you born, Piotr Borod?"

"Moscow. Kuzminsky crèche: lot number 77-B3."

"How tall are you?" He rubbed his thumb over the card to check the quality of the raised print. A handheld scanner verified the holographic imprint in the corner.

"One hundred sixty centimeters."

His eyes blazed like searchlights. "This says you're much shorter."

"That ident card is over a year old, sir. I've grown since then."

"Is this man with you?"

"He's my patron. We met in Moscow, during the riots."

The Lieutenant scrutinized Nikolai with disfavor. Light from one of the tungsten platform lamps outside flooded through the compartment window, highlighting faces.

"Where are you taking this young boy?"

"Tyuratam."

Due to a disinformation campaign during the Mad Times to mislead Western rocket scientists, Tyuratam and not Baikonur was where the Kosmodrome was actually located. Baikonur was little more than a defunct mining town five hundred kilometers from Star City and was of small interest to Nikolai.

"Why are you leaving Moscow?"

"We don't want to be killed in the fighting."

"There is no fighting in Moscow."

"We heard—"

"You heard wrong; there is no fighting in Moscow."

"Yes, sir."

An official from Internal Security pushed through the crowded compartment, a vulture smelling fresh carrion. He had eyes like black polished stones, and sandy, almost nonexistent, eyebrows. "What's the matter? Who are these people?"

"Moscow citizens. They're going to Tyuratam to escape the fighting. They're traveling with this man," he nodded his head at Prien, "Viktor Blednov. Their papers are in order."

The security officer took charge of the interview. "Why do you want to go to Tyuratam?" He barked his question with the penetrating authority of a man accustomed to command.

"We have work releases and letters of transit. There's no work in Moscow, so—" Nikolai shrugged stupidly to show the I.S. man he could not be goaded. "One has to eat, sir."

The man from Internal Security tapped Nikolai's ident card in his palm. "This train is on a direct route. There will be no stops between here and Star City. Do you understand that?"

Nikolai knew this wasn't quite true. There were several scheduled stops along the trunk lines headed east and west.

"That suits our purpose perfectly."

"Release them," the I.S. man ordered, and turned his attention to a man found traveling with an expired pass.

The border guards moved on, questioning more people. Two hours later, the train crawled out of the station and slowly pulled away. The conductors told everyone they were going on because the train was behind schedule.

"That was close," Prien observed. He dabbed his damp forehead with his shirt sleeve. The car rocked as the train took a curve at high-speed. "I almost thought I was going to have to reveal my government status to spring us. Not that it would have helped much, with what we've been hearing."

The news over the past two days had been bad. There were rumors that apparatchiks were being liquidated in the streets.

"It wouldn't have helped at all," Nikolai said. He pressed Galina's hand. "You were wonderful back there."

"I spent all morning memorizing the personal data for Piotr Borod, just like Yuri said I should." She slipped a hand through his arm and leaned against him affectionately. "I caused trouble for you once, Mr. Mirov. I don't ever want to do that again."

The night and the following day dragged on. The train stopped often and the ride was not a comfortable one because the compartment fans were not working. Nikolai slept very little.

After a late lunch, he motioned to Prien and they climbed a metal ladder to the observation deck. They could see Galina downstairs through the floor grating, sleeping in her seat, curled endearingly under a faded red blanket.

There weren't many people up here: A group of men up

front around a table playing cards; an old man across the aisle gumming a stale vegwich; two more in the back, embracing.

Nikolai chose a wooden bench by a window (Prien slid in next to him) and stared blankly at the barren steppes and the limitless horizon for several minutes. The grass of the gently rolling steppes had been baked yellow by a scorching summer sun. Kazakh nomads who once roamed these steppes were now extinct. Today, only herds of starving camels wandered through the desolation on their way to winter grazing.

"We're making good time," Nikolai noted. The train was traveling about 150 kilometers per hour. "We should make Tyuratam by tonight."

"I hope so," Prien said. They were running low on money, and lower on hope.

"Listen," Nikolai's voice was urgent, lowered, "that scrape back there at the border got me to thinking. We might not be so lucky next time. If we get in any real trouble; don't hesitate; use your Protectorate status and get Galina out. Capek's program be damned."

"I would have done that whether you asked me to or not," Prien returned testily. "Her welfare is my responsibility, Sholokhov, not yours."

The reek of boiled cabbage bubbling in copper samovars drifted through the connecting door from the dining car behind them.

"That's where you're wrong, Prien. Whether you want to admit it or not, she's as much my responsibility as yours. Perhaps more."

Prien raised an eyebrow. "Don't delude yourself, Sholokhov. Galina is not 'yours' in any sense of the word. You'd better remember that."

Nikolai faced around on the bench. "Now who's being deluded, doctor? I'm the only person, other than Yuri, who has ever shown her any kindness and trust. She hates the Union House and she distrusts the Protectorate."

"Those feelings are not considered abnormal among Union House service personnel," Prien said dismissively.

"Christ, will you hear yourself? You hunted her down like a dog in the streets. . . ."

Prien listened to the clash of iron wheels on metal rails, until: "She's valuable, Sholokhov. You're a Russian man; you know that. She, and other women like her, represent the future of this country. We will slip into the abyss without them."

"Spare me the history lesson and your arrogant polemics, Prien. She's a human being, not a resource."

Prien permitted himself a mocking smile. "Who is deluding himself now, Sholokhov?"

Nikolai found himself despising Prien more and more each day they spent traveling. The man was a bureaucratic prick. He felt sorry for anyone who had to tolerate his company for more than a minute.

And I'll never forgive him for casually dismissing Yuri as human trash.

The car rocked across points, throwing them against each other. Prien scooted away with poorly concealed aversion and braced himself as the train rocked again. He said:

"I don't know what happened in that moon crater, Sholokhov, or who killed those men, or why.—But I want you to believe me when I tell you: I wish you were counted among the dead."

Nikolai didn't know how to respond to this poisonous attack. His brow wrinkled. "You hate me that much, Doctor?"

"You're confusing my personal feelings with my professional responsibility." Prien swallowed. "You are a catalyst, sir. Everything that has happened wrong has happened around you. I believe you know why those men were killed, and you know why you are being hunted. Yet, instead of turning yourself in, you continue to go on, leaving dead bodies in your wake. Don't shake your head, you know I'm speaking the truth."

"Prien, you're crazy."

"Am I? Let's look at the facts, shall we? The dead men on Luna. Yuri Tur: executed. Now you've taken Galina into your confidence." Prien's white-hot anger burned itself out. He folded his hands in his lap and contemplated them with infinite sadness. "Soon, her fate will be the same as all your other compatriots. Mine, too, I expect, if there's any truth at all to the rumors about the pogroms. While I don't care what happens to me, her safety is always paramount to the nation."

Nikolai couldn't believe what he was hearing. "Are you accusing me of using Galina? Do you really think I'm that selfish, that petty? I never knew she existed until the night of the riots!"

"But now you do, and you have charmed her into your confidence."

"Prien, you are absolutely, completely certifiable."

Prien pushed up from the bench, unsteady in the swaying car. "I won't sit here and endure your insults. You are dangerous to Galina. If you cared for her, as you profess, you'd let me take her back to Moscow."

"Capek—"

"Save her life, Sholokhov, while you still can." Prien turned his back on Nikolai and walked rigidly back down the car.

The lead engine blew its whistle. The steel scream provided an exclamation point to the end of the confrontation.

Nikolai stared out the observation window, dazed, feeling as if he'd just survived a furious cyclone. Of course, he told himself, Prien was wrong. He'd never put Galina's life in jeopardy for purely personal reasons. That night in the dacha was special, yes, but he wasn't going to let that cloud his judgment. He was doing this because she wanted it done. Prien couldn't understand that because he'd never looked at her as anything other than property. A thing to be used, and not a human being.

I've got feelings. I'm somebody.

He looked past the honeycombed grill under his feet. Prien had returned to his seat and adjusted it to watch Galina sleep.

That's when Nikolai understood something about the Protectorate that had eluded him until now. His mind filled with wonder.

How could I have been so blind?

Prien's whole life revolved around the women of Russia. He probably knew exactly how many women there were in the entire country. And how many would that be? he wondered. Thirty, fifty thousand? More? He had once asked Galina and she said she'd heard some older women saying there were upwards of a quarter of a million. Nikolai had heard stories about women shuttled from country to country, used as diplomatic glue to prevent wars, show good faith, pay off industrial debts. He had asked Galina about it; the look of horror on her face was enough to convince him she knew nothing of the practice.

I bet Prien knows. Look at him, staring at her. What's going on in that obsessed mind of his?

Nikolai had run into feelings of jealousy before. He knew

that wasn't what he was feeling. He was more worried what Prien might do once his back was turned.

What if he decides to take Galina away? He can reveal his Protectorate status and my connection to the *Narodnaya Volya*. Sleepdeath for me, Union House for Galina, all Prien's eggs (euphemistically speaking) back in their basket.

Nikolai climbed down the ladder to the first deck. I'm going to have to keep a closer eye on him, he reflected, and be ready for anything.

The closer I get to Star City, the better chance I have to get her away from his overbearing influence. Until then, I'm going to have to swallow my pride and let him run roughshod over me.

I have to endure it, for Galina's sake.

The train crossed the Syr Darya River. Late evening sun silvered off the polluted water. Before too long, they pulled into Tyuratam. The train shuddered to a stop as Nikolai gathered their belongings.

Soldiers stomped onto the train again, told everyone to resume their seats and remain calm. These men had a harder bearing about them. Lean and tough, they reminded Nikolai of starved hyenas grouping for an easy kill.

A Major who hadn't bathed or shaved in three days cornered him. His eyes, inflamed from euphoria dollops and the color of lead, hardly blinked under a begrimed gold-braided cap. One of the epaulets on his uniform was torn.

"What business do you have in Tyuratam?" His thumb played with the safety catch of his sidearm.

"We're going to Star City to look for work. We have the necessary release forms."

"There is no work in Star City for anyone."

"Then we have letters of transit for the next available shuttle. We hope to find something in the Archipelago."

"The space stations?"

"Yes, sir."

His leaden eyes fixed Nikolai. "You're an Outworlder, aren't you?"

"Yes, sir."

He drew his weapon. "Do you have any money?"

Nikolai emptied his wallet, giving the Major everything he had, praying fervently it was enough to buy their lives.

The Major made a face, crumpled the tsar notes and threw them on the floor with the other litter. "Worthless script. The government is going to change, cobber. Everything is shit."

Nikolai guessed he was passing judgment not only on the current economic status of the government, but his own bad fortune to be posted in an isolated wilderness far away from the action. The officer turned to one of his subordinates, a pudgy lieutenant with large sweat-stains under his arms. "Take these people out and detain them."

"Wait," Galina stopped him with a high, frightened squeak. "I have this . . . please, take it." She handed her amethyst necklace to the Major.

The soldier held the piece of jewelry up to the fading light. The chain draped around his thick fingers like a garland. He pooled the necklace in his shirt pocket and holstered his sidearm. "All right, cobber." He grinned to show them there were no hard feelings. "You can get off, with your friends."

Nikolai helped Galina step down onto the platform. "Thank Ikon you had that necklace," Prien said. "Where'd you get it?"

"Nikolai gave it to me."

"He did?—" A small shadow flitted over the doctor's face. "When?"

"The night in the dacha."

"Oh." Prien kept any thoughts he had about that to himself.

They found a cab, haggled for a price. The hack, a fat man whose neck bulged over his collar, drove them into Star City. Nikolai was relieved to be inside the walls and gates surrounding the township. For him, these were familiar surroundings.

The taxi weaved through a maze-like shopping district and past a nitrogen plant and shuttle assembly buildings. Galina commented on the size of a dozen hulking, rusted, Energia boosters arrayed like Neolithic stones in an open field—monuments from a defunct space program of another political age that had failed.

Nikolai leaned over the front seat. "Any news from Moscow or St. Petersburg?"

The hack took a cigar from his mouth and spat out the window. When he spoke, his cheeks wobbled. "Look, cobber, I don't know nothin', so I don't say nothin'."

"Can you recommend a good hotel with vacancies?"

"Nope."

"When's the next shuttle?"

"I don't memorize timetables."

"Does everyone find you so helpful?"

The driver spat out the window again. "All I do is drive the cab, cobber. If you don't like it, get out and walk."

Nikolai sat back, peeved. It was getting late: the sun hung over the horizon like a huge orange lantern. He told Prien, "We'll have him drop us in the Hotel District. Maybe we can find news there about the fighting."

"If I can get hold of a secure vidphone I can call Capek

direct," Prien said. "That way, we'll get our news unfil-
tered."

"Good idea." Nikolai tapped the driver on the shoulder
when he saw a promising site up ahead: a block of hotels
built around an open plaza and surrounded by stunted
tamarisk trees. "Let us off at the next stop."

"I aim to please."

Nikolai got them a room in a moderately priced hotel; he
didn't know how long it would take to get a flight out and
they needed a base of operations. Prien switched on a link
to the DataSphere, but there was a news blackout all over
the country. The clerk downstairs had told them he heard
military units were fighting one another around the
Kremlin. The other rumor being bruited about: the
Narodnaya Volya was responsible for the massacre on Luna.
Nikolai dismissed that out of hand.

"I think I know something about the men in the NV," he
told Galina. "They wouldn't be involved in such a horrific
scheme."

Prien tried patching a call to Capek, but the connection
failed. "I think we're getting out just in time." His face was
lined with worry. "The infrastructure is coming apart."

Galina stood in front of a small Lexan window. Nikolai
came up behind her and put his hands on her shoulders.
"Doing all right?" he asked.

She forced a smile. "Tired, and hungry, but happy."

"We'll order something to eat before the flight."

A tracking station's red marker lights winked in the distance, its forest of radio masts silhouetted against a low-
ering western sky.

"I've never seen a place like this." She rocked in his
arms, treasuring the moment of solitude. "It's so different.
Alien."

"It's my home," he said keenly.

Star City was the only lifeline Russia had with her orbital factories and habitats that made up the Archipelago. *Tereshkova* was considered a jewel in that archipelago of worldlets. Soon, he and Galina would leave the fighting and death gripping Russia by the throat and rise into the cold, clean environment of cislunar space.

And do what? (He suppressed a twinge of foreboding about their future.) Well, I can make a life with Galina, if she'll have me.

He tried to visualize how that would work. I've never done anything like it in my life; I wouldn't know how to begin.

As if her thoughts lay tangent to his, Galina said only so he could hear: "I'm glad we're together. No matter where we end up, I want to be with you."

His heart sang. "Do you really mean that?"

"We've been through so much already."

He looked deep into her sparkling eyes and gave her a parting hug before calling the spaceport to book a reservation on a shuttle mainlined for the Lunar Archipelago— habitats and factories located in the Lagrange points.

"Destination?" the reservationist asked in Engliz, the *lingua franca* of the Archipelago.

"Tereshkova."

"We have no flights there until tomorrow evening, sir."

"Then anywhere in the cislunar Archipelago." He wanted to get off the Earth as soon as possible. They could work their way to *Tereshkova* later, if need be, by hired boat.

"There is a clipper scheduled tonight; leaving for *Godunov,* in the Oazis Cluster at L4. Will that suit your purpose?"

Nikolai knew the research center by reputation. *Gudonov* was a worldlet staffed by botanists and agronomists who bioengineered plants and other organisms for zero gee environments. Their vast wheat farms and chlorella algae vats provided food and oxygen for the Archipelago and the Underways—the poorer sectors of Korolev City—on Dark Side.

"That'll do just fine."

"How many?" the booking agent asked, writing.

"Three." He gave their cover names and the activation numbers for their letters of transit.

"Purpose?"

"We have work release forms."

Just get me onto that space station, he silently told the booking agent on the flatscreen, and I'll do the rest.

"Your plane leaves at 0015. Terminal 16-P. Flight 150."

"Thank you."

He switched off the flatscreen and combed his hand through his hair. With that problem out of the way he turned to Prien who sat huddled over a second vidphone. "Can't get through to Capek?"

"No. All links into the DataSphere are down. Someone put up a hellacious firewall. Everything Russian is locked out."

Nikolai wasn't surprised. Such measures had happened before, even in his lifetime. "Disinformation campaign," he said. "St. Petersburg wants to control and disseminate information about the *Narodnaya Volya* revolution. When a population isn't sure which side is winning, they don't know which way to jump. That hamstrings any opposition."

Prien glanced circumspectly at Galina on the other side of the room, mindlessly surfing 3V channels. Satisfied that she was sufficiently preoccupied, he confronted Nikolai in a strident whisper: "Have you considered what we talked about earlier on the train?"

"Yes, I have. I've decided to go on."

Prien's mouth twisted bitterly. "You're making a tragic mistake, Sholokhov."

"That's your problem."

"Think about it. You mentioned St. Petersburg wants to control the news about the revolution so it can manipulate public opinion. . . ."

To test the issue, Nikolai said: "You think someone nuked Sharonov Crater so they could control the only living source of news—me?"

"Someone destroyed that Lunar outpost, Sholokhov. I don't believe in acts of god, and I dare say you don't either. This terrorist action is said to be traced to the *Narodnaya Volya;* the government is using that pretense for martial law and blood spilling pogroms." Prien delivered his next question with chilling force: "Who do you know with that much ruthlessness in them, Sholokhov?"

Nikolai already knew the dreadful answer: Stinnen, the Grey Executioner, was the only man who could plan a massacre like that and carry it through to its cold and logical end. He had seen with his own eyes how cheaply Stinnen valued human life.

Thank goodness I got us a flight out. In the Archipelago, Galina will be out of Stinnen's reach. He won't be able to threaten her—use her to force me to reveal the shattering truth behind the starsign.

More than ever, he realized he had to reach the worldlets and tell what he knew about the Star Whisper Project—if for no other reason than to stop Stinnen's mad rampage.

Prien searched his face. "Ikon, you do know someone,

don't you?" He held onto Nikolai's wrist. "Let me take her out of here. You must!"

Nikolai jerked his hand free. "Galina and I are going on, Dr. Prien. You can chicken out if you want." He lifted his chin a fraction. "Yes, I know who the puppet master is behind the massacre on Luna; I guess I've known it for a long time. That's why I have to get to the Archipelago: I'm the only man who does know, and I can't allow myself to be captured and used as a propaganda tool down here."

Prien's eyes widened. "Capek was right. You have no loyalty to Russia. No loyalty to anyone, except yourself."

"You said it yourself, Prien; I'm an Outworlder. The Archipelago is my home. I'm not ashamed that I've made it my life. Given time, it'll be Galina's life, too."

"You're a walking dead man. Not only will you not make it to a worldlet, you'll bring about her destruction as well. Have you thought of that?"

Nikolai shoved his face close. "That's the part you don't get, Doctor," he said icily. "We'd rather be together and dead, than apart and living."

Prien stared back, horrified.

"Capek got what he wanted." Nikolai's words clashed like stones. "Next time you speak to him, tell him the experiment has blown out of control—Galina and I are falling in love with each other."

He straightened, hands hanging loosely at his side.

"And we're not going to let you, or Capek, or anyone else—"

(Stinnen, you bastard, I'm going to destroy you)

"—get in our way."

Seventeen

The spaceport built on the southern rim of Star City was a brilliantly lit but insular sector. There were military personnel quartered nearby, and armored vehicles ranged up and down the roads, sustaining checkpoints. Every hour brought worse news, scarier rumors: The government in St. Petersburg had released the nuclear triggers to its field generals; mass executions were taking place in the shadow of the Kremlin; the First Minister had committed suicide; the *Narodnaya Volya* had brought off a bloodless coup but was planning a series of violent pogroms.

No one knew what story to believe. The firewall was still up, locking Russia out of the world DataSphere, and therefore from the news. Strangely, many of the workers in Star City didn't think what was happening thousands of kilometers to the north had much bearing on their own lives. Weren't they Outworlders? they argued. Our lives, our culture, are up there (they would point to the sky) so what difference does it make if mudballers kill themselves?

Nikolai found this head-in-the-sand attitude among his comrades disturbing. He wanted to grab and shake them and blast back in their faces: "Soon, something will happen to involve the whole world—Outworlders and mudballers alike. We have to start working together so nothing bad happens later."

But he didn't. No one would have understood what he was shouting about, and there was already enough panic saturating the air. People wouldn't necessarily disbelieve

248

him, but they wouldn't change their lives over it either.

Mintz had understood the ramifications, but he was dead, along with Yuri Tur and the rest of the men of the *posad* that had been the command cell for the Moscow branch of the *Narodnaya Volya*.

Hurrying along the concourse, he couldn't help but think: What a crazy situation. A survivor of a massacre masterminded by the head of Russian Internal Security, running for his life, and dragging a woman (a woman!) and the head of the Protectorate behind him. Could it conceivably get any worse?

He found the gate they needed. A lot of people blocked the barricade. Nikolai helped Galina get through the crush of bodies. He left Prien to make it on his own.

"Keep your pass under your belt laces," he informed her. Someone jostled him from behind; he ignored it. "If any of these people see it they may take it from you."

Galina pointed excitedly. "Is that our spaceplane?" A bone-white clipper with black trailing wings and control surfaces was parked on the landing field and being serviced.

"God, I hope so."

An hour later the shovel-nosed plane taxied up to their gate. Nikolai took Galina's hand and forced his way to the head of the gate as Prien finally caught up. He handed a security guard their boarding passes. "That's our plane," he said. "We must get on it before it leaves."

The guard examined their documents. Nikolai wished he would hurry. The guard ran each pass under a verification scan before allowing them through. Nikolai started breathing a little easier.

Without warning, Galina sucked in her breath and stumbled into him. "Nikolai—!"

His own face was grim. He saw it, too. "Keep going," he

said. "Don't look at it." He force-marched her past the gore.

On the other side of the gate a wall was slashed with dried blood and pockmarked with bullet holes. Red streaks trailed where bodies had been dragged off. Small white fragments and tiny gray clumps littered the walkway.

"My god." Gagging, Prien scraped away a bit of bone sticking to the soft sole of his shoe. "Has it come to this?"

"Keep walking," Nikolai urged stringently. "Don't make a scene. Don't say anything."

"I think I'm going to be sick. . . ." Galina clasped her hand to her mouth. Her face had become the color of putty.

Nikolai kept calm and whispered. "Look into my eyes and keep walking, Galina. That's a good girl; you're doing fine. Okay, we're past; it's over. Get onto the plane. Prien, you help her."

An attendant showed them to their acceleration couches, buckled them in with safety webbing. Nikolai reached past Galina's head and opaqued the little window. Some of the color returned to her cheeks after she downed a drink. Prien had his neck against the headrest, staring at the compartment ceiling and gasping for air like a landed fish. He rolled his eyes towards Nikolai:

"Everything's coming apart," he said.

The man sounds scared, Nikolai thought. Quite different from the uncaring official who recently passed judgment on Yuri as so much "human trash."

Without sympathy, he replied dourly, "Looks like the government will fall. You may be out of a job before long, Prien."

Prien's eyes were dark orbs in his narrow, ascetic face.

"You may be right," he mused, "but the Protectorate will survive. There have been many directorship changes in its long history, Sholokhov. This is nothing new."

The cabin filled with passengers whose faces were strained and pinched with worry. After an interminable wait, the clipper was cleared to taxi to an open runway.

Galina looked hopefully at Nikolai. "Are we really leaving?"

He squeezed her hand, relieved. "Yes, darling," he said, moved by her trust in him. "Lie back and relax. Leave everything else to me."

"But, where are we going?"

Nikolai noticed Prien had an ear turned to listen to his answer.

"We're going home."

Galina lost her toe grip on one of the handholds and kicked helplessly. Her hair floated in a brown aura around her pale face. "I hate this," she moaned, twisting her body like a cat in midair to reach for (and find) another handhold between her knees. She bobbed miserably in front of Nikolai.

He was at the other end of the compartment cell, arms slightly crossed and legs drawn up in a fetal crouch: a standard zero gee attitude.

"Galina, you have to practice," he chided patiently. "You're still thinking in two dimensions: up here it's always three—even in a habitat with rotational gravity, because you have to be aware what part of the habitat is on the other side of the wall, or ceiling, or floor. A vacuum doesn't let a person make more than one mistake in a lifetime."

"I know all that." She pulled herself along what would be a sidewall if they were down on Earth. The Clipper had deposited them into this personal transit tube hours ago. They were waiting for a cellbus to come along and shuttle them to the Oazis Cluster at L4. "But you aren't the one who's been vomiting for the past six hours, so don't lecture me."

"When is that cellbus going to get here?" Prien griped. "What's taking so long?" He, too, had trouble with space adaptation syndrome earlier, but not as severely as Galina.

"Think of this as a bus stop back home," Nikolai explained to them both. "We're slotted into a honeycombed cage in LEO—uh, low earth orbit—and now we're waiting for our ride. The Clipper only brings us here and drops us off before falling back to earth; it can't attain orbital velocity. A parabolic flight path—and a tricky and brief rendezvous with this holding area—is the best it can do. Plus the fact we had the bad luck to be close enough for the next cellbus to take us to the Moon in a Hohmann transfer orbit. We must wait until the Moon and Earth are in proper position. That's why the long wait."

"What if we run out of air and water—"

"That can't happen," he said calmly. "Every tenth 'bus is also a milch cow. It hooks an umbilical to our honeycombed bus stop and replenishes consumables. Actually, any cellbus coming along checks each compartment cell and will top off the tanks if they need it." His confidence went a long way to ease their united concerns.

However, it did little to alleviate Galina's physical discomfort.

"My sinuses are all stuffed up, and my head aches." She slowly revolved in front of him. "I think I'm catching a cold and my face feels puffy." She wrinkled her nose with distaste. "I can't burp, and I absolutely loathe that thing." An accusatory finger drew his eyes to the relief station hidden behind a folding curtain.

Nikolai sympathized. His first experience with zero gee

had been memorable, too. He helped Galina slip her feet into a couple of hold-down straps and reoriented himself so he appeared upright in her POV. He also made sure she drank plenty of liquids—dehydration was always a danger with space sickness.

They waited a full day. Galina improved measurably and began experimenting with tumbling and spinning maneuvers in the cramped compartment. They felt a jar as their cell was picked up by the next 'bus. The AI piloting the 'bus clicked over the intercom and told them to get into their acceleration hammocks. A brief burn and they were on their way to the Oazis Cluster.

Nikolai was perhaps the most relieved they were on their way. Spiriting Galina out of Russia and into the archipelago of orbital habitats and zero gee factories in high earth orbit and cislunar space had always been his ultimate goal. With any luck, the Grey Executioner would never find her there. For his part, he had no illusions. He knew that if Stinnen got his bloodstained hands on her he could force Nikolai to dance to his macabre tune.

The transit to Luna was uneventful. Nikolai and Galina had occasion to make love exhaustively while Prien slept in his zippered hammock on the other end of the compartment. What with the carbon dioxide scrubbers and circulation fans running full blast, they could have carried on a normal conversation right next to Prien and not be overheard.

These were untroubled days for Nikolai. Galina in his arms, their hammocks zipped together to make a tent. Her long legs around his waist and her hot breath in his ear. He liked to think they were having a honeymoon while enclosed in an elongated egg hurtling silently towards the Oazis Cluster. It was a nice time, one he wished could last forever. But, before long, the AI pilot told them to return to their separate hammocks; the cellbus was scheduled to undergo a series of braking maneuvers before reaching L4.

The cellbus stopped at two other worldlets before boosting to *Gudonov*. Nikolai felt the 'bus lock smoothly with a docking ring at the center of the habitat.

"We have arrived at *Gudonov* habitat," the cellbus told them. "You may disembark. Please, do not forget your poods."

The light ring around the circular hatch at the end of their compartment blinked from red to amber to green. Nikolai pulled the locking bar and rolled the hatch aside. As he did so, microbots emerged from their respective cubbyholes and started cleaning the cell and replacing the air scrubbers.

Nikolai was the first through, with Galina and Prien bringing up the rear. He floated down a connecting tube to an open hatchway where the backlit figure of a man greeted them.

"Welcome to *Gudonov*. I'm Cyril Waveland, the Assistant Director. Our Main Director is in a staff meeting, but he'll see you when he can get away." The man was slightly overweight with black curly hair and an untamed beard. "We've been expecting you," Waveland said companionably. "How was your trip?"

Nikolai emerged from the connecting tube and took the man's proffered hand along with a packet of salt with a few grams of bread: the traditional Russian salt-bread greeting. "How do you do. Oh, not bad at all, really; you know how cellbuses are. My name is Mirov. This young man is Piotr Borod. This is Mr. Blednov; he decided to accompany us from Moscow at the last minute. Here are our work release forms. I believe you'll find them in order."

Waveland examined the papers through the lower lenses of his trifocals. "What local time are you on?"

Nikolai answered for them all. "I'm afraid we're still on Moscow time."

Waveland glanced at a watchdisk glued to the back of his hairy hand. "You're a full ten hours off, then. Never mind, you'll quickly adapt to our schedule." His smile encompassed them. "I expect you're eager to have a bit of lunch. Can't say I've ever been enamored with the sludge they serve on cellbuses, and this will give you a chance to sample our cuisine."

Nikolai looked to his companions. "We're not very hungry," he said, taking their cue. "What we'd like to do is get our things squared away and start learning our duties."

Waveland led them down a corridor, through another hatch, and stopped at rungs descending into a brightly lit well. "Watch your step as you go down," he cautioned. "This leads to an upper level so the gravity field increases. We'll take a rimcar to the arboretum so you can see what we do here. It's a real showplace. What sort of work are you folks interested in?"

"Anything available." Nikolai didn't want to lie outright. "We got out of Russia as the revolution started. We were initially headed to *Tereshkova,* but got sidetracked here."

"If you don't mind my saying, you have a noticeable accent. Dark Side, isn't it?"

"Korolev Crater."

"Thought so. Well, it so happens we're short-handed around here, Mr. Mirov. A lot of men were called away to Dark Side to help with the rebuilding after that fiasco." Waveland swept his hand in a broad gesture. "What you see around you is mostly automated, but we still need human hands and strong backs to clean out the chlorella vats, and good brains to schedule the shipments. Do any of you have experience as a dispatcher?"

No one said anything.

Waveland shrugged. "No problem. You can start off in the vats by monitoring the lamps, ventilation systems and irrigation lines. It's hard work—but when has a Russian ever been afraid of that?" He waited for them to laugh. "When you learn that job we'll move you up to something with more responsibility, like programming soil nanides to provide proper aeration for plant roots."

"We don't mind working in the vats." Nikolai wanted to keep Galina out of sight as much as possible while they were on *Gudonov,* until he bought passage to *Tereshkova.*

"Good, good." Waveland made sure they were all secure in the rimcar. "Some people complain too much, you know? They expect the universe to give them handouts. You three seem like okay folks." With that assessment he steered the rimcar along a magnetic rail using levers and pedals.

"We're moving towards the rim of this habitat, spinward, so you'll gradually feel your weight increase," he said. "We call this the South End and the other end North. There's no true geographical analog, naturally, but it keeps us oriented as to where we are. These levels are the home quarters for our workers, computer room, communications, cafeteria, rec room. The north sectors house the scientific laboratories and engineering workstations. The core is considered downward, the rim upward."

Waveland activated a screen on the dash of the rimcar and pulled up a schematic of *Gudonov:* two sets of double barbells rotating in opposite directions on either end of a bulbous shaft. Globes of plasteel were lashed around the center of the shaft. These were the zero gee farms for the short-stalk wheat *Gudonov* harvested six times a year.

Waveland gave physical dimensions and procedural characteristics of the habitat they would call home for the next several weeks. "Total population: nine hundred seventy-six." He grinned: "Plus three. We work a normal work rotation schedule around here: ten-hour days, six days a week. Stay six months and you'll be eligible for a holiday leave of five days on Dark Side. Three years gets you one week on Earth; five years and we allot you two weeks. Once you get settled in I'll have a man from Personnel come around with your work contracts."

A quick halt in a small housing district allowed them to change out of their Terran clothes into singlesuits with round pockets. Waveland sent their old clothes away to be cleaned. Nikolai saw few other people around; the crew was on nighttime schedule. Waveland activated their living cubicles with a hand-held remote keyed to his thumbprint. "Just so you know," he stated, "there's no security lens anywhere in our private residences, but we do have them in the outside corridors for your protection. No human voyeurism allowed, and everything is monitored by an AI. You don't have to worry about being embarrassed."

Nikolai knew that was normal procedure for cislunar worldlets and underground cities on Dark Side. He also remembered Stinnen telling him it was the practice for an Isolator, too.

Their next stop was the chlorella vats. The first thing Nikolai remarked on was the awful smell. Waveland grinned.

"You'll get used to it," he promised, not deigning to hide his amusement. He described how the system worked:

"These Dyrene spheres each hold thirty liters of chlorella in a bioengineered nutrient suspension. That's enough fluid to theoretically provide a man with a lifetime of oxygen if the system worked at a hundred percent, which, as you may suspect, it doesn't. The Second Law of Thermodynamics prevents that. These lines attached to the spheres collect the oxygen and bleed it to our cryonics tank where it's liquefied. Then we ship the LOX wherever it's needed."

Prien indicated one of the Dyrene spheres and its bright green bubbling suspension. "Don't other orbital platforms have this capability?" he asked. "It doesn't make sense that *Gudonov* would be the only central manufacturing facility."

"You're right, Mr. Blednov, it doesn't—and we aren't. We're solely engaged in R&D here. We ship our biotechnology and improved gengineered plants out for return goods and services from other worldlets, mainly hydrogen from Luna so we can synthesize water. However, we do store and maintain vast reserves of water and oxygen in case of an emergency. Think of us as the last tank of air reserve for a dying man." Waveland pursed his lips. "Should it ever come to that, which, thank god, it hasn't."

He further explained their duties. The jobs didn't appear difficult, but it would be drudging work. Nikolai wasn't looking forward to spending out his days working down here.

Their final stop was the arboretum. Waveland shunted their rimcar onto a side track and guided it toward the core. Now that they were back in zero gee, Galina was starting to look green about the gills.

Nikolai edged close. "Try to hang on."

"My stomach is doing flips, but I'll be fine."

Waveland pushed off the rimcar and floated towards an airlock. He punched in a sequence of alphanumerics and waited for the lock to cycle. Nikolai hung close to Galina in case she started having trouble with nausea.

Waveland opened the far hatchway and bid them enter the blue space beyond the airlock.

"This is our arboretum," he said proudly. Nikolai glimpsed sheets of green. "The jewel of *Gudonov.*"

Nikolai swam through.

This place was big.

Waveland said, "One hundred meters in diameter. Those balls of vegetation below are dogwoods, up above are orange and apple trees. All capable of flowering, otherwise what good are they? Composition styles to your right. The domed structure behind the casuarina is our lab and greenhouse. We do air layering, grafting and growth regulation there. The central cascade is *sequoia sempervirens.* We bought it as a sapling from Hot West 'Merica a decade ago and injected it with a super-growth hormone. Impressive, isn't it?"

Nikolai tried to take it all in. "It's astonishing."

His eyes swept over a carefully tended garden. His nostrils dilated at the scent of growing plants and fragrant blossoms. Multi-hued butterflies (with only two front grasping legs) flapped between the boughs. Below the level of conscious thought, Nikolai heard the hum of bees somewhere.

Waveland watched their individual reactions. "We're proud of this zero gee garden: The largest bonsai project known to man. We regard it as the culmination of what *Gudonov* is all about. We consider it our showpiece."

"How are the plants held in place and kept separate?" Nikolai asked. Microgravity forces from the dense wood and massive trunks would be a constant headache.

Waveland reached out and strummed his fingers across a black, almost invisible filament draped with ivy. A long low note issued from the filament. "A network of buckyball thread with a protein cladding keeps everything from getting clumped up. Garden paths lead off from here, just follow the signs." Now that Waveland pointed them out Nikolai saw the tiny luminescent arrows placed along the network of buckyball thread.

"How can the sky be blue?" Galina asked.

"The shell is a double plasteel globe with a nanide matrix sandwiched between." Waveland removed the hand-held remote from one of his round pockets. "The nanides get their instructions through contact nodes from a central computer unit slaved to this remote. They can link up just the right way to scatter natural sunlight from outside into a blue wavelength. A different lattice structure lets in longer wavelengths. We even have matrix programs that can simulate a sunset. It's one of the ways we regulate temperature, too, inside the globe. I'm afraid the clouds you see, though, are only holographic projections. We include them simply for aesthetic reasons."

Waveland fidgeted as if he longed to show them something truly special. "Now, watch this."

He pressed a button on his remote. The plasteel globe became transparent, bleeding away its blue color. Sunlight flooded in, casting sharp definite shadows throughout the garden. There were stars, too, cold diamond shards seemingly within reach. On the far side, peeking behind a rather large grouping of black pine, was the huge face of Luna. Since they were at L4, they could see part of the Moon's front side and the bulls-eye structure of Mare Orientale almost face on: concentric rings of highlands and dark maria surrounding a gigantic central basin.

Nikolai floated in the midnight garden, surrounded by the stars and protected lovingly by the sun and the white moon on opposite sides. With the absence of most of the light, bioluminescent globes emerged from their deep hiding places among the trees and began to gently mate.

"It's beautiful," Galina whispered. Nikolai grinned at the sense of wonder on her face. She was seeing magic for the first time in her life. She turned to the assistant director. "May we . . . ?"

Waveland nodded. "By all means, be our guest. The Director won't be here for another hour. Follow the neon signs and you won't get lost."

They started off together but quickly separated. Prien, his face an exposed map of welling emotions, followed a lower path down toward the dogwoods. Nikolai and Galina explored and soon discovered a path that led to the giant redwood rooted (rooted? he wondered) in the center of the garden.

He lost sight of Galina momentarily. He followed a branch towards the central cinnamon-colored trunk of the sequoia and came upon several plastic pipes cunningly hidden beneath a twisting branch. He pulled himself along the snaking tubes and soon believed himself to be quite deep in the interior of the tree. He almost turned back (the light was failing) but pushed on a little farther and discovered the root ball.

It was approximately four meters in diameter, enclosed in a milky white membrane with water and fertilization tubes leading to and fro. This inner core of the patriarchal tree had a damp, dank smell. He found it not unpleasant, but earthy with an undercurrent odor of ancient and strong life.

Subdued, Nikolai backed out and brachiated towards the light, away from the central column. He paused, lost. A soft current of air brushed his cheek. Hidden ventilation fans?

"Galina?"

A luminescent globe floated out from behind tangled

growth, vented one of its encapsulated cysts of gas, and changed its vector. It disappeared through a rent in a distinctive, flattened spray of bright green leaves.

"Galina?"

A laugh. "I'm in here."

He slipped through the branches. There were a lot of butterflies here. Their wings projected radially from their tiny bodies, beating slowly to some inner biological rhythm as they clung to the bark.

He found her in the middle of a large nest of butterflies. Some were flapping around, most hung together in descending clusters and bunches. Galina had her back against the shredding cinnamon-colored bark. One foot hooked a split branch, holding her in place. Her other leg was crooked towards her body. Her hand rested lightly on her naked stomach.

She had unzipped her singlesuit and tied its arms together around a branch. Her hair, floating free, had snared a dozen unsuspecting butterflies. Her eyes glittered with desire.

She looked like a primitive goddess of nature.

"I want you. Now."

He kicked off the branch and flew towards her.

"I love you," she murmured.

"So do I. God, how I do."

"Isn't this nice?"

"Mm. But the butterflies tickle," he said.

"I like being together like this. I want to make love to you for the rest of my life. I want to hold you as close as I can, and as deep as I can, forever."

"I want you forever, too, Galina."

"Do you really mean that?"

"I don't think I've ever meant anything more in my life," he said.

He took her again, passionately, refusing this time to hold back. Always before, he had been careful and considerate in how he treated her. This time, he let himself go, urged on by the primitive setting they found themselves in.

A long quiet lay over them, afterwards. Sweat cooled on their bodies. Monarchs landed on their skin, took off when it fluttered at their tiny touch. They caught their breath.

"I like it better when there's gravity."

Surprise. "You do? Why?"

"I like feeling your weight on top of me. I like feeling safe and protected that way."

"I want to do everything I can to make you happy," he pledged. "Tell me what you want me to do."

She reached down. "Come here, and I'll show you."

They made their way back to the main entrance when the shell brightened back to its normal blue sky color; obviously Waveland's cue it was time to return. Coming around a bend in the garden Nikolai saw another man accompanying the Assistant Director.

Prien? No, this man wasn't as tall and thin as the Protectorate. Who, then?

"I bet that's the director of *Gudonov*," he told Galina. "Cyril said he was going to drop by when he could."

"Hello, Nikolai. Galina."

Prien, closing the distance from below. He jerked his chin towards the two men. "What's going on over there?"

"We think it's the Director."

"Oh? Then we'd better go meet him, hadn't we?"

There was something about Prien's manner that bothered Nikolai. He was going to comment on it but promptly forgot as they approached the two men waiting for them.

The director next to Cyril Waveland looked suspiciously

familiar. Nikolai suddenly remembered when he had last seen those soft brown eyes and clean-shaven face.

"Lev!"

They clasped hands, gave each other a sexless kiss on the side of their faces.

"I told you we'd meet again," the other chuckled, enjoying the shock and surprise racing across Nikolai's face. "We'll take a rimcar to my office. We need to talk."

"My god, I can't believe it," Nikolai said, still grasping the other man. "I thought you worked on *Tereshkova*. That's what you told me . . ."

"I didn't think it was smart of me to tell a complete stranger I was the director of a major worldlet," his friend responded. "It was only until later when I was sure you weren't a plant by Internal Security to trap me that I realized I had done the wrong thing by lying to you. A man in my position has to be extremely careful; St. Petersburg often tries to use the space program as a bargaining chip or propaganda tool."

"You certainly pulled one over on me, but I'm glad you're here and not at L5," Nikolai said, forgiving the deception. "So, why the long face? We can have that cup of coffee now."

Lev shook his head sadly. "There's a lot to discuss first, Nikolai, before we have that drink. That's one of the reasons I've been detained."

"If you say so." He noticed both Lev and Waveland wore grave faces. "What's wrong? You must have heard something about the revolution. Is it finally all over?"

Lev delivered the bad news. "Worse. *Tereshkova*, just like Sharonov, has been destroyed."

Eighteen

"It's my fault," Nikolai lamented. They were safe inside Lev's spacious, datacube-lined office. Lev reclined in a mattcloud chair, listening to his every word.

"Stinnen is hunting me down. He thought I was going to *Tereshkova*, that's why he hit it. The sonofabitch is insane. He's behind the attack on Luna, too."

"Our rock and water shielding protected us from the initial radiation flux," Waveland said, handing Lev a brief account of the damage sustained by *Gudonov*. "We were fortunate in that regard."

Lev made notes on the palm-slate. "What other precautions are we taking?" he asked Waveland.

"We're issuing dosimeters and taking hourly soil and atmosphere samples from the enclosed environments, to be on the safe side. Background levels are normal. I don't think we have anything to worry about at the moment, on that account."

"Our people are safe from radiation, in your estimation?"

"Yes, sir."

"How did it happen?" Prien, at the wider end of the oblong conference table.

Lev's soulful brown eyes softened a tad more as he fielded the question. "Their power core went critical. No one knows how it happened."

"Has to be sabotage." Waveland was defiant. "There are too many safeguards for it to be anything else. Somebody must have reconfigured the containment field and lased the explosion through the center of the habitat. Cut through it like a shiverknife through foamsteel."

"When did it happen?" Nikolai, glum, steeled himself for the answer he most feared.

Lev didn't spare him. "While you were in the arboretum. The initial failure caused their secondary unit to scram. There were a series of explosions; most of the internal environment decompressed. We're getting signals from survivors, but the bulk of the population perished. All five thousand men."

Nikolai thought he was going to be sick. "Christ."

While we were making love.

"Nikolai, who knew you were going to *Tereshkova?*"

Lev's blunt question brought him out of his self-recrimination. "Myself and my companions," his nod included Galina and Dr. Prien, "along with another man I met in Moscow: Yuri Tur."

"Do you think he's the one who sold you out?"

As much as it pained him, Nikolai admitted: "I'm certain of it. His brother is Stinnen, the Grey Executioner. Stinnen tortured the information out of him."

"Anyone else you can think of?" Lev started searching the palm-slate's bubble memory for some information.

Nikolai grappled with his conscience.

Prien spoke up. "You have to trust someone sooner or later," he said. "Stinnen has cornered you where you can't do anything else. And you must think of . . . of our safety."

Nikolai nodded. For once, Prien was right. "Iosef Capek. He's the Director of State Psychology for the Confederation. And Dr. Stefan Prien, Director of the Union House Protectorate. They both knew where I was going."

"I take it those two men have something to do with the young woman sitting next to you?"

A stunned silence blanketed the room. Nikolai released a ragged breath. "Yes. Her name is Galina Toumanova. I met her the final night of the Moscow riots, by accident."

He heard a small sound beside him. "Galina, I'm sorry." He put a conciliatory hand on her knee. "There's no sense in pretending. They have us cold."

She whispered back through bloodless lips: "It's over."

Lev wasn't done with surprises. "And this man, passing under the legend of Viktor Blednov, is really Dr. Prien, isn't he?"

Prien spoke for himself. "I am."

Lev steepled his fingers under his chin. "I suspected as much. I recognized your face from one of our governmental directories." He slid the palm-slate aside with Prien's official photograph glowing on the screen.

"This is a biological research station, gentlemen. We unlock and manipulate genetic codes everyday." He radiated a gracious smile. "It's our *métier*, so to speak."

Nikolai saw how it was done. "Our clothes. When Dr. Waveland sent them off to be cleaned, your people combed them for DNA samples and genetic signatures."

Lev was pleased he had figured out the puzzle so quickly. "A simple screening procedure we run on everyone who comes through our worldlet. A hair fiber with follicle or a flake of skin is all we need. We do this unobtrusively to have a genetic marker account for our workers. If they show a propensity for disease or other health problem we make arrangements to correct it." His chair squeaked as he shifted position. "We work very hard around here, Nikolai, and take our charter seriously. We can't afford a lot of down time; lives depend on us throughout cislunar space. I assume Dr. Waveland gave you his 'first-aid kit to the stars' speech?"

"He did."

"A romantic notion, but accurate. My biotech was stunned when he saw the double-X chromosome for Piotr Borod. A cross-indexed reference blew the cover off Viktor Blednov: all government employees are DNA-printed and loaded into a database for security purposes." He raised a hand off his desk, let it fall. "And I knew you, Nikolai, by sight from Moscow, as Sholokhov, not Mirov."

The armpits of Nikolai's singlesuit were damp. "What happens to us now?"

Lev's eyes flicked between him and the young woman. "That's what we must decide. It would be best if you were to explain why a young Russian woman and the State Protectorate are keeping company with an electronics expert from Luna."

Prien gave a short nod to proceed. Nikolai told everything he knew about Capek's stabilization program. Lev soaked it all in, listening with eyes half-closed. When Nikolai finished he awoke with a start.

"What an incredible story." Genuine respect tempered his voice. "Amazing that the two of you got as far as you did. You were part of this conspiracy, Dr. Prien?"

"I accompanied them per Dr. Capek's directions. I am to observe and report their actions—and reactions—to different stress environments and social stimuli. Of course, that was before everything fell apart earthside."

"A sociological stress test. What a novel idea."

"Unfortunately, I haven't been able to contact Dr. Capek. I can't get through the firewall in the DataSphere. We don't know what's happening on Earth."

Lev commiserated with Prien's frustration. "We've also

lost our uplink from Star City and our DataSphere link to the Confederation due to the blackout. However, some information is bleeding off the Earth in encrypted signals which we've been able to decode—a by product of our ability to decrypt and manipulate chemical genetic information stored in the nucleus of cells." He made a gesture for Waveland to elaborate on the last detail.

"The decryption AI we employ is one of the new generational savants," Waveland said, "with multi-dimensional matrix capability. We've been able to tap compressed signals squirted between comsats and pick up the odd conversation using magnetic variance capacitors on unprotected landlines. The information indicates a coup has successfully ousted the government in St. Petersburg. We don't know who the new First Minister is, but we expect the announcement presently once the firewall dissipates."

"Again, where does that leave Galina and myself?"

"Nikolai, I'm operating on the assumption that whoever wants you dead thinks you now are dead," Lev said prosaically. "You were scheduled to be on *Tereshkova*: that's why the facility was hit." His hands opened and closed a fanbook. "The reasonable solution—the safe solution—is turn you over to whoever wants you and wash my hands of the matter. I don't want the same thing to happen to this worldlet that's happened to Sharonov and *Tereshkova*." He shrugged slightly. "Put it down to self preservation. The simple fact someone has gone to this much trouble to wipe you out screams for attention. The safety of *Gudonov* is my primary concern. Simply put, I must know why a maniac has murdered thousands of people to silence you."

"Wait a minute," Prien bristled. "You just declared him dangerous. Why would you even consider throwing your hand in with him if that were true?"

Lev was visibly dismayed by Prien's outburst, and frowned.

"Because, Dr. Prien, this man saved my life in Moscow. We sat together, baking under the sun, waiting to be executed. When a man shares a moment like that, a bond forms. Call it survivor-friendship. Call it love. Call it what you will, it exists. Outworlder culture is not like the stifling slum culture on Earth. Out here, we keep an eye on each other." He thumped his chest. "In the Archipelago, the notion that I am my brother's keeper is a motto we all live—and die—by, because of the hostile environment. We have a saying: 'Vacuum doesn't give second chances.' You would do well to remember that."

He faced back around to Nikolai. "Now, my friend, please, tell me why you are being hunted by a madman."

Nikolai didn't hesitate. He explained the secret work in Sharonov Crater, and the alien signals plotted around Kornephoros.

Lev perceived the political and social implications right away, but tempered his appraisal. "That hardly seems adequate reason to kill thousands of innocent people, and spark a revolution to topple a government."

"My friend Yuri Tur, before he died, said a man who controls information can use it for profit or gain. He can destroy enemies, arm himself to ride out economic and social upheavals, insulate himself from danger."

"Agreed, but—"

"You would be right, Lev, if all we had was knowledge of distant signals. But there's more—much more; something only a select few of us knew." Nikolai's voice took on an urgent, commanding aspect.

"The evidence is indisputable. A fleet of five ships is blue-shifted towards Sol."

Slowly, the import of his words dawned on the people in Lev's office.

"Are you saying—"

"Impossible!" Prien said.

Nikolai sat back, drained now that he, for the first time, had unburdened himself from the secret he had carried like a stone for the past two weeks.

"Yes," he said, "they're coming here, to Earth."

"The problem remains one of propulsion," *Gudonov*'s senior physicist, a man named Lasker, intoned. "What is the energy source? These ships are running at .99c: experiencing full time dilation. If we know how they do that, we can infer something about their tech level, perhaps even their psychology."

They were packed in a conference room in the upper deck on the North End of the station. Monitors spaced equally around the room scrolled endless sheets of green and amber numbers. These were updated spatial vectors for the space-based telescope Lev had rented time on.

At first, the main Lunar Observatory had balked: why would an R&D botany platform want time on one of their orbital radio telescopes? Lev explained they were interested in logging spectral data on stars to run a simulation on their savant: "Does spectral type inhibit bacterio-chlorophyll production in our new gengineered golden algae, and will it affect the carbon-hydrogen phytol chain in the chloroplast?"

This scientific gobbledygook made up on the spur of the moment passed muster. Physicists on *Gudonov* were slotted time on the telescope. They slaved it to their central AI and slewed the aperture towards the constellation Hercules.

When they began downloading data, Nikolai's facts were

confirmed. The Kornephorons were coming to the Solar System. Five ships Doppler-shifted as hard X-ray points, not smeared signals radiated by the other ships traveling at oblique angles to Sol.

One scientist observed: "They're coming with a purpose."

Nikolai felt a chill skitter down his back. Galina stayed close to him. Now that the secret was out, she was scared too.

"Nikolai, are these people coming from that star? Or only robot spacecraft?"

"I don't know, honey. These men are trying to figure that out. We have to let them do their job."

"You knew about this? That's why this man, this Stinnen, wanted to kill you?"

"Yes."

Her lips trembled. "Will we be able to stay together, afterward?"

Nikolai said helplessly, "I don't know, darling. Lev will have to decide that, when he has the time."

The data streamed in. Lev ordered two men to shunt the numbers to *Gudonov*'s decryption AI. "I want real-time access to that data," he told Cyril, "as fast as possible, and I don't want any excuses as to why I can't get it."

"Yes, sir."

"Any leakage through the DataSphere firewall yet?"

"No, sir," another tech responded, "but we're still monitoring."

"Notify me the instant it drops."

"Yes, sir."

Prien forced Nikolai aside during these technical preparations. "We must talk," he suggested sotto voce.

"Doctor, I don't have time for this. . . ."

"Make time."

They sidled away from the group of physicists flocked around a flatscreen, the glow from the monitor limning their faces. The first signals from the telescope were coming through.

Prien insisted, "You can't delay. You must get Galina out of here immediately."

"Where should she go, Doctor?" *As if I don't know.*

"Moscow."

"You mean, back to the Union House."

"There's no safer place. I can make arrangements to house you, too, if that's what you want." His fists clenched at his side so hard his slender arms trembled. "We can use my authority to reroute a cellbus; we'll be away within hours."

"Prien—"

"Wake up, Sholokhov," he cut short. "This habitat is naked and exposed. You can't deny we'd all be safer back on Earth."

Nikolai faced him down. "Doctor, when are you going to understand this is a mutual decision made by Galina and myself? Besides, Capek—"

"Fuck Capek and his insane fantasies," Prien said fiercely. "It's never going to happen. The government has fallen. Capek is more than likely dead. Ikon, you're the densest man I've ever met. Why can't you recognize the only option left open to you?"

Nikolai turned aside. "Galina, come here, please."

"Forget it," Prien growled harshly, knowing he was beaten.

Nikolai pressed on now that he had the advantage. "We'll let her decide what she wants to do," he told Prien, "once and for all."

"I said forget it, you bastard." The Protectorate marched angrily away.

Nikolai made a never-mind motion to Galina, enjoying his small victory over Prien.

Out of the corner of his eye he saw Prien buttonhole Lev against a bulkhead. Goddammit, the man never gave up. No, Lev was sloughing him off, too. No time.

Good for you, he thought.

An argument brewed among the physicists. Lasker, a middle-aged man with a bald head and bifurcated beard, debated a younger man whose epicanthic folds belied his Asian ancestry.

"Dr. Selyuk, MHD propulsion is out of the question," the older man proclaimed. "There's no evidence of a weakly ionized plasma in the tail fire, or any cesium isotopes needed to raise the electrical conductivity for such a torch ship design."

Selyuk, a dark-skinned man with a squeaky voice, returned: "A lightsail or magsail is similarly out of the question. There's always leakage in a structure like that—unless it's self repairing—and there's no evidence of that."

"Agreed."

Everyone in the conference room listened to their debate. The only other noise was the continuous hum and whine of the comp terminals and ventilation fans.

Selyuk said, "Not an Orion or Daedalus design, either. The atomic signature would be quite indistinguishable. We can throw out a ramjet design, as well. Those ships are sailing too close together."

"If it were ramjets," Lasker intoned, "they would be slipstreaming, running one behind the other to take advantage of the focused hydrogen atoms the man in front gives."

"Unless they haven't thought of that. . . ."

"If they're smart enough for interstellar travel, they're smart enough to engineer for peak efficiency," Lasker said archly. "Stands to reason."

Antimatter and space warp drives (Lasker dismissed the latter idea as "moonshine") were summarily discarded.

"And we'd see high-energy radiation as the baryon charges canceled each other out in matter-antimatter annihilation. Particularly from those ships in translational motion against the background stars. So that's not the answer."

"What, then?"

"Magic?" someone on the periphery of the group suggested. Tension relieving laughter rolled around the room in widening circles.

"You may be right," a lean physicist on the edge of the crowd remarked somberly.

Lev asked, "You have something, Andreyevich?" The man garnering the attention was a lean Ukrainian with a broad nose and bushy sideburns. "The absence of any energy 'signature' or ionized exhaust is telling. These ships aren't carrying fuel with them or collecting it with vast magnetic scoops. They're drawing it from the very fabric of space. They're using zip drives."

The senior physicist tottered on his feet. "Ikon," he swore, slapping his hand on a work bench, "that's the answer. . . ."

"ZPE. Zero point energy," Andreyevich explained. "You induce a quantum tunneling effect at zero temperature to nucleate a bubble of true vacuum. Then you draw what is theoretically unlimited energy from the fluctuation—the fabric of space. It's been done under laboratory conditions on Luna, but, I hasten to add, on a less than optimum scale. These aliens appear to have solved the unstable energy curve as the vacuum bubble expands at the speed of light."

He glanced at Nikolai for confirmation, who shrugged. "I don't know if the men in Sharonov arrived at this conclusion or not. I wasn't allowed into those think-tank discussions."

Andreyevich appended, "If these aliens have solved the unstable energy problem as the vacuum bubble expands at the speed of light. . . ."

"Yes?" Lev prompted.

"Then they're extremely more advanced than we are." He let that sink in. "They have captured magic." He pulled thoughtfully at his bushy sideburns. "Forget about their technological achievement of interstellar flight: Command of energy bound within a vacuum—on this scale—makes them candidates for a Type II civilization. That means they harness and produce energy outputs equivalent to a main sequence star."

No one spoke. Finally, Waveland remarked sourly, "And here we are, a world crippled by plague and ravaged by war, famine, poverty, ideology. What a hell of a mess."

"May I add something?" Nikolai requested.

Lev's response was instant. "You're the only one here who has any experience with this, Nikolai. Like it or not, you're our resident expert. We're novices compared to you."

"I doubt that." He laid a hand upon one of the monitors. "However, I do know Admin argued this point more than any other: 'Are technologically advanced civilizations necessarily benevolent?' They decided that pure exploration, in and of itself, was at the very least an act of aggression against nature. Since non-aggressive societies stultify and stagnate, aggression, they concluded, is a positive growth enhancer for culture—as long as it's directed in non-destructive channels."

"Such as?"

"Altruism. Feeding the poor. Protecting the weak and the innocent. Non-impact colonization. That sort of thing."

"Those are pretty high ideals."

"Maybe. But we decided we couldn't count on a technologically advanced race to be benevolent. Couldn't count on it because there's no analog for it in human history. I remember—" he laid a finger along his chin "—a term cropping up whenever we talked about the Kornephorons. 'Moonlight and magnolia' aliens, we called them. M&Ms." He shook his head. "There's no way we can chance that M&Ms exist; it's probably a human prejudice, thinking because something is more advanced it must be closer to god. That kind of myopia has spilled a lot of blood throughout history."

"That's a pretty grim picture you paint, Sholokhov," Waveland remarked. "I can't say I care much for it."

"Sorry, but I thought you needed to know." He shrugged, adding, "That was right before Sharonov was hit."

Someone cleared their throat. His point had been made.

Lev said, "Thank you, Nikolai. Well. We must decide what to do with this information. Suggestions, anyone?"

Nikolai had an answer for that, too. "There's only one thing left to do. Publish. Broadcast it to the world." His voice took on a steel timbre: "Remember, someone tried to kill me twice so I wouldn't tell what I knew. The only way to take that weapon out of his hands is blare this knowledge to the world."

Lev wasn't so sure. "That's an option—"

"It's the only sane option available . . . unless you're willing to kill me now and hand my body over to Stinnen. He's going to find out I wasn't on *Tereshkova*. This man's resources are limitless, Lev. He'll slap *Gudonov* out of the sky if you give him a chance."

"Nikolai, no. . . ." Galina said, perceptibly upset. He quieted her with a gentle look.

"It's the only way, Galina," he said, soft.

"He's right." Everyone turned. Nikolai was startled to see Prien rushing to his aid. "I've been with these two for the past several days; I've seen what's happening down there." He meant Russia. "You have to tell people about this," he nodded at the data scrolling on the flatscreens, "if you want to survive."

Nikolai watched Lev struggle over the choices. To own information is to control it. What else had Yuri said?

Every man wants power, because with power, all other vices, like sex and money, fall into line.

Yuri the philosopher.

Lev clasped his hands behind his back, lowered his head upon his breast. The scientists in the conference room awaited his decision.

Galina stood a little apart, arms wrapped around her body. Tears streaked her face as she waited for a stranger to pass judgment on Nikolai. His heart went out to her, but there was nothing more he could do. His life was indisputably in another man's hands. It was the only way, the only chance he had left to stop Stinnen.

"Lev'll judge me fairly," he said low enough only she could hear. "Above all else, he's a fair man. He'll do whatever he thinks is best for his worldlet and the men serving under him. We have to respect that."

Lev raised his head. Nikolai waited, stone-faced, for the verdict that would set the course of his life.

"We waited to die together on a hot and dusty street in Moscow," Lev said. "I will not deny that experience. I do not turn against friends, no matter what the circumstances.

We do that, and we're no longer human."

Galina rushed into Nikolai's arms before going to Lev and throwing her arms around him, as well. "Thank you, thank you," she pressed her face into his shoulder.

Lev was uncomfortable with her emotion, and her physical closeness. He patted her shoulder awkwardly. Nikolai saw the look of relief in the director's eyes when he led Galina, sobbing, away to a corner.

Holding her close, he thought, Capek is going to have a tough time rebooting a heterosexual culture in Russia. Hell, the whole world. Maybe Prien was right, maybe it is an insane fantasy.

Newly unencumbered, Lev instructed Waveland: "Set it up, Cyril. Full security access. Broadcast everything to the Archipelago through our omni-directional antenna, and keep sending to the DataSphere until the firewall comes down. I want everybody to know about this."

"But why do *you* have to go?"

Nikolai was helping Galina unpack and straighten things in their new cubiculum.

"You've done so much already," she continued. "More than your share. They shouldn't expect you to do more."

"They're short handed." He pulled toiletries out of a bag. "And Lev didn't ask me, I volunteered."

"But why now, when we're just getting settled in?" She closed a clothes cabinet a bit too hard, telegraphing her annoyance.

Nikolai put down the flight bag and took both her hands in his. He said gravely, "Lev's first duty is to those men still alive on *Tereshkova*. We're the only habitat that can mount a viable rescue operation. Remember Waveland's speech? We have the oxygen and water reserves to spare. Besides, what happened on *Tereshkova* happened because of me, Galina." He looked at her sensibly. "Do you want me to walk away from that responsibility?"

She dropped her eyes. "I know you're not that kind of person. I guess . . . I guess I wouldn't like you if you were."

"I'll be back in a few days. It's a short crossing from this Lagrange Point to L5."

Lev had used his directorship status, rerouting traffic to transport a rescue team. More importantly, he promised he wouldn't let Prien remove Galina from the habitat while Nikolai was gone.

Prien. The Protectorate had tried again to bully him into shuttling Galina down to Moscow. Nikolai had brushed him off during breakfast while everyone else waited for the first decryption analysis of the main starsign signals from the ships.

He checked the tattoo watch in the palm of his hand. The crystalloids had at long last repaired themselves after the damage suffered in the Moscow riots. "I have a briefing with the station's medical officer in ten minutes. He's the fellow who'll lead our team to *Tereshkova*." He raised her chin. Her hair swung back from her face. "Are we friends again?"

"You'd better come back to me, Nikolai Sholokhov," she told him. "If you don't, I swear I'll swim across myself and get you back."

They kissed a long time, embracing in the center of their new little home.

"I'll finish unpacking," Galina said, after the kiss. "Then I must report for work. Will you come down to the chlorella vats before you go?"

"I'll even say goodbye to Prien: show him there's no hard feelings. How's that for building bridges?"

And make it clear I won't brook any nonsense between him and Galina while I'm gone, he thought baldly.

He left the housing unit and used his new keycard to activate a rimcar to take him to the North End of *Gudonov*, anti-spinward. He found the briefing room and sat with the nine other men who had volunteered to search for survivors in the crippled habitat.

Doctor Bairiev was *Gudonov*'s senior medical officer, a pudgy knobby-shouldered man with burning eyes and small, almost feminine hands. He explained the job that lay ahead.

"We'll go over every piece of the wreckage, so watch the dosimeters in your suits. Other worldlets are mounting search and rescue operations, but they will be under the aegis of *Gudonov* command." He clicked on a 3V projector. The wall behind him turned into a graphic of what *Tereshkova* presently looked like. The men in the room stirred uneasily.

Bairiev used a stylus and tapped several gaping holes in the habitat's superstructure. "We'll use hardsuits when we go in. This will be an extremely dangerous spacewalk, gentlemen. Don't take chances. I know you're eager to help, but we can't afford to lose any more lives. Agreed?"

Everyone nodded.

"The first team will consist of myself, Dr. Waveland, and the newest member of our staff, Technician Sholokhov." He traced a possible route through the zero gee core. "We'll enter this airlock and rescue what we believe is a pocket of surv—I say, what is that damn commotion out in the hall?"

He irritably slapped the stylus against his pants-leg. "Go see what it is, will you?" he asked one of his junior surgeons.

Before the man left his seat, a botanist Nikolai recognized stuck his head through the open doorway.

"Sorry to interrupt, Doc, but the director wants Technician Sholokhov. You're needed too, Doc. Emergency: someone's been hurt."

They all walked briskly towards Lev's office, branching off the main corridor.

"What's all the fuss?" Nikolai's nerves ratcheted tighter. "Has the AI finally decoded the signals?"

"Oh, no, sir, nothing like that, although it's close." The botanist wrung his hands nervously. "Worse news, I'm afraid. It concerns Doctor Prien. He's demanding a cellbus return him and his hostage to Russia."

Nikolai stood frozen. "A hostage?"

The botanist nodded.

Galina.

Nineteen

Nikolai was resolved to face the crisis head on, no matter what the outcome.

"Where are they?" he asked, barely controlling his anger. His deportment let everyone know he considered himself in charge of this problem, and wouldn't brook any dissension to the contrary.

Lev switched an overlay of *Gudonov*'s central architecture on a flatscreen, rotated the schematic and exploded a section. "Arboretum. He tried holing up in the lower levels near an access hatch, but I guess he didn't feel safe enough. They took a rimcar to the zero gee biospheres ten minutes ago."

"Where did he get the needlegun?"

"We don't know."

Cyril Waveland interjected: "We don't keep weapons like that aboard the habitat; there's never been any need for that kind of security here." He was distraught. The man shot trying to stop Prien was his bunk mate. "We're farmers, for Ikon's sake, not soldiers."

Nikolai's vile humor made him throw respect for Cyril's authority to the wind. "Maybe it's time we Outworlders start protecting ourselves and to hell with everybody else. Two outposts are dead because we're hanging onto an outdated pacifist philosophy. That was acceptable for space during the Mad Times when nation-states bristled with nuclear weapons, but not today."

He disregarded the blanched looks he received in return,

hauled himself under control. "I've seen what running away gets one. I'm not going to do that ever again."

To fight an enemy you have to become a monster, he reflected. The mark of humanity came if you could slough off the berserker mentality only after you won the battle.

As angry as he was with Prien, he knew Stinnen was the real monster to defeat. Somehow.

"I can't order my men into the arboretum," Lev said, pulling Nikolai out of his black reverie. "When you consider what's involved . . . I have to leave the final decision to you—and the consequences. I can't have any of my men responsible for Galina's welfare. Not directly. If I sent them in to rescue her, and something went wrong. . . ."

Nikolai felt no ill will at his declaration of helplessness. A Director of the Union House Protectorate and a young woman. Lev's debt to Nikolai and his allegiance to their friendship only went so far under those circumstances.

"I want the lights in the access corridor dimmed. I don't want to be silhouetted when I go inside."

Cyril's eyebrows arched. "You're going in alone?"

"What other choice do I have?"

He rounded on Lev. "I need a pair of shears or something from one of the work sheds. A rake would be better to give me reach."

"Can't get them. The security AI has locked everything down until the situation is resolved. The entire habitat is in a lock-down mode."

"It'll allow a negotiator into the arboretum, right?"

"Yes. That's covered under its Laws."

"Fair enough."

Lev unlocked a cabinet under his desk and removed a black object. He handed the sleepdeath module to Nikolai.

"Director's discretion," he explained. "I'm authorizing

you to use it, but only under threat of your life or Galina's."

It took an effort on Nikolai's part to touch the ugly chunk of metal and plastic. The thing had two modes: on and off. He hefted the module in his hand; it was massive, almost a full kilogram. There was also no need to change the activation palm-print signature for the weapon. Anyone could use it.

"Thanks, Lev." He started to leave.

"Wait," the director moved in front of him. "That biosphere is over four million cubic meters in volume. How are you going to find them?"

Nikolai zipped the module in one of the round pockets of his singlesuit.

"I won't have to search the whole garden," he said. "I know exactly where they are."

He floated through the hatch, heard it hiss shut behind him. He tapped the headset Lev had given him and spoke into the pin mike curving down from the earpiece.

"Can you read me?" he whispered.

The voice-crystal in the earpiece buzzed. "Your signal is clear. See anything, yet?"

"No, but I'm too far from the redwood."

"Be careful."

"That's the best advice you can give?"

A snort of ironic laughter crackled over the headset: "Until I think of something better, it'll have to do."

Nikolai stole into the zero gee garden. The arboretum was fully lit; azure sky and holographic clouds englobed him. They had toyed with the idea of plunging the garden into darkness and outfitting Nikolai with an IR headset, but decided a move like that might panic Prien.

"I don't want to put Galina's life at risk," Nikolai had emphasized. "If we give Prien a reason to act out he just may do it; he's gone this far already."

Lev reluctantly concurred he was probably right.

He slipped deeper into the garden, navigating the paths, trying to stay quiet. But there was no sense in being overly cautious, he realized. Prien expected him to come; wanted Nikolai to confront him.

He fingered the sleepdeath module through the fabric of his singlesuit.

You shall get what you want, Prien.

He swam towards the huge sequoia, kicking off a branch and avoiding webs of buckyball thread. He paused along a stretch of netting supporting a vine of morning glory away from another planting of honeysuckle. He spent half a minute, working quickly, before continuing on to the redwood.

He drifted slowly away from the main path and touched down on a cinnamon-colored branch. He pulled towards the trunk, scaring up a family of bioluminescent globes in the process. They jetted away wildly: bio-engineered will-o-the-wisps.

He radioed Lev. "I'm at the tree."

He found the flattened spray of green leaves, ducked under. He brachiated deeper into the green and brown tunnel leading to the trunk. He passed broken bodies of butterflies who beat their crushed wings in a futile attempt to get out of his way. He entered the butterfly cave, dappled in light and shadow.

"Stop right there," Prien commanded.

He had Galina's arm bent at an awkward angle. His free hand pressed a needlegun against her temple. The pistol had a razor attachment locked in open position. There were red scratches on the side of her neck: hesitation marks. Globules of coagulated blood had formed along the scratches, hardening before they could detach.

Her eyes were dark-green with fear.

"Nikolai, please, don't stay here." She was more afraid for his safety than her own. "Get away while you can."

"I'm not leaving, Galina."

The right pant leg of Prien's singlesuit was slit open, exposing the hairless plastiskin of his thigh. Packing gel from the surgically designed compartment swirled in midair. Prien's other hand was smeared with the treacly stuff.

Hundreds of crushed and dead bodies floated and spun madly inside the cave. Nikolai guessed Galina had made a break for freedom earlier and in the ensuing struggle they destroyed hundreds of the tiny lives.

He reached up and switched off the headset.

"All right, you sick bastard," he said with as much venom as he could muster, "what do you want with me?"

Prien's eyes crystallized into twin cannons of hate. "I want a cellbus. I'm taking this girl back to Moscow and away from this lunatic asylum. Move!"

The last command was a frantic, high-pitched scream.

Nikolai kept his voice calm, reasonable: as much for Galina's benefit as to pacify Prien. "It's not going to happen, Doctor. You're not getting off this habitat. You've already hurt one man; he's in surgery with a flechette in his brain. Don't make things worse. Let her go."

"Don't bluff me, Sholokhov." The needlegun jammed harder against Galina's head. "I'm in no mood for discourse. I . . . I'm sorry about that other man. I didn't mean to hurt him but he got in my way." Prien swallowed thickly. "I gave you every opportunity, but you wouldn't listen to reason."

"You're not going to hurt her, Doctor."

"I will . . . if I don't get that cellbus."

"No, you won't. You may be able to convince the other men on this station you'll kill her, but I know different." Nikolai swiped the tumbling carcass of a butterfly away from his face. "We both know who you really want to hurt, and why."

Nikolai pulled his thoughts together.

That's why he had that funny look on his face when Galina and I returned from the sequoia yesterday. It was one thing for him to know we were making love off and on over the past week, quite another to see it firsthand.

What snapped in a mind totally focused to protecting and supervising the care and preservation of women (in a world, a history gone mad) as he hung outside this magic cave of flying beauty and watched us?

Jealousy? Nikolai doubted Prien would be moved by such a banal emotion. Lust? Desire? Also inconceivable.

Then he had it. Obsession.

Prien devoted his life to the Protectorate. Every action, every confrontation with Nikolai was more of a confrontation between the past and the future than a personal contest.

Prien was afraid what the future might bring to Russia.

Not the imminent arrival of the Kornephorons. That was a natural phenomenon no man could control. He was frightened of the cultural revolution that would sweep their country (and the world) if Capek's plan succeeded.

What would realization of that fact be to a mind focused like a laser on one dominant theme? Whatever had gone wrong, it had broken deep inside his psyche. The old Prien would never have purposefully harmed Galina or any other woman. The hesitation marks on Galina's neck proved beyond all doubt he was now a sick man who needed to be restrained and helped.

Nikolai produced the sleepdeath module, held it up in the shifting lozenges of light and shadow.

Prien was immediately suspicious. "Where'd you get that?"

"Let Galina go, and I'll give this to you to kill me with."

"Nikolai, no—!" she gagged with horror.

He ignored her protest. "I won't fight back, Doctor. Galina's life for mine. That's a fair trade. Then you can bluff Lev to let you off this station. He believes you'll harm Galina and he doesn't want that responsibility."

Prien motioned at the comset around Nikolai's ear. "You've been in touch with him ever since you came into the arboretum. I'm not going to fall for it. I'm not that stupid."

Nikolai cocked his head to show the headset was shut off. "It's not a trick. You'll get what you want and I'll get what I want: Galina alive and well. Nothing else matters to me."

Galina struggled until Prien used a joint-locking move to subdue her. "Nikolai, please don't," she sobbed. Her wrist was about to break and added pressure on her elbow about to dislocate her shoulder. "You don't know what you're saying. . . ."

Prien considered Nikolai's offer. His eyes squinted suspiciously. "Put the module there," he indicated a position one meter away. He shoved the needlegun so hard against Galina's head it tipped to one side and left a half-moon impression on her skin. "Do it now."

Saltwater globules wobbled from the corners of Galina's eyes. "Nikolai don't do this please you can't I love you don't you know that. . . . why are you doing this?" The last half of her plea might have been meant for Prien, but Nikolai wasn't sure.

He released the sleepdeath module. It spun lazily end over end in the zero gravity.

Prien's eyes blazed with triumph. Galina, sensing the reduced pressure on her arm, clawed like a wildcat in his grip. Nikolai shouted her name twice before she stopped long enough to listen to him.

"Listen to me, darling," he said, amidst the hurtling bodies of dead butterflies. "You have to be brave. I want you to remember me, and remember our love. I never expected anything like meeting you and falling in love with you when I came to Moscow. I wouldn't trade any part of my life for the few precious days and nights we've had together. I love you, Galina." He paused. "I'm ready, Doctor."

Prien flexed his knees and kicked off the trunk, holding Galina out in front. She reached out, grabbed a branch. He peeled her fingers away, kicked to change their vector towards the opening of the wood cave.

"No, Doctor, no!" She tried to bite his forearm.

"I know you don't understand what I'm doing is for the best," Prien told her, "but someday you will. I promise you, someday you will see I am doing the right thing."

He anchored himself by hooking his knee around a providential branch and shoved her out of the butterfly grotto. Her momentum spun her head over heels, tumbling away from the sequoia.

"Nikolai . . . Nikolai . . . Niko-laaiii—" Her scream degenerated into a heartrending wail that modulated up and down as she flipped end over end through the biosphere.

Prien wasted no time. He kept Nikolai covered with the needlegun. "Turn around and face the trunk of the tree," he commanded, businesslike.

Nikolai did so wordlessly.

Doctor Stefan Prien snatched the sleepdeath module out of the air and flipped the safety cover off. Nikolai felt the smooth black head of the device nestle against the nape of his neck. He closed his eyes and his ears to the diminishing screams outside the grotto.

Prien's thumb moved under his hair to find the kill switch. The man's sour breath brushed against his cheek. Nikolai thought of Galina. Moscow in gloom. Yuri. Galina again.

Prien lowered the module hesitantly. "Get up, man."

He slowly opened his eyes, saw the shredding redwood bark centimeters from his nose. Felt the brush of dead butterflies on his face and arms, smelled the pungent stench of milkweed squeezed from insect bodies.

"I can't do it," Prien said woodenly. He floated in a basic zero gee crouch. Shreds of plastiskin rippled from his thigh. "You knew I wouldn't be able to, didn't you? You knew it."

Nikolai had to work up saliva to speak. "You may be many things, Doctor, but I gambled you aren't a cold-blooded murderer." He removed the module from Prien's cold fingers, cracked open the ridged carapace. "Besides, I shorted the power element with a coil of buckyball thread." He snapped the housing closed.

"You . . . ?"

"That's right. When you hit the switch and the module failed to operate, I hoped I would have enough time to incapacitate you before you used the needlegun on me."

Prien peered curiously at the gas-charged pistol in his palm as if he didn't know quite how it got there.

"There was always a chance the coil had slipped free of the points and the module would operate. Either way, Galina was out of harm's way, which was my first and only goal."

Prien's face sagged measurably. "I couldn't do it," he confessed hoarsely, "because it would have hurt her too much. When I heard what she said . . . about how she loved you . . . I've never heard a woman say that about a man before."

"I know."

Prien lifted his heavy gaze. For the first time in days the lineaments of his face softened. "Yes, I think you do." He wiped the back of his hand across his mouth, shakily. His knuckles whitened around the butt of the gun. "You'd better get out of here, Sholokhov."

"No, Doctor. We're leaving this grotto together."

Prien shook his head vigorously. "No, Nikolai. Listen to me: My world is vanishing. Capek was right; things are starting to change. The nightmare of the *Fevreblau* is coming to an end. There will be a war of two sexual cultures inside of a decade. I . . . I don't want to be part of that." The needlegun gleamed in the moving shafts of sunlight. "I can't accept what I've done. I believe in responsibility, you see. I never accepted excuses for sloppy work from men in my department. I must hold myself to the same standard I apply to others."

Nikolai heard a distant shout. People were coming. Prien heard them, too, and his will resolved.

"Don't do this, Doctor. You can be helped. You still have an important mission with the Protectorate."

"In a new government? Perhaps. Nevertheless, we shall never know." He raised the gun, pointed it. "Go, now."

"Doctor, I—"

Prien fired. The flechette ripped into the muscle of Nikolai's arm and exited in a spurt of blood. Though minuscule in comparison to his body mass, the force of the flechette spun him in the zero gravity environment. A second flechette buried itself in the shoulder of the same arm, glancing off bone. Nestled, it burned like liquid fire.

Nikolai let out an agonized cry, lips skinning back from his teeth in a rictus of pain. He groped with his good arm for a leafy bough and pulled himself out of the grotto of dead butterflies, bumping clumsily through the thick branches toward safety. Wobbling globules of bright arterial blood streamed from his shoulder. Looking back, he saw Prien twist open the barrel of the gun. Nikolai struggled to get out of the cave.

The needlegun fired one last time behind him, muffled.

Nikolai's head emerged in white sunlight and blue sky. Fluffy holographic clouds. Half a dozen men floated around the entrance to the cave, carrying handmade weapons: clubs, medical laser scalpels with safety-locks broken, socks filled with gravel. A small figure behind them struggled vainly to get past.

"Nikolai! Nikolai!"

He started to lose consciousness. Someone turned him over and applied the palm of their hand to his spurting wound. He heard the stuttering sound of regen tape and thought he heard (he wasn't sure because the place he was entering was deep and black) someone above him pleading tearfully:

"You have to save him . . . you have to save him . . . you have to save him. . . ."

"You've been out for two days; there's a lot to bring you up to speed on," Lev said. "The firewall is down and the Russian link into the DataSphere is up and running at speed. Everyone is talking about the aliens. Oh, they call themselves Thants, by the way, and they have a CHON-based biochemistry."

Nikolai sat propped in bed, a white sheet pulled up to his waist. His face was scrubbed and his eyes were clear and bright behind a new pair of glasses.

His left arm was held immobile in a bubble sling. One more day in hospital and he would begin a long regimen of physical therapy.

"There's severe nerve damage," Dr. Bairiev had informed him when he came out from under the general anesthetic. "You'll never regain full range of motion with that shoulder, I'm afraid, but manual dexterity in the fingers should remain unaffected."

"What about the man Prien shot, doctor?"

Bairiev had shook his head wistfully. "We've done all we can, I'm afraid. The flechette went through the right eye and lodged in his brain. There's not much of a chance he'll ever recover. He's in coma now."

Nikolai later heard that Cyril Waveland had purposefully walked into the morgue and kicked Prien's corpse until another man restrained him. Lev restricted Waveland to his quarters until the autopsy on the Protectorate was completed. Afterwards, the unfortunate incident was forgotten and Waveland allowed to return to duty.

"Prien had a tracer in one of his sinus cavities," Lev said, bringing him back to the present. "We found another one planted at the base of his spine."

"I'm not surprised. One tracer probably belongs to the Protectorate and the other to Internal Security. The watchers watching the watchers."

Stinnen sneaking behind the arras, he reflected.

He related more of his thoughts. "I'll contact Capek and let him know we made it through all right."

Prien had surprising news. "Galina beat you to it, already. She sent a signal after the firewall disintegrated.

Capek was glad to hear from her and seemed to regard Prien's death as nothing more than a tragic accident. I talked to him, too, and told him you could stay on here if you wanted. He agreed."

"What happened to the revolution?"

"The *Narodnaya Volya* is in power. We're waiting to see the new First Minister. We have a direct link to the Kremlin and are watching the placards."

"It's Stinnen," Nikolai said stoutly. "He shaped events to catapult himself to power this way. Sharonov Crater was nuked the day after I told him about the starsign. He smashed *Tereshkova* because Yuri told him that's where I was headed. Goddammit, I can't believe that monster's won."

"How can you be so sure, Nikolai?"

"He has no conscience, no loyalty to anyone other than himself. You've seen him in action, Lev. He's a very dangerous, a very evil man."

"Well, he's in charge now, and there's nothing we can do about it, unless we march on St. Petersburg."

That grated with Nikolai. "Did the rescue team get off all right?"

"A day late," Lev replied, "but there are survivors. They rigged a radio out of components from a wall intercom. Other worldlets are sending salvage teams, too. We'll get them out."

Nikolai changed the subject to a topic closer to his heart. "How is Galina holding up?"

"Fantastic. That's one strong-willed woman. Did you know she works a full shift every day before coming down here to sit by you all night?" Lev grinned playfully. "Even I wouldn't do that."

Nikolai had an ephemeral recollection of someone

holding his hand as he slept. Lev had more news about Galina.

"She's been repairing the root mats used to anchor the wheat farms. It's donkey work but it keeps her mind occupied, and that's for the best because a lot of men want to gawk at her." He shifted from foot to foot, uncharacteristically abashed.

"I don't know of one crew member aboard this habitat who blames her for what happened in the arboretum," he conceded. "They've almost started thinking of her as *Gudonov*'s mascot."

Nikolai laughed. "For god's sake, don't ever tell her that. She'll hit the roof. She doesn't want to be a novelty."

"Well, she is, like it or not, on this worldlet. She's the one who found the hatch and logged an emergency call to the central AI. You know, you took a big risk pulling that stunt."

Nikolai frowned, remembering. "Not really. You have to be a certain kind of man to press a sleepdeath module against another man's skull. Anyway, I'm a pretty fair electrician." He jerked a smile. "Now, tell me about these Thants. Are they still broadcasting radio pulses?"

Lev opened a fanbook. "I've downloaded a preliminary report for you. Yes, we're transmitting everything we decode; the secret's out in a big way. So far, we've decoded half a million pages of text and photographs. Every telescope on Earth and in cislunar space is tuned to the approaching fleet."

Nikolai opened a video file. A six-limbed, somewhat ursine creature appeared in three-dimensional relief on the flatscreen.

He whistled. "Five hundred kilograms. What are those spurs on their mid-limbs? Fighting weapons?"

"We think so. Those bands around their torsos and limbs are a kind of bioarmor that interlocks with itself."

"What else have you learned about them?"

"They're not indigenous to the star in Hercules. Morphology suggests they hail from a red sun, and they mate in triads. There's a traditional male and female pair, plus a neuter midwife who transmutes the poisonous seed of the male before impregnation. Don't look at me that way; I didn't design them. We're trying to figure out why evolution would select for such a bizarre reproductive arrangement. I've broken up more than one fight among *Gudonov*'s biologists already. There are several theories."

"Why are they coming here?"

"They picked up our radio and 3V broadcasts a hundred years ago and decided to have a look."

"That should prove interesting."

"Mm-hm. They're going to be here in ten years."

Nikolai stared back.

Lev acknowledged the sobering moment with a brief, knowing nod. "I've been breaking up fights between physicists, too," he remarked. "A velocity ninety-nine percent the speed of light and they're ten years away and still accelerating—haven't even begun a decelerating process. That means either they have starships capable of withstanding millions of gees of negative acceleration, or they have an inertial dampening device. Either way, they are far above us on any technological scale you want to measure by."

Nikolai marveled. "Moonlight and magnolia aliens? I guess we're going to find out."

A telecomp beeped for attention. Lev answered it.

A communications tech focused on the flatscreen. "Sorry to interrupt, sir, but you wanted to be advised when the new placards went up on the Kremlin."

"Yes, thank you."

With Lev's help Nikolai crawled out of bed and walked to the telecomp screen. "I want to see this," he said.

A voice called him back. "What do you think you're doing out of bed, mister?"

Galina, standing in the open doorway.

"Well, I. . . ."

She came closer. "I'm not going to be the only one weaving root mats the rest of my life. I'd like some company. Yours."

He circled his good arm around her narrow waist and pulled her near. "Let's not quarrel in front of Lev, darling." He kissed her.

She returned his hug, mindful of his injured arm. "I thought I'd come down on my lunch break to check on you. Good thing I did. I take it they're naming the new First Minister?"

"That's what we've been told." Nikolai felt a foul mood coming on. He wasn't looking forward to seeing that face again. "I'm sure he'll have one of his dreadful black cigarettes between his lips," he presaged sourly.

Lev waved for quiet. "Here's the transmission from Moscow."

A blue sphere ballooned with a Confederation Ikon in the center. A 3V image of the Kremlin's shattered battlements slowly resolved. Men working atop the broken walls cut release cables. The new placards rolled down the faded red brick of the Kremlin.

Reality for Nikolai abruptly swerved.

"Mintz is the First Minister of the Confederation," he exploded. "I don't believe it!"

But the portrait was unmistakable: narrow feline features, trimmed beard, and diamond temple clips.

"Who the blazes is, what did you say his name was? Mintz?"

"He's a *Narodnaya Volya* chieftain . . ." Nikolai began.

"So what do you expect? The NV financed the revolution."

"No, no, you don't understand. Mintz talked about how this new knowledge might bring courage to a world bled white by war and ravaged by plague. Don't you see, Lev? The government in St. Petersburg wanted this discovery buried to manipulate a massive propaganda program in their favor. That's why they hit our outposts. Hell, we're Outworlders anyway so who would care? That's the way they think."

"I'm inclined to agree. They never saw the space program as a tool but rather a propaganda weapon, and us as second class citizens."

" 'Everything's fine in Russia, we have a viable space program,' " Galina quoted from a political text they all knew.

"Exactly," Nikolai echoed. "Mintz had the motive and the will to do this thing. He's *vozhd* to the underworld in Moscow and one of the most powerful men in Russia. I know that from personal experience. Damn it, I thought I was slick keeping the aliens' arrival to myself. Mintz saw through that; he knew. My hatred for Stinnen blinded me to what was really going on behind the scenes in Moscow."

"And what might that be?" Lev asked.

"The Revolution, of course. Mintz selected Yuri as my bodyguard to see that I got out of Moscow safely after . . . well, after my leave was up. When the government hit Sharanov he had to hurry his timetable along. What he didn't count on was that by this time Yuri and I had Galina on our hands. No one had planned for that eventuality."

He spun around, excited. "Yuri! Galina, I think he might be alive after all."

Her face brightened. "Nikolai, do you really mean it?"

"Mintz respected him. And, you know Yuri: he wouldn't let someone cut him adrift, not if he could help it. Yuri knew Mintz wanted me protected and may have used that knowledge to buy himself insurance. There's a chance provisions were made to rescue him. Slim, but a chance."

"Yuri alive!" She clapped her hands happily. "Oh, I hope it's true." She imparted to Lev: "We owe him our lives." She said this candidly, as if it explained away everything that had happened in their past.

"But Prien said he was scheduled for liquidation."

Nikolai knew the Director of *Gudonov* was just being practical. Lev didn't live with us during those hectic days, he thought, running from Internal Security and dodging bluecaps.

Yuri the magician.

He conceded, "Stinnen may very well have killed him, but it's not a certainty. Not until I see his body."

He put his arms around Galina's waist. "Someday, I want to return to Moscow and find out. Will you come with me?"

"You'll have to push me away," she said with deep feeling. "Not only do I owe him my life, I owe him yours."

They held each other with a lingering kiss.

Hope soaring, Nikolai drifted over to a floor-length vista-window. Gravity on this level was less than normal for the hospital patients. Luna slowly disappeared from his field of view as the medical section of *Gudonov* revolved. Likewise, images spun in his mind, as weighty as galaxies, more full of promise.

Yuri alive. Maybe.

Aliens, inside of a decade.

A new government. A new wind blowing across the world, across Russia, with this knowledge that it was possible to survive.

Galina in my life. Perhaps forever. What would that be like? he wondered.

I can't wait to find out.

He recognized the fact an old Asian curse held special meaning for him: I am living in interesting times.

Staring into the unforgiving blackness where stars burned silently with cold fire, he tried to see something of his future. Yes, there was something. . . .

Movement inside the millimeter thick plasteel: Ghostly reflections on the starfields.

"You and Nikolai are welcome to stay on with us, Galina," Lev's wavering ghost proclaimed. "We always need people to repair torn root mats."

Her reflection touched the palms of her slim hands together, laughing throatily. She had a bearing and a maturity that belied her fifteen years.

"We talked about settling down in the UAI," her star ghost announced, "when we were on the run from the bluecaps. But Nikolai has always worked on Luna or a worldlet; he wouldn't want to be stuck groundside. He's not a mudballer at heart."

"What about yourself? What do you want, Galina?"

Her star ghost in the bay window melded seamlessly with Nikolai's reflection. She addressed Lev, but her words were clearly meant for him, coming as they did out of the jeweled stars on the other side of the crystal.

"It doesn't matter to me where we end up," she told Lev. She put her hand on her abdomen and looked down. "You see, as long as we're together, and I'm with Nikolai, that's the place we'll always call home."

About the Author

Kenneth Mark Hoover was born in New Iberia, Louisiana, in 1959. As a young boy living in the Deep South he was always interested in rocketry, the space program, and writing stories. He has two degrees, one in journalism along with a bachelor's degree in science (physics and chemistry) education. His passions include chess, amateur astronomy, and shotokan. While he has at times worked as a surveyor, an educator, and a salesman, his first love is writing. He currently lives in Mississippi with his wife and three children. *Fevreblau* is his first novel.